PAUL G. KALOYEROPOULOS

# A NATURAL KILL

PAUL G. KALOYEROPOULOS

A
NATURAL
KILL

ARCHWAY
PUBLISHING

Archway Publishing books may be ordered through booksellers or by contacting:

Archway Publishing
1663 Liberty Drive
Bloomington, IN 47403
www.archwaypublishing.com
844-669-3957

Because of the dynamic nature of the Internet, any web addresses or links contained in this book may have changed since publication and may no longer be valid. The views expressed in this work are solely those of the author and do not necessarily reflect the views of the publisher, and the publisher hereby disclaims any responsibility for them.

Any people depicted in stock imagery provided by Getty Images are models, and such images are being used for illustrative purposes only. Certain stock imagery © Getty Images.

Scripture taken from the King James Version of the Bible.

ISBN: 978-1-6657-5903-8 (sc)
ISBN: 978-1-6657-5905-2 (hc)
ISBN: 978-1-6657-5904-5 (e)

Library of Congress Control Number: 2024907600

Print information available on the last page.

Archway Publishing rev. date: 05/22/2024

# ACKNOWLEDGMENTS

It is my belief as a writer that my task is to walk the tightrope between the carnal, and the Godly, of what is and what can be; to tell the tale of the sinner and the saint, and to ultimately reveal Devine truths found in the life of Jesus Christ. With that said, I first want to thank the Father, Son: Jesus Christ, and Holy Spirit. God, Who is the beginning and the end, the source of all creative thought.

I would like to thank my father, mother, and sister: Gus, Ellen, and Gigi who have long since passed on, for their unconditional love and guidance.

Love and thanks goes to my dear aunt Sofia who believed in my talent and motivated me to push on and finish this labor of love.

My brother Perry and sister-in-law Sharon provided me with a beautiful safe haven in which to write and also encouraged me. Jason, Robin, Christopher, Collin, Jennifer, James and Jon, the family, were an ever-present example of what a loving, caring, family should be, thank you. I drew much inspiration from their lives. Special thanks to James, the computer genius in the family, who helped with the technical and word processing challenges I faced.

Thanks to Jennifer for the many hours she put in on the first edit.

Special thanks to my friend John Cummings for his input.

Valuable feedback and assistance came from; my cousins Maria and

George Georges, Stanton Manolakas, also Hellene Liatsos, Ed Vaks, Mary Lloyd, Leo Lau, Earl Douglas and Rick Edwards.

Trish, much love, and thanks for the memories.

My many years of friendship with Frank Naley provided me with a treasure chest of humor and wit for the novel, thank you.

John Quern, a great friend, provided me with valuable character insights, thanks.

Thanks to my dear friend Steve Crenshaw for his invaluable advice and technical assistance.

Thank you to my friends and fellow believers at Saint Sophia Cathedral and Saint John the Divine Church.

This book is dedicated to my aunts,

Sofia, Pat, Georgia and my mother Ellen,

All of whom loved and nurtured me.

And

To my brother Perry and his family,

The inspiration behind this novel

# CHAPTER 1

THE SMALL, SPARSELY DECORATED HOSPITAL ROOM HAD JUST ONE BED. Dr. Peter Kalos rested his arms on a narrow countertop as he examined a patient's chart. Nurse Gilda entered with an armful of supplies. Peter was in his midthirties, handsome, with a chiseled jaw, patrician nose, and dark features. His large, brown eyes displayed compassion, kindness, and concern, reflecting the traits of a conscientious emergency room physician. He also held the added responsibility of being the director of that division. Gilda walked over to the counter next to Peter and unloaded her medical accessories. "How's it going, Doctor?"

"Just fine. How 'bout you, Gilda?"

Gilda was a stout woman in her fifties with salt and pepper hair. "I had a great weekend. My grandkids were with me. We spent the day at the beach on Saturday, and then on Sunday we did a little bowling." Gilda began to restock the supplies.

"Sounds like fun. I love the beach, especially Manhattan. I can never get enough of the ocean," Peter said.

"Anything exciting happen over the weekend for you?"

"Actually, there was a memorable incident. Steph and I were at the grocery store picking up a few things on Saturday when we ran into

Samantha Olson. I don't know if you remember her. About a year ago, she was in here and had her appendix removed."

"Yes, I remember Samantha. Petite, attractive blonde."

"Yes, that's her. She was about to get married."

"To an army sergeant, right?"

"Yeah. You've got a good memory. Well, she's all happy to see me and meet Stephanie, but I couldn't help noticing her stomach was protruding and that she had gained about thirty pounds. She was even wearing one of those blouses that are pleated to give you more room around the waist, so I assumed—"

"You didn't."

"I got as far as 'Congrat—' when Stephanie pinched my leg, and this was not a 'Pinch me. I'm Irish' pinch. These were the pincers of death. Do you think I got the hint? No! I had to say, 'Congratulations on your pregnancy.' You would have thought I told her her cat died. She mumbled that she knew she had put on some weight. I immediately apologized, but I had already shoved my foot in my mouth, and I went deep. I mean deep! I almost came in here to have it surgically removed. She even thanked me because now she would get serious about dieting. Yeah, thank you for ripping my heart out and leaving my self-esteem in shreds, especially in front of your wife."

Gilda was laughing, almost in tears. "Stop already."

"Her compassionate doctor said this. So yes, it was a great weekend. The downside is one of my patients is on a suicide watch, but hey, my diagnostic skills are improving."

The door to the examining room opened slightly, and Nurse Josie, a petite African American woman, stuck her head in. With urgency in her voice, she said, "Dr. Kalos, we have a child with multiple traumas in exam room 3."

Leaving his chart, he quickly walked out of the room, followed by Gilda. Peter entered exam room 3, where Nurse Josie and two other medical staff members were standing hunched over the child. Joined by Gilda, he walked over to the boy. The sight before him was horrific. The boy appeared to be about five years old, but it was hard to tell through his injuries. His head and face were swollen to almost double in size, and blood was everywhere. The child was unconscious. Although shocked by what he saw, Peter's instincts kicked in.

"Let's get him on the larger gurney," Peter said to Josie, who was standing opposite him. They each grabbed the sheet beneath the boy.

Peter began to count. "One, two, and three." On "three," they transferred the child to the gurney.

Removing the stethoscope from around his neck, he applied it to the boy's chest and listened for a heartbeat. He quickly removed it and barked, "Get an ET tube; we need to intubate him." After Peter put on sterile gloves, Josie quickly handed him the tube, which he deftly eased down the boy's throat.

Peter then looked up at Josie and asked, "What happened here?"

"He fell down a cement stairway," responded Josey.

"I want a CBC, Chem panel, a CT scan of his head, and C-SPINE x-rays. Get a pediatric neurosurgeon and respiratory down here *stat!*" bellowed Peter.

Taking his eyes off the child for a moment, he scanned the room for a parent. He couldn't miss Phil Darso; he was a mountain of a man standing six feet, five inches, and weighing about 250 pounds, all muscle. His head was shaved, and he sported a trimmed goatee, which further added to his menacing appearance. His bloodshot, teary eyes and his distraught look intimated that he was the boy's father. Peter approached him.

"Are you the father?"

Phil's voice was hoarse with emotion. "Yes."

"I'm Dr. Peter Kalos," Peter said, extending his hand.

"Phil Darso," replied Phil, reciprocating with a handshake.

"How did this happen?"

"Jimmy must have been up and down those steps a hundred times. He was playing on the landing near the stairs. I took my eyes off of him for a moment; it couldn't have been more than a couple of seconds. I just went to answer my cell I'd left in the office. He screamed, 'Daddy!' When I got back, he was at the bottom of the steps." Phil broke down sobbing. "I should have been there."

Compassionately, Peter put his hand on Phil's shoulder. "Accidents happen; I have a young son myself. You can't be there every second."

"Dr. Kalos, he's coming to," Josie blurted out.

Peter and Phil moved quickly to the side of Jimmy's bed. Looking closely, they saw slight twinges in his hands and legs; with a low groaning voice, Jimmy uttered through the ET tube, "Ah … ah."

Phil leaned over him. Talking just above a whisper, he said, "Jimmy, it's Daddy."

Suddenly, Jimmy's eyes opened wide, bulging in terror. He took quick, staccato breaths and began to hyperventilate. The monitor that had previously given off a steady beeping sound was now giving off a loud, rapid alert noise.

Peter turned to Phil. "Phil, you have to leave." When Phil didn't move, Peter added more firmly, "Please, just step outside." Nurse Gilda grabbed Phil's arm and nudged him toward the door. He left hesitantly.

Shouting out orders, Peter yelled, "I need two syringes: one amp epinephrine and one amp of calcium chloride!"

Josie responded by thrusting the syringes into his waiting hands. He injected the drugs, one after another, into Jimmy's arm. There was no response. "Give me the paddles; charge to one hundred." Gilda appeared at Peter's side and she quickly complied. He shocked the boy, to no reaction. "Charge to two hundred!" He shocked the boy again—still no life signs. "Give me three hundred." He jolted Jimmy once more.

—ɷ—

Phil was in the critical care waiting area, pacing. There were a few other anxious people scattered about the room. A large clock on a nearby wall read 7:30.

—ɷ—

Back in exam room 3, Peter and his staff were busy trying to revive Jimmy. Manipulating an airbag inserted in the tube over the boy's mouth, Josie continued trying to resuscitate him. Peter, with a stethoscope in hand, listened for a heartbeat. In the background, the constant flatline beep of the monitor was heard, breaking the concerned silence in the room.

Jimmy's eyes were closed; a serene, peaceful look enveloped his face. Peter looked up from the boy to the other nurses in the room: Gilda and Josie. "We're not going to bring him back," he said softly as tears welled up in his eyes. Looking up at the clock, he said, "Time of death: 8:32." As a tear rolled down his cheek, Peter made the sign of the cross and rested his hand upon Jimmy's forehead. "You're in God's hands now."

Gilda looked at Jimmy and then at Peter with teary emotion. "I'll never get used to this. It's all so sad." With a mournful look upon her face, she exited the room.

Josie stared thoughtfully at Jimmy. Then she turned to Peter and with determination said, "Doctor, I need you to look at something. When I removed Jimmy's clothes, I noticed this." She gently turned the boy to his side and pulled down the sheet covering him. There were black-and-blue welts in horizontal bar shapes across his back, legs, and buttocks. The assumption was that they were the result of being beaten with a leather strap. Josie moved the boy onto his back again.

Peter angrily blurted out, "That son of a bitch!" He gently cradled Jimmy's head in his hands, turning it to the right and to the left to do a closer examination. There were bruises everywhere. "The trauma to the head looks like the blow came horizontally from the side, as if he was punched or backhanded. I want an autopsy. Was there an officer with the ambulance?"

Josie nodded. "Yes, there was."

"Would you please find him and send him in here?"

"Sure," Josie replied, and then she departed the room.

—m—

Uniformed officer Bill Parsons was standing at the far end of the hall talking sports with an orderly as Josie approached. His close-cropped, sandy-blond hair, blue eyes, and youthful good looks made him look more like a college-aged surfer than a police officer. Fresh out of the police academy, he had been on duty for only two months.

"Officer, did you come in with the little boy that fell down the stairs?" Josie asked.

"Yes, I did."

"I'm Josie Windell," said Josie as she extended her hand.

"Bill Parsons," responded Bill with a handshake.

"Dr. Kalos would like to see you. Would you follow me please?"

"All right." Bill turned to the orderly. "I've got to go, but I'd still put my money on the Lakers if I were you."

Officer Parsons followed Josie into the urgent care room where Peter was involved in a thorough examination of little Jimmy's body. With gloved fingers, he prodded for broken or extended bones and other injuries. Josie jarred his concentration. "Dr. Kalos, the officer is here."

Peter looked up, pulled off his latex glove, and extended his hand. "Hi. Peter Kalos."

"Bill. Bill Parsons," said the officer as he shook the doctor's hand.

"I'd like you to take a look at this." Peter lifted the boy's body and turned it over then removed the sheet from around the shoulders. Bill was horrified by what he saw. Shaking his head in disbelief, voice cracking, he said, *"This didn't happen from him falling down a flight of stairs?"*

"No, it didn't. He was beaten, beaten severely. I'd say with a leather belt. It looks like he was also punched," Peter responded somberly.

Peter turned the body over again. He pointed to the boy's cheek, "And his jaw is broken. That's not a typical injury from a stair fall."

Bill grimaced and continued to shake his head. "I've never seen anything like this; it's … it's brutal."

"I know. "We need to find Phil Darso, the boy's father," Peter replied.

—∞—

Peter was the first to enter the trauma waiting room. Phil, who had been expecting him, immediately approached. He anxiously blurted out, "How is he?"

"Jimmy died at 8:32 this evening. I'm sorry."

Phil contorted his face as if in extreme pain. "No, no!"

Officer Parsons entered the waiting room, with Josie following close behind. Phil saw them enter but concentrated on Peter only. "Can I see him?

It was unnatural to keep a father away from the body of his dead child. Although he would not be able to harm the boy any further, Peter's inner feelings screamed at him to keep this monster away. Taking a deep breath and exhaling as he spoke, Peter said firmly, "I'm sending Jimmy's body for an autopsy."

By now Bill and Josie were standing next to Peter. Phil looked intently from one person to another, his eyes throwing daggers as they moved from Peter to Bill to Josie and back again.

"What the hell is going on here? Are you telling me I can't see my dead son?"

Bill stepped forward and said purposefully, "Mr. Darso I'd like you to come down to the station and answer a few questions."

"Are you arresting me?" Phil asked with attitude.

"It's just for some questioning."

Phil hesitated. He turned and looked at Josie. Then he turned and his eyes zoned in on Peter. His stare was chilling. Peter could feel the hairs on the back of his neck rise. Finally, he turned back to Bill and stared intently and coldly into his eyes. Bill locked on, eyeball to eyeball with him; taking a hard swallow, he tried to hide the fear welling up inside his body.

"All right," Phil said in a matter-of-fact tone. Phil was no fool. A quick analysis of the situation told him that his best course of action was to acquiesce for now so he could come back and fight another day.

There was an almost simultaneous sigh of relief from Josie, Peter, and Bill.

Peter and Josie watched as Bill escorted Phil out the door.

—ɷ—

Peter entered through the front door of his cottage-style home. His wife, Stephanie, was sitting at the dining room table. She was a natural beauty. Her long, sandy-brown hair was twisted above her head and held in place with an unsharpened pencil. Stephanie's large hazel eyes were the perfect complement to her hair shade. High cheekbones, a small, upturned nose, and full, sensual lips completed the composite of her facial features. She was slim, but not model thin; her ample breasts, bubble butt, and strong, muscular legs made her more curvaceous than petite. She was casually dressed in a pair of aged blue jeans and one of Peter's old blue oxford cloth shirts, sleeves rolled up and collar unbuttoned.

Looking up from her laptop, she tipped her tortoise shell glasses downward, peered over them at Peter, and said, "Hi!"

"Hi, sweetheart," said Peter with a forced smile. He proceeded into the hallway then down the hall. He stopped in front of a closed door and slowly opened it. The room was dimly lit with a golden glow provided by a small Winnie the Pooh nightlight. His three-year-old son, John, was fast asleep. Peter walked over and knelt at the side of the bed. He stared at his son, mesmerized by his cherubic face. Wavy brown hair, long eyelashes, full cheeks, and a small, impish nose produced a portrait of the classic Norman Rockwell child. One of John's hands was extended on the bed. Peter tenderly lifted it and cradled it in his own. He continued to gaze upon his son as tears welled up in his eyes and began to stream down his face.

Barely audible, he prayed, "Dear God, thank You for this gift, this beautiful child of mine. Forgive me if I've ever lashed out in anger, physically or verbally, at him. I'm truly sorry. Please give me the wisdom to discipline him fairly, with love, and give me the strength and courage to right the evil that has been done to that poor boy who suffered so greatly. I love You, Lord." Peter bowed his head and kissed John's little hand.

Gently closing the bedroom door, Peter headed toward the living room. He went over and sat in his favorite chair, an oversized rocker with large leather cushions. He stared off into the distance as he methodically rocked back and forth. Stephanie, who was still seated at the dining room table, watched him intently. After a few moments, she rose and walked over to him. Peter stopped rocking as she gently sat in his lap. Stephanie snuggled up to him and slowly began to rub the back of his neck and shoulders with her hands. Peter put his hands around her waist.

"What's wrong?" asked Steph.

"A child was brought in today, about John's age, which we were told had fallen down a cement flight of stairs."

"My God!"

"His head was so swollen it looked almost double in size."

"Oh, honey."

"We couldn't save him. Then Josie has me take a look at his back." Peter paused. "He was beaten black-and-blue with a strap." Voice cracking, Peter struggled to continue "He had been beaten so badly that in some places his skin was broken and scabs had formed."

"No!" cried Stephanie in disbelief.

"I can't believe someone could harm another human being like that … and this was a child.

Stephanie looked into his tear-filled eyes. "Is there anything I can do, sweetheart?"

"Just having you close is enough."

He laid his head against her chest, and she enveloped him in her arms. Slowly the rocking chair began to move. Peter could hear the steady beat of her heart like the rhythmic sound of waves crashing against the shore. Lulled by this, as well as the unbroken back-and-forth motion of the rocker, Peter grasped the sacred beauty and purpose of this godly creation, his wife and soulmate. With their hearts entwined, beating together as one, in sync with the divine heartbeat of the universe, he found peace.

# CHAPTER 2

PHIL DARSO WAS SEATED ON A WOODEN BENCH OUTSIDE A LARGE OAK door with a sign above it that read, "Judge's Chambers." Seated next to him was Mark Tribecca, a thirtysomething man dressed in a suit and tie. He was short with a slight body frame and jet-black hair and wore wire-rimmed glasses. Basically, he looked like Woody Allen with Wayne Newton's hair. Phil, with a newspaper in hand, scanned a headline that read, "Explosion and Fire Destroys Autopsy Lab; Arson Suspected."

He turned to Mark. "Sharky, in this fire at the autopsy lab, did any bodies get destroyed?"

Mark looked at him shocked. "They didn't ... You don't know?" He paused and then continued. "Your son's body was burned beyond recognition."

"No!" said Phil with the slightest hint of insincerity in his voice.

After a long moment of silence, Mark spoke. "Phil, this may not be the right time—"

"That's Mr. Darso," interrupted Phil.

Mark sighed. "Mr. Darso, my name is Mark Tribecca, not Sharky. I get the not-so-subtle comparison to an undersea killer, and to be honest, it's offensive."

Phil feigned sincerity. "Oh you're offended." His voice took on an angry tone. "With the amount of money I'm paying you, I'll call you whatever I damn well please."

Mark stared back at him silently.

In a more placating tone, Phil continued. "I did have another nickname for you. It was kind of a toss-up between Sharky and ... well, does Numb Nuts work for you?"

Mark looked away, quietly fuming.

Phil went on. "Get over it. There are more important matters to deal with. What's on the plate here?"

Mark snapped back into attorney mode, and he was more than capable at his profession. "They can't use the boy's body for evidence because of the fire. There are no x-rays. The only ammunition they have is their witnesses: the nurse, the doctor, and the police officer. This is only an arraignment. You have no prior arrests, you run a successful company, and you are a member of numerous business and charitable organizations. You'll be out on bail; however, I do believe it will go to trial. The district attorney wants you in the worst way. This is an election year for him, and child abuse is a passionate issue with everyone."

Phil, deep in thought, digested the information and replied in a pensive tone, "OK."

—⁜—

It was midmorning when Peter entered the hospital. Dressed in casual attire, he approached the assignment desk where five of his fellow colleagues—three men and two women—were gathered. They looked up from assorted charts and paperwork simultaneously. The melancholy looks on their faces was unmistakable. Peter picked up on this and responded, "Why the long faces?"

Rita Witherspoon was the first to speak. "Obviously you haven't heard." She took a deep breath. "Josie was killed last night by a hit-and-run driver."

Peter was overwhelmed by the news. "No ... not Josie!" He hung his head in bewilderment. "God, no."

Randy, an orderly standing nearby, took a beat then quietly interjected, "There's some men here to see you, Dr. Kalos; they're waiting in the cafeteria."

"Thanks, Randy," responded Peter. He looked at the rest of the group and grimaced. "I miss her already."

Peter turned and headed for the cafeteria.

—∿—

Peter entered the cafeteria, which was sparsely populated. The presence of four men seated at one table caught his attention. The men's names were Vince Darelli, Max Freeman, Nick Warsinski, and Darrel Washington. Vince Darelli was the charismatic district attorney. He had a movie star persona characterized by a strong jawline, sculpted nose, piercing brown eyes, and premature silver hair. Vince was lean and fit. Legend had it that at one time he was a mean amateur middleweight who was talented enough to go pro.

Max Freeman was the chief of police. He was not a particularly attractive man with his large nose and bristly eyebrows, but Max was a principled, shrewd leader of men.

Seated next to him was Nick Warsinski, all 230 pounds of him. He was built like a fireplug: short at five foot, nine, but with wide, powerful shoulders and a lower body to match. His waistline was thirty-eight inches, but he wore thirty-six-inch pants that allowed his stomach to protrude over his belt.

Finally, there was, Darrel Washington, an African American with the archetype model's face and classic Adonis body. His phenomenal athletic appearance belied a childlike innocence.

Peter approached the table. Vince was the first one to stand; the rest followed suit.

Vince extended his hand. "Dr. Kalos?"

"Yes."

"I'm Vince Darelli, the district attorney."

"Hi. Peter Kalos."

"I'd like you to meet," he turned toward the group and pointed, "Max Freeman, chief of police." Peter and Max shook hands. Vince continued. "This is Detective Nick Warsinski and Detective Darrel Washington."

Peter then shook hands with Nick and Darrel. "Pleasure to meet you."

"You too," Nick replied.

"Hi," Darrel responded.

Vince motioned with his hand to an open chair. "Doctor, please sit down."

"Sure." Peter sat down with the men.

Vince looked intently into Peter's eyes and began. "You are aware of Josie Wendell's death?"

"Yes."

"My condolences to you and your staff."

"Thank you."

"You may not be aware that Officer Bill Parsons was murdered last Friday."

"That's the officer that helped us report the abuse incident."

"Yes, and I believe Josie's and Officer Parsons's deaths are related."

Peter took a moment to comprehend. "How?"

"Phil Darso is how. He's the largest narcotics distributor on the West Coast."

"*He is?*"

"Yes, he uses minors … the younger the better, kids thirteen and under to distribute the drugs." Max Freeman interjected. "We can't touch him. There's no way to prosecute adolescent drug offenders as adults, and without stiff prison sentences, these kids get a slap on the hand or some juvy time and are back on the streets."

Darelli, in an obsessed tone, said, "He's bright and vicious. His middlemen are afraid of him. We haven't even come close to nailing him with a drug conviction, but with the child abuse, we could get him on murder two. I want to bring this dirtbag down. Will you help me?"

"Sure, I'll do anything I can," said Peter.

Vince leaned in closer to Peter, "I'd like to place you and your family in the witness protection program."

Vince's request caught Peter off guard. The surprise registered on his face as he said, "Whoa … whoa. Hold on. Let me get this straight. You think Darso had Josie and Bill Parsons killed, and I'm next?"

Shaking his head yes, Vince acknowledged his statement.

Peter continued. "I want to help, but what you're asking me to do is life-changing. If I testify and go into the program, my family and I would get new identities, we'd be out of here, new home, new state, new everything, right?"

"Yes," Vince replied.

Peter shook his head in bewilderment, running his hand through his hair. "I've got to think this over."

"I understand. We'll keep you and your family under twenty-four-hour surveillance as a precaution," Vince cajoled.

Chief Freeman added, "Detectives Warsinski and Washington will take the first twelve-hour shift; they're among our finest officers." A slight smile appeared on both Nick's and Darrel's faces. Peter turned his gaze toward the two men. Nick was the first to speak. "We'll be there for you." Darrel interjected, "Watching over you and your family … We'll protect you."

With gratitude in his voice, Peter said, "Thanks."

Peter drove his newer model sedan into the driveway of his house and parked. Darrel was seated on the passenger side next to him. A dark, nondescript Chevy following close behind stopped in front of the house. Nick was behind the wheel. Darrel exited the car then shadowed Peter to the front until he entered his home. Nick joined Darrel at the entrance.

"I'm going to check out the back of the house," said Darrel. "Good. I'll canvas the neighbors' homes on either side," quipped Nick.

Darrel approached the rear of Peter's home and discovered a six-foot privacy wall surrounding the backyard. He pulled himself up and peered over the seven-inch-wide barrier. He scanned the nicely manicured yard filled with lush green shrubs and brightly colored flowers. Nick, without being too obvious, investigated the frontal expanse and sides of the house. Back in the car, Darrel told Nick what he discovered. "We hit some good luck; they have a six-foot privacy wall surrounding the backyard. In the morning I'll get surveillance out here to set up some cameras."

"There's a lot of clearance space between the houses, which is also a plus. It looks like the big electrical van will work for a base of operations," stated Nick.

"Yeah, it's just that I hate wearing those coveralls all day," replied Darrel.

"You! On our last stakeout, I had to have a tailor put extra fabric around the waist on mine."

"I hope this case goes to trial soon."

"It should. Darelli will move it along."

"I'd hate to be in Doc's shoes," Darrel continued.

"I know. If he chooses witness protection, everyone he knows—his friends, his family, even the place he works—becomes nonexistent for him. If he chooses not to testify, they might kill him anyway just to be sure."

"And there's always the possibility they could target his family."

"It's a no-win situation."

"Yeah."

As Nick pondered Peter's plight, he turned his attention to the new pair of black lace-up leather shoes he was wearing. He licked the two fingers of his right hand and rubbed a small scuff mark off one of the shoes. Darrel observed his actions.

"New kicks," said Darrel.

"Yep … That's better." Nick turned to Darrel and continued. "Can you believe these are eleven-and-a-halves?" Darrel shook his head from side to side in response. Nick resumed, "I used to be a ten. My feet have grown one and a half inches in two years! *Why can't my dick get bigger as I grow older?*" Darrel laughed; Nick joined in.

"Bro, you've put on thirty pounds since I've known you. No wonder your feet are getting bigger. Why don't you mix in a salad once in a while?" Darrel chided.

"Thank you! I appreciate that you noticed. You know, I never say anything about you being the only black guy on the face of the earth that doesn't get laid."

"Don't go there. *Don't.*"

"I mean, look at you. The way you're built, you could probably bench-press this car. You could have any girl you wanted. But I get more action than you do, and I only win that by default because you don't get any."

"Stop while you're ahead."

"My partner is St. Darrel of Englewood, the patron saint of the never been laid."

Darrel pursed his lips and shook his head. "That's it. That's it."

"What are you going to do? You're a saint. You can only admonish me verbally."

Darrel, smiling, said, "Verbally on the side of your head." Darrel paused to reflect. "Call me crazy, but—"

Nick interrupted. "You're crazy!"

"Ya knucklehead, let me finish. I want sex to be special, in the bonds of marriage. I want it to be right with God. I've got nothing to prove. You can have the record. Nick Warsinski is *the ass bandit.*"

"Once, every ten years … *do I fall into that category?* Please say yes," Nick said with a smile. They both laughed.

Peter hung his jacket in the hall closet and headed toward the kitchen, drawn by the aroma of simmering vegetables. He entered the kitchen where Stephanie was stirring the ingredients of her famous beef stew. Her eyes lit up as she saw him. "Hi, sweetheart," she said. Leaving the stirring spoon in the pot, she walked over and planted a big kiss on his lips.

Peter responded, "Hi, that was nice."

"Good day at work?"

Peter looked around. "Where's John?"

"He's sleeping. I kept him home from preschool today. He had a slight fever."

"How's he doing?"

"The fever's gone. He'll be fine."

"That's good to hear."

Peter walked over to the stove and turned off the burner. In a somber tone, he said, "Sit down, hon." They walked over and sat at the kitchen table. Stephanie was wide-eyed with concern.

Peter spoke with gravity. "I found out today that Josie was killed by a hit-and-run driver."

"Oh my God!"

"And the young officer that helped me with Darso, the abused child's father, was murdered."

"No!"

He nodded his head and said, "Yes. I met with the district attorney and the chief of police today; they believe Darso was behind both deaths."

Stephanie grabbed Peter's hand. "You're scaring me."

"It gets worse. Darso's a big-time drug dealer who uses young kids to push his drugs."

Stephanie shook her head in disbelief. "What a lowlife."

Peter took a deep breath and exhaled. "In a nutshell, the district attorney and chief of police believe that Darso is capable of anything, and I mean anything. They want us to go into the witness protection program."

Stephanie was stunned. "What if you don't testify?"

"I guess I'm in danger either way. He may want to hedge his bet even if I don't talk."

Peter's eyes begin to fill with tears, angered. "This sucks! I want to testify. I want to put this creep away, but now I've put you and John in danger."

"What about you?"

"Yes, and me too."

"Witness protection means we leave here and come back after the trial?"

"No, there's no coming back. It means name changes, living in a different state. I don't even know if family members can see us again or if I could still continue to practice medicine."

"But if he's convicted, why would we need to hide?"

"Retribution, payback, call it what you will, he's scum."

Stephanie was lost. *"Do we have a choice?"*

"There's two detectives parked out front as we speak … Twenty-four-hour police surveillance for the rest of our lives or some form of that."

"I can't believe this, not to see Mom and Dad, pretending we're somebody we're not. This is the worst!" She broke down crying.

Peter got up from his chair, walked over to Stephanie, and cradled her in his arms. "I know, sweetheart. I know."

There was a prolonged silence, then Stephanie pulled away, looked directly into Peter's eyes, and in a clear voice said, "I'll leave it up to you. Whatever you decide I'll respect and follow … I know you'll make the right choice." She hugged him close. "I love you."

The enormity of her words hung heavy in the air as Peter contemplated their fate.

The hallway was dark as Peter entered. He turned on a small wall sconce that bathed the hallway with a dim, almost candlelit glow. A large cross and a few icons came into view. The largest icon and most dramatic depicted a crucified Christ on the cross with the Virgin Mary weeping at his side. Peter knelt in front of the picture, clasped his hands in prayer, looked up at the figure of Jesus, and poured out his heart. "Lord, have mercy on me and my family. I don't know what to do here. This Darso guy is evil. Do I go with the witness protection, or do I stay and hope the police can protect us? I just don't know, Lord, and so much depends on what I decide. Please, I beg You, give me an answer. I love You. Thank You for all your blessings."

From the hallway, Peter walked into the master bedroom and turned on the light from a small lamp that was located on a table perched between two wingback chairs. He pulled a drawer open from beneath the table, retrieved a well-worn Bible, King James Version, and sat in one of the chairs.

Peter clutched the Bible to his chest and softly said, "Father, I ask in Christ's name, through the power of the Holy Spirit, that You guide me as I open Your book so that I might find the answer to my prayer. Will we be protected if we stay, or should we go into the witness protection program? Please Lord, please let me know."

Peter randomly opened the Bible, and his right thumb alighted on the beginning of a verse. The verse was the ninety-first psalm.

> He that dwelleth in the secret place of the most High shall abide under the shadow of the Almighty.
>
> I will say of the Lord, He is my refuge and my fortress: my God; in him will I trust.
>
> Surely he shall deliver thee from the snare of the fowler, and from the noisome pestilence.
>
> He shall cover thee with his feathers, and under his wings shalt thou trust: his truth shall be thy shield and buckler.
>
> Thou shalt not be afraid for the terror by night; nor for the arrow that flieth by day;
>
> Nor for the pestilence that walketh in darkness; nor for the destruction that wasteth at noonday.
>
> A thousand shall fall at thy side, and ten thousand at thy right hand; but it shall not come nigh thee.

Only with thine eyes shalt thou behold and see the reward of the wicked.

Because thou hast made the LORD, which is my refuge, even the most High, thy habitation;

There shall no evil befall thee, neither shall any plague come nigh thy dwelling.

For he shall give his angels charge over thee, to keep thee in all thy ways.

They shall bear thee up in their hands, lest thou dash thy foot against a stone.

Thou shalt tread upon the lion and adder: the young lion and the dragon shalt thou trample under feet.

Because he hath set his love upon me, therefore will I deliver him: I will set him on high, because he hath known my name.

He shall call upon me, and I will answer him: I will be with him in trouble; I will deliver him, and honor him.

With long life will I satisfy him: and shew him my salvation.

With his eyes wet from tears, Peter prayed, "God, thank You. I am so blessed, thank You." He stood, with one hand still clutched on the Bible; he made a fist with the other and waved it in the air.

"Yes, yes! We stay!" yelled Peter.

# CHAPTER 3

THE OPULENT DEN HAD A DEFINITE MASCULINE TONE WITH ITS DARK mahogany leather chairs, oak wooden floors, and forest green, burgundy, and black plaid wall accents. Phil Darso was watching a football game on a massive state-of-the-art television when Caesar Farintoni entered the room. Caesar was a stocky muscular man who stood five foot, eight, with thinning dark hair and a bulldog face. The two went back a long time, to the old neighborhood in the Bronx. Phil rescued Caesar from drowning back in their teen years and the two were inseparable ever since. Caesar presented Phil with a handful of mail. "Boss, here's the mail. I dumped all the advertising crap," he said.

"Thanks." Phil muted the sound on the TV as he took the envelopes. He laid the letters next to him. "Caesar, sit down." Caesar slid into a chair nearby. "I was checking last month's profits out of East LA. They're down by 5 percent; what's going on?"

"I don't know, boss. The economy is down; there are a lot of guys out of work. That's my guess."

"You think someone's skimming off the top?"

"Not after what you did to BB Smacks. No one's got the 'nads to go against you."

Phil pondered his statement. "Let the network know I want some free samples given out, the good stuff. Start with the junior highs. That's twelve- and thirteen-year-olds, right?"

"Yeah, I think so."

"Go with the coke and ecstasy, and not too much. Just what it takes."

"You got it." Caesar stood. "Do you have anybody taking care of that doctor guy from the hospital?"

"It's done." Phil sat back with a wide grin.

"Same way as the other two?"

"No ... no, that's barbaric. I want it to look like he died of natural causes.

"How are you going to do that?"

"I've hired the Black Stallion."

"The Black Stallion! I thought he was just a rumor."

"Oh no, he's very real."

"That's a hell of a name for a hit man. Why not Dr. Death or the Grim Reaper? The Black Stallion, that's a kid's story."

"Caesar, the problem with you is you've got no imagination. Dr. Death and the Reaper are pro wrestler names. The Black Stallion is special. The horse represents death. This beautiful thoroughbred gallops into your life and when he leaves, your essence, your being, is carried away with him. Now that's class!"

"Whatever you say, boss, but how's he make it look like the guy died naturally?"

"That's the beauty. Using surveillance, he observes and listens to his prey, finds a weakness that he can utilize, and then strikes. Sometimes he'll make it look like an undetected carbon monoxide leak; other times it may be a deadly allergic reaction he's uncovered. He's brilliant. My guess is he has already set up minicameras and sound sensors where this Dr. Kalos lives. From what I've heard, he's a master of all kinds of disciplines. When it comes to science, he's skilled in biology and chemistry. He has top-notch experience in computers, mechanical engineering, cameras, electrical and sound technologies, even makeup. It's been said he did some of the alien makeup on the old *Star Trek* series. If he's faced with a physical confrontation, his talents vary from martial arts to marksmanship, arms, and demolition. The guy's got it all."

"How did you contact him?"

"Even that's first rate. There's this old bookstore in Pasadena called the Bookmark. You walk to the back of the store and on top of a weathered bookshelf, to the far right, is a tattered leather volume titled *The Art of War* by Sun Tzu. This Chinese military genius wrote the ultimate book on fighting strategy. You slip a three-by-five card with the typewritten name of your victim and a work or home address where they can be found."

*"That's it?"*

"That and $50,000 in $100 bills that you put into a large leather-bound book to the left of the Sun Tzu book. The inside of the book is hallowed out for that purpose."

"Fifty thou! Isn't that a little pricey?"

"It's about 10,000 more than I'd pay for a regular hit, but he's never failed, and it always looks like a natural death."

"What's so important about the doc looking like he died of natural causes?"

"It's going to drive Darelli nuts. His only witness dies, and they can't figure out how it happened. The satisfaction of busting that asshole's balls is worth every penny of the ten thou. Ahh, to be a fly on the wall and see the expression on his face when he gets the news, especially when he knows, in his gut, that I had something to do with it."

"Yeah, I can see how that would get him riled. How'd you find out about this Stallion guy?

"Like I'm telling you, someone told me."

Caesar shook his head in disbelief. "I'm blown away." He started to get up. "I'm going to get a beer. Do you want one?"

"No, but I'll take a glass of merlot."

"You got it, boss."

Caesar arose and headed toward the kitchen. As he approached the archway to the hall, his eyes alighted on an end table that displayed a small, framed photograph, and immediately a cloud of memories engulfed him.

The photograph was of Jimmy, and he had taken it. They had visited the zoo that day, just the two of them. He had never married or fathered a child that he knew of. Jimmy was like a son to him and the only person on earth who had ever uttered the words "I love you" to him. Caesar's mother had deserted him at birth, and he was left to be raised by his father. Later his dad remarried, to a woman who resented his presence. Hale, his father, was a mean-spirited drunk who despised his lot in life as a janitor. He took his anger out on those closest to him, namely yours truly. Caesar had left home and was living on the streets by the age of fifteen.

Caesar smiled to himself when he thought of how Jimmy called him "Unkie CeCe." Jimmy had trouble pronouncing Caesar. He also loved the way Jimmy's soft little hand fit into his thick, oversized paw. What he missed most, however, was the way Jimmy would take his small hands and cup his face, stare into his eyes, and say, "I love you, Unkie CeCe." The sorrow was like a dagger thrust deep into his heart. How that boy possessed so much love when he was so brutally treated by Phil was nothing short of miraculous. Phil's weapon of choice was a two-inch-wide leather belt he would use at the slightest provocation, but he also used his open hand and fists when incensed. Suddenly hairs on the back of his neck stirred as the memory of that night enveloped him.

Caesar had not been in the room when Jimmy was beaten so unmercifully, but he could hear Jimmy's screams from the kitchen. Caesar had learned early on not to interfere with Phil when he was disciplining his son. He had tried once to intervene and had taken two vicious body shots from Phil that laid him out. He had long ago figured out that Phil was a psychopath. Darso's mastery of martial arts and his sheer strength made for a lethal combination that was no match for Caesar, even with his considerable street fighting experience.

Once Caesar had entered the living room, the visual of that poor child with his bloodied face lying on the floor groaning was a recollection he would never forget. He despised himself for his cowardice and what he had become, a high-paid lackey. His bringing up the doctor to Darso was his way of showing Phil that he was looking out for his interests and that he could still be trusted. He was such a wuss. Actually, he admired the doctor. At least he stood up for what he believed, even though it was going to get him killed.

Was the money really worth it? It was a couple thou a week, tax free. What did it buy him? He had a great-looking car and sex with drop-dead gorgeous women. He adored attractive women who had all the curves. Sometimes he had two go down on him. He liked that, but it was expensive, and after he shot his wad, there was that feeling he couldn't explain. When he shut his eyes, a dark emptiness permeated his very being. The lyrics from an old sixties song came to mind. 'Is that all there is?" No woman had ever told him, "I love you," only a small, abused, little boy who he had abandoned when he was most needed. Caesar wasn't sure he believed in a God, but somehow Jimmy was proof that He existed. The little boy's pure goodness and sacrificial love spoke of a higher presence. Caesar knew evil; his name was Phil Darso.

—m—

The study was sleek with a modern motif. Black and mandarin red were the accent colors with stainless steel and silver the connecting color tones. Metallic and black hues integrated the desk, shelves, and chairs together in harmony. The computer, sound, and visual equipment were state-of-the-art. A huge TV hung over the desk, which acted as the main monitor. Surround sound speakers and additional smaller monitors were tastefully displayed nearby. All the electronic equipment was controlled through a powerful bank of servers. There was a clarity of style that exuded from this habitat.

It was his eyes that you first noticed. They had that deep blue color of the Aegean Sea. When he was out of the house, he mostly wore brown contacts. That came with the territory for Clint Wolf—part of his persona as the Black Stallion. Brown hair, rock-hard jawline, a nose that was wide at the bridge from a break that was never set right, and wide, full lips came together in a face that was rugged yet handsome. Combined with his lean, muscular body, this was not a guy you wanted to meet in a dark alley. Not so much because his physical presence was so menacing, but there was something in his eyes; there was icy coldness exuding a crazed calm that chilled one to the bone.

Clint looked up at the large screen where six images of six different rooms were projected. He pressed a numeral on his keyboard and the screen displayed the living room where Peter, Stephanie, and John were watching television. This part of his profession he truly enjoyed was getting to know his prey. This was the research part of his job. No hit man he knew of went to lengths he did to study his victims, but then no hit man ever guaranteed that the hit would look like death from natural causes. Looking at the Kalos family, he was impressed by how attractive they all were. He pressed another button on the keyboard and the camera zoomed in for a closer shot. He reflected on the day he had installed the cameras. He had posed as a heavyset, black, gas meter inspector. He had cased the house for two weeks and knew their routine, entering from the back of the house when it was empty. The cameras, sound equipment, and tools were all completely stored in his fat pads. The setup was finished in a record two hours.

Thankfully he had been hired before the police became involved in the case. Cameras and sound equipment were also installed in both Kalos cars. He had completed that on the evening of the same day he had installed the other electronics. It was another instance of too much junk in the garage, so the cars were parked out front in the driveway. They had made it easy. There were no complications, the job was textbook, and the reception from all systems was excellent. Clint made sure the cameras and voice monitors in both the house and cars were hidden well.

The Kalos family was watching a *Sponge Bob* cartoon. The little boy was seated on Peter's lap, his head resting on his father's chest. Stephanie was snuggled up shoulder to shoulder with Peter. John had his Spider-Man pajama top on and a white diaper for the bottom.

Clint couldn't remember ever sitting on his father's lap. His father deserted the family when he was seven. The only memory of his father was a face contorted in anger yelling and calling him stupid. Of course, there were also the open-handed slaps to the face.

Back at the monitor, he saw John slip out of his father's lap and walk toward the television. "John, where are you going?" said Peter.

The little boy slowed his progress toward the set. "Don't even think about going behind the television," continued Peter.

John slowed his movement again.

"We've told you we don't want you going behind there; there are electrical wires. It's very dangerous."

John took a quick look at his parents and then darted behind the television.

"John!" yelled Peter as he rose from the couch and headed toward the set. "You know better."

Suddenly John bolted from behind the television and yelled, "I do it, Daddy. Bad boy! Bad boy!" As John ran yelling, "Bad boy! Bad boy!" he began spanking his own bottom.

Stephanie and Peter couldn't help but laugh at their child.

Clint produced a wide grin as he witnessed John's antics.

Peter shaking his head and with a smile said, "You're right. You are a bad boy. If you ever do that again, I'll help you out with that spanking. Understood?"

"Yes, Daddy. I sorry," John said apologetically.

Peter scooped him up in his arms and held him close to his chest. "It's time to go to bed, son." He turned to Stephanie. "Coming up for prayers?"

"Of course," she replied. The three exited the living room.

The camera in John's room revealed Peter, Stephanie, and John on their knees in prayer at the side of the bed. John was in the middle, his arms intertwined with Stephanie and Peter. Their individual hands clasped together skyward in the classic position of prayer. "And God bless Mommy and Daddy. I love You, Jesus, amen," said John.

"Let's do our cross," Peter directed as he, Stephanie, and John made the sign of the cross with their hands.

"OK, pumpkin, get under the covers," encouraged Stephanie. John scrambled under the blankets. Peter stood, leaned over, and kissed John's forehead. "I love you." Stephanie kissed him on the lips, "Good night, sweetie. Love you."

"I love you, Mommy and Daddy," said John.

Before Peter turned off the light, he added, "Happy dreams."

The honey-coated slice of life that Clint had witnessed on the monitor was totally alien to him. He had not been brought up in a loving family or taught to believe in God. In those early years when his father and mother were together, he could only remember the punches, the beatings, and the hateful, harsh, venomous words being spoken. He had heard his father call his mother a bitch so often that before he knew what it meant, he thought it was a nickname. That was until he used it once while talking to her. Pain is a very quick teacher. You wouldn't think someone could get that angry over one word.

Actually, he was pleased when his father left. His mother belittled him, but nowhere near as much as his father had, and she rarely struck him. She was so tired when she came home from the ten-hour days at the factory that she pretty much left him alone. Most of his lessons came from the street. She catered more to his younger sister, Ann, who was mentally a little slow and very needy; consequently, she got more attention, and there's something to be said about the mother/daughter relationship. Once he enlisted into the military, he never looked back. He hadn't seen or talked to his mother or sister in over a decade, and that was just fine with him.

When it came to God, he just didn't buy it. You created your own destiny. There was no omnipotent being looking over him. Clint was master of his existence. Life was a commodity in his line of work. Being a hit man was empowering; control over life and death was its own kind of high. However, there were those moments when a golden-hued sunset at the beach made him wonder how it all came about.

He pressed a number on the keyboard and Peter and Stephanie were framed in the bedroom monitor. Peter removed his shirt as Stephanie walked over to the dresser and pulled out some sleepwear then proceeded to the bathroom. Peter removed his shoes, socks, and pants. After storing them in a nearby closet, he pulled down the covers on the bed. The door to the bathroom opened and Stephanie appeared in a knockout negligee that revealed all her glorious curves. "Wow," said Peter smiling. "You're such a babe!"

"You like?" Stephanie replied as she turned, doing a slow 360.

"Even though you're only going to be wearing that for two seconds, yeah."

Stephanie walked over to Peter, engulfed him in her arms, and kissed him passionately. As she pulled away, she said, "Let's say our prayers."

"*Now?*"

"Yes, now," she said smiling.

The two dropped to their knees at the side of the bed and intertwined their arms in prayer. Peter began. "Thanks, Lord, for everything. I love You. Amen."

"I want you too, but come on."

"I don't have to recite the liturgy, do I?"

Stephanie gave him that look. Peter began anew. "Father, Son, Holy Spirit, my God, thank You for all Your many blessings. Thanks for all the angels who are protecting us. Please continue to watch over and bless the people I love: all my friends and family. I surrender them unto You, Lord. And Lord, thank You for my son and this amazing, beautiful woman at my side, who I love so much. Who am I that I should be so blessed? Forgive me for my sins, and have mercy on my soul. I ask this in Christ's name. Love You. Amen."

He turned his head toward Stephanie. "All right, sweetheart, go ahead."

"Same for me, Lord."

"No … no, none of this 'same for me.'"

She snuggled her cheek into his neck. "Oh, be quite." She then wrapped her arms around Peter, and he responded by lustfully kissing her.

Clint turned off the monitor and stared at the black screen. He had never been a watcher. There was something about observing a couple making love that made him feel uncomfortable. Even watching pornos elicited that same feeling of weakness. He preferred performing when it came to sex rather than peering at others as they consummated the act.

What he found enthralling was the relationship that Peter and Stephanie exhibited. They sincerely seemed to care about one another—a sharp departure from the relationship his parents displayed, but it was the regard that they held for God that truly blew him away. To kneel down before anyone or anything was beyond his scope, and to profess love for this person or entity was ludicrous. They seemed sincere though. Love, he thought, was such a cheap word; however, their bond seemed to define the concept. He found that troubling, especially when he thought of the relationships he had encountered.

Sex was more animalistic for him. There had not been any complaints, but then he was not one to make a woman feel comfortable enough to share intimate thoughts. Almost all of his sexual partners were strippers. He found them attractive, and likewise, they usually had the hots for him. It was easy. The bar scene was time-consuming and presented intrinsic complications. Woman he met there would eventually guide the conversation toward his employment status. That was one of the reasons he never drank. No person he had ever known knew what he did for a living, and he was going to keep it that way. "Sales" was his initial response when asked, and then he would move the conversation in a different direction. Table dancers were effortless, and that worked for him. They never gave him the third degree.

There was one girl though, Stacy; she was different. She was a waitress at a mom-and-pop diner near where he lived. Stacy knew him by name, Rod. Well, one of his names.

She was beautiful. Not a glamorous kind of beauty, but she had that "no need for makeup" good looks. Her long, golden hair, piercing blue eyes, and strong jawline accented a petite nose and rosy cheeks. He would arrive at the restaurant near the end of her shift, and she would sit and talk to him after she signed out. Stacy made him smile. She was young, bright, self-assured, and vibrant. Her dream was to own a restaurant, a bistro. The menu would be eclectic: burgers and steaks for the meat lovers and major vegetarian fair for patrons who prefer to pet animals rather than eat them.

He had never had sex with her. He had never gone out with her. There was quality about her that was so real. He found it hard to lie to her, but of course he did. That was one of the reasons he never asked her out. She had purity, and he did not want to destroy that. Life would thrust upon her soon enough its dark side, but for now the glass was half full. Maybe with her, in an alternate universe, he might have found the kind of love that Peter and Stephanie possessed. It was getting late, and thoughts of finding true love made him feel uneasy. In this universe, he was a hit man. That was his reality.

—⁂—

Clint was standing in front of the monitor in his office, viewing the Kaloses while chomping on half a sandwich. The other half of the sandwich was on a plate nearby. Peter and his son, John, were sitting on the floor in the living room, playing with a wooden train set that was arranged before them. A phone ringing could be heard in the distance.

Stephanie entered the room while holding a cell phone. She handed it to Peter, saying, "It's the hospital."

Peter took the phone and said, "This is Dr. Kalos."

John pulled on the sleeve of his shirt and shouted, "Daddy play!"

Peter stood so he could concentrate on the call. Talking into the cell phone, he said, "Yes, I understand."

Stephanie addressed John's concern by commenting, "Honey, Daddy's working."

"Be sure to give him plenty of fluids," responded Peter to the caller as he paced the floor.

"I working too," said John as he stood, put his hand to his ear, and began to pace, mimicking his father.

"Yes, that'll work," replied Peter to his caller.

"Yes, that work," said John.

"Yes," answered Peter to his caller.

"Yes," retorted John, talking into his hand while he continued to pace.

"Yes, that's good," acknowledged Peter to his respondent on the phone. He walked the carpet oblivious to his son's corresponding actions.

"Yes, that good," echoed John while he continued to impersonate Peter's pacing.

Stephanie laughed at John's caricature of his father.

Clint found himself smiling at John's performance; and it felt good. Playing the consummate professional killer role grew old sometimes. He had to be careful though. He couldn't start liking this family. That had never happened before, and caring could make him slip up. He defined himself by his craft. Yes, it was a craft involving many diverse skills and he was proud of what he had made of himself. *Proud* struck him as a strange word to use in this context, but it was the only word that expressed how he felt. This was his life.

# CHAPTER 4

Nick, Darrel, Peter, and John were seated at the kitchen table. The two detectives were dressed in city worker coveralls. Stephanie was standing next to the stove.

"Nick, Darrel do either of you want these last two pieces of bacon?" asked Steph. Nick was the first to pipe up. "If nobody else wants it, I'll take it." On hearing Nick's words, Darrel responded, "Dr. K, you're going to have to bring a set of those paddles home for Nick and give him a charge when his arteries jam."

"Hey … hey, it's protein. There's a whole diet based on meat. Right, Doc?" countered Nick.

"Yes, the Atkins diet," said Peter.

"That diet doesn't include the two pounds of hash browns you've eaten or the three pieces of toast you've scarfed up," replied Darrel.

"Picky, picky, picky," Nick responded with a smile.

"Doc, what's on the agenda for today?" asked Darrel.

"No big plans. I thought I'd stick around here and …"

"We're shopping for a jacket today. Your navy one is stained and has holes. Kerns is having a sale," Steph said, cutting him off.

"You heard the lady. We're going shopping," conceded Peter.

"That works for me. We can get out of these da-d-darn … jumpsuits," said Nick, catching himself.

Clint was seated in front of his large monitor, observing the scene. He looked at his watch, turned off the visual displays, and exited.

—⁓—

Kerns was an upscale department store. The men's department bespoke sophistication from its dark, paneled mahogany walls to its wooden hangers and racks of fine clothing. The displays featured riding gear seemingly aimed at the polo crowd but actually zeroing in on the wannabes. Even though Darrel was dressed in a suit and Nick wore a sport coat combination, they seemed out of place gazing at neatly displayed cabinets lined with pants and suits. Stephanie with John in hand was inspecting a bar of leather coats while Peter examined wool jackets on another rack next to the leathers.

An odd-looking professor type sauntered into the area. He had a pointy nose, hair parted on the side, sporting rimless glasses, and wearing a Brooks Brothers' argyle vest with a club pattern bowtie. This was one of Clint's favorite disguises. The nose tip and slight chin implant were a snap to apply, and he enjoyed the collegiate look even though he had never been to college. He went immediately over to the dress shirts and perused the broadcloth button-downs.

Nick was the first to spot Clint and moved tactfully near him, drawing little attention. Darrel was close behind but came in from the opposite direction. Clint could feel their eyes x-raying his body. They were looking for any abnormal bulge that might spell danger. He was not packing— at least nothing obvious like a gun. His five-inch throwing knife was concealed in his belt. It was attached to the buckle. It was his invention and could be drawn and thrown in less than a second. From as far as thirty feet, he was lethal with it.

These two guys were good, he thought. Old school. They'd have checked out a silver-haired, eighty-year-old grandmother with the same intensity. They would be on him like flies on shit until he left the department. Now that he thought about it, he wasn't particularly fond of that analogy given he was the *shit* part of it. They would be on him like bees on honey. Better!

Stephanie, turning to Peter, said, "Sweetheart, come look at these leather coats." As he moved toward the rack, a silver-haired salesman dressed in a dark suit and tie approached.

Darrel stepped in front of him and the two collided. "I am so sorry," cajoled Darrel as he frisked the salesman discretely. Clint was impressed. These guys had it down. He would have to be careful. No slip-ups. He'd have to stay one step ahead of the detectives.

"Let me unlock those for you so you can get a better look," said the salesman as he moved toward the tiered rack of leathers.

"Thank you," said Steph.

The salesman unlocked the jackets, and Stephanie pulled a coat from the group. "I don't know, hon. Leathers are expensive," stated Peter.

"They're half-off this weekend with the sale," the salesman interjected.

"It's still a lot of money and definitely not in the budget," commented Peter as he examined the sales tag.

"You never spoil yourself. Try it on," Steph prodded as she held up the coat. Peter slipped on the leather. The jacket was car coat length. "It is soft, feels real good," said Peter as he began to walk with an exaggerated strut.

"It looks great on you, sweetheart, even with the attitude," interjected Steph.

"The leather is of top quality," the salesman added.

"I like it, Daddy," chimed in John.

"Well then, we'll just have to get it," said Peter with a smile.

"Yea!" yelled John.

—⚒—

Peter entered the kitchen and was greeted by Stephanie, John, Darrel, and Nick. The detectives were wearing sport coats with accompanying dress shirts and ties. They were seated at the kitchen table sipping coffee. Stephanie, who stood by the sink, was the first to speak. "Morning, sweetheart. You up for eggs this morning?"

"Thanks, hon, but I think I'll go with a bagel and cream cheese today," replied Peter.

John chimed in, "Happy morning."

Peter responded, "Happy morning to you, champ."

He walked over and kissed John on the forehead.

Nick entered the conversation. "Doc, you're going to notice a real distinct difference in your two cars. We thought it would be best for security reasons to darken the windows of both the Saab and the Volvo."

"When he says darken, he means black out," interjected Darrel.

"It sounds like my rides will be lookin' big in the hood," said Peter.

"As hip as you're going to get with a Volvo and Subaru," Darrel countered.

"That hurt, Darrel. Did I get new rims?" Peter continued with a smile.

"That would be a no, but nice try, Doc," said Nick with a grin.

"Hey, it was worth a shot," remarked Peter. He looked at his watch. "It's getting about that time," he continued.

Darrel and Nick stood up and said their farewells to Steph and John, then waited for Peter outside. Steph left the kitchen and emerged with Peter's new black leather coat. She helped him put it on. "You look so handsome."

"All right now, I'm going to get a swell head if you keep that up."

"Well, you do." Steph gave him a kiss. "I love you."

"I love you too, but you spoil me too much."

A week had passed since the detectives dropped their disguises as city workers. The white van was still nearby, and a crew monitored the cameras that surrounded the Kalos home twenty-four/seven, but Darrel and Nick were on the day shift as detectives and were attired as such. The department had wisely decided to heck with what the neighbors thought. Peter and his family needed to be protected and if it was obvious, so be it.

Darrel had finished checking under the Volvo using a mirror attached to a rod when Peter approached. The trio entered the car. Nick sat in the driver's seat and Darrel accompanied Peter to the back as they headed for the hospital.

Nick's voice invaded the solitude. "Doc, we didn't mention this while in the house where Stephanie could overhear, but just so you know, the darkened glass in both cars is bulletproof."

Darrel interjected, "And they also inserted steel plates in all four doors on the two cars, just in case."

"Oh … OK … Thanks," responded Peter. The danger of his situation was beginning to dawn on him.

The Volvo continued its journey through the sleepy suburban community toward the city and hospital.

Nick's voice broke the momentary silence. "Doc, I wanted to get your medical opinion on the health of my mother. She's eighty-four, been losing some weight recently, has stomach pain, she gets confused, is urinating a lot, and her eyesight is getting sketchy."

"Has she been in to see a doctor recently?" said Peter.

"You know the routine. She's had tests done, but I think she's falling under the radar … Know what I mean?"

"I get off at six. If you want to swing by her place after work, I'd be happy to examine her."

"You would do that for me?"

"In a heartbeat, Nick. You're putting your life on the line for me and my family. That's the least I can do. I'll call Steph and let her know I'm going to be late."

"Thanks. I just hope it's not cancer."

"From what you've described to me, it sounds like it could be the early stages of diabetes, and with medication, you might see a dramatic improvement in her condition."

"God, I hope you're right, Doc."

"I'll say a prayer for her too."

"Appreciate that," replied Nick, a little teary-eyed.

The car pressed onward through the city when Nick came to a stop for a red light. To the right of the Volvo, sitting on a bench, was a haggard homeless man. The temperature that morning was about forty-five degrees and this dirty disheveled man had pulled his lightweight jacket tight over his head to keep warm as he shivered violently. Both Darrel and Peter noticed the man and his plight. Darrel was the first to speak. "Poor guy, he should be in one of the shelters."

"Nick, could you unlock the back door on my side, please?" asked Peter.

"Sure, no problem," replied Nick as he unlocked the door.

Before Darrel could react, Peter had opened the car door and walked over to the transient, taken off his leather coat, and wrapped it around the man. He then quickly returned to the car and slammed the door. "OK, we can go," said Peter.

Nick was halfway out of the car with his revolver in hand as he blurted out, "What's going on?"

"It's all right, Nick. There's no danger," Darrel responded.

"What happened?"

"The doc just had a little house call. That's all."

Nick, still a tad confused, returned to the driver's seat and continued on to the hospital. Peter stared off to his right, taking in the scenery. Darrel gazed intently at the man sitting next to him, overwhelmed by what he had just witnessed.

Darrel was not the only one to be astounded by this act of charity. Clint was perplexed by what he observed on the monitor. Why had Peter done that? He had really wanted that coat. Clint did not like loose ends and this episode that he had beheld was disturbing.

Nick's mother, Sally, had a small bungalow home in Glendale. It was cozy with a traditional flair. She had that "let's put some kind of framed picture in any open space available on the wall syndrome." Consequently, there were twenty or so framed pictures of Nick from the age of six months to forty years. That in itself was a little scary. Sally had silver-gray hair, a petite figure, and a twinkle in her brown eyes. This was a good day for her; she was coherent and in good spirits.

She had lived alone since the death of his father five years earlier, and that was area of concern for Nick. He had seriously been thinking of giving up his apartment and moving in with her. It wasn't like the apartment was this big love nest. Although that was exactly what he was wishing for when he rented it. He was hoping that he might get lucky with one of the women at the local pub nearby, but that hadn't happened yet. Hope springs eternal. So it was his routine now to stop by after work and see how Mom was doing.

When Nick, Peter, and Darrel entered the house, Sally struggled to stand.

"Mom, I'd like you to meet Dr. Kalos, and of course you know Darrel," said Nick.

"What a pleasant surprise. Nicky said he was bringing his friends over, but a doctor! How nice," replied Sally.

After the introductions were made, Sally returned to her seat and preceded to make small talk. "Nicky, it looks like you're losing weight."

"Really! I have been eating more salads," Nick proudly announced. Darrel, who was sitting across the room next to Peter, whispered to him, "That's Nick speak for he had lettuce and tomatoes on his bacon cheeseburger." Peter smiled. He enjoyed being one of the guys and felt honored that Nick and Darrel had so quickly included him in their inner circle. They made a good team, and the love and respect they had for each other was evident.

He was also touched by the affection and esteem that Nick showed toward his mother. Here was this barrel of a man being so gentle and caring. The way he took her hand as he guided her through the house caused Peter to ponder on the ironies of life. It seemed to him that when parents reached the sunset years in their lives, the child/parent relationship reversed. The child became the adult and the parent became the child. It was the eternal circle of life.

Peter engaged Sally in conversation, eventually getting to the topic of her health. Once she felt comfortable with him, he eased his way into the exam, which seemed to confirm his initial suspicions of diabetes. She would need to come in for tests, but he was sure they would find her sugar to be high. The small platter of candy she had on the coffee table would have to go. He told Nick to pick up some sugarless candy for her. That way she wouldn't feel deprived, and it would help her to make the transition to a sugar-free diet. Nick, of course, was thankful beyond words, and Sally was relieved to know the reason for her physical ailments.

The three headed back to Peter's house. It had been a long day, but they were in good spirits.

—ɯ—

The routine at the hospital had changed for Peter. He was now permanently shadowed by Darrel and Nick while at the hospital. The staff had adapted well to the change. The detectives were appropriate; they would allow Peter privacy with patients, but only after they were screened. Even then, the boys were always in close proximity in case of a threat.

Clint was cognizant of the fact that the hospital was probably his best chance for a natural kill. The proximity of drugs and anesthesia and the deadly diseases that were found there made it ideal for his purposes. He had forged certificates and letters of recommendation and the phone contacts he provided were linked to associates who could falsely vouch for him. He was "Pano," the Filipino orderly. The black, dyed hair, the almond-eyed makeup technique he used, and his strong grasp and talent for dialects made for the perfect disguise. He could have faked being a doctor, but a new doctor on staff would have drawn suspicion. Clint would just have to deal with the stigma associated with orderlies.

He continued to be awed by Darrel and Nick. They bought his Pano disguise, but only to a point. The detectives deep down held to the belief that not all was as it seemed. They would've in a heartbeat blown his ass away if they truly thought he was an assassin, dialect or no dialect.

He had worked at the hospital for over three weeks, starting a week before Nick and Darrel came on duty. Clint had been able to sidestep some of the less palatable jobs like changing bedpans by giving misinformation to subordinates, but eventually Clint had to empty a bedpan; in life as in hospitals, shit happened!

—⁂—

Peter was in the hospital filling out charts as Darrel and Nick stood nearby. Sally was there also, for the test that Peter had recommended. Nick's concentration was not the usual 100 percent. This was his mom, and he was an only child. Their relationship has always been close. He could talk to her about almost anything. For example, she knew what a muscle car was, and in her younger years, she was able to change the oil in the family car herself. Sally knew her way around a hammer too. When he was thirteen, the two of them had erected a white picket fence in the front of the house. It was only recently that it had to be taken down because the wood had rotted. His father, who he respected and loved, had worked in the local airplane factory. He worked the afternoon shift and would take all the overtime he could get. His dad was a kind, able provider; however, he was rarely at home. It was only after his father retired that they truly bonded.

His mother's health had improved dramatically since Peter's visit. Medication and the absence of sugar in her diet seemingly had done the trick, but he was still concerned. Sally was in great spirits and all smiles.

Loretta was the nurse assisting her. She was an attractive, petite brunette with ample breasts, large, beautiful hazel eyes, and a winning personality. Sally and Loretta hit it off instantly and pretty much had talked nonstop since she had entered the hospital. This pleased Nick because he was secretly enticed by Loretta. Peter had made the introductions a week ago, and she had given Nick an inviting smile. He did not want to read into it because he knew he was not the heartthrob kind of guy that women desired, but still there was something in that smile that said she was interested. He wondered if Loretta's fascination with his mother was partly due to interest in him. He didn't have to wait long.

"Nicky, come over here!" yelled his mother.

"Mom, don't call me Nicky. It's Nick at work," said Nick as he walked over to the two women.

"This is Loretta. Isn't she beautiful? And she's single," stated Sally.

Nick smiled shyly. "We've met … and yes, she is beautiful." Nick usually didn't respond with such candor and self-assurance when talking to women.

"Thank you, and I like Nicky. It's cute," Loretta responded with a smile.

"Yeah, but I'm not a cute kind of guy" was Nick's comeback.

Sally pinched Nick's leg. "Ask her out for a cup of coffee or something, son."

"Ouch! Mom, stop it," said Nick. He then turned to Loretta. "That's actually a good suggestion though. Would you like to go for coffee or get a bite to eat sometime?"

Loretta hesitated, and Nick could feel his blood pressure skyrocketing.

"Yes, I'd like that," replied Loretta.

Nick was ecstatic. True, his mother had forced the issue, and he wasn't proud of that, but he'd be going out with Loretta, and she was a babe!

# CHAPTER 5

IT WAS SUNDAY AND THE KALOS FAMILY WENT TO CHURCH ON THE Sabbath. They attended St. Sophia Cathedral, the golden jewel of the Greek Orthodox community, located on the corner of Normandy and Pico in Los Angeles. The church was a sumptuous feast for the eyes. A cornucopia of gold leaf, crystal chandeliers, imported marble, dramatic mosaics, and exquisite frescos that depicted the life of Christ. Peter was dressed in a charcoal-gray suit and textured white shirt that was accented by a tasteful blue and yellow tie. His son, John, was sort of a "Mini Me" version of Peter wearing a small dark suit with a white shirt and a clip-on tie similar to his father's. Stephanie was beautifully attired in a navy two-piece outfit. Unlike the custom of most churches where the dress was casual, Peter felt you should wear your finest in the house of God. Only the best for the Lord, and his family followed in kind. Most of the congregation was dressed up as well.

Richard, Jim, and Sam were the detectives on assignment that day. They were all affable and highly competent. Peter had been a member of St. Sophia's for over ten years and a current member of the parish council. Steph was a convert originally from the Episcopal church.

Peter and Stephanie had met at a bus stop. That's where their love story began. She was new to California and was without wheels at that time.

Peter was an undergraduate, and his car was in the shop for repairs. There was an empty seat next to Steph and Peter immediately secured it. His opening words to her were a little less than brilliant. "Looks like it could rain." There were two small wispy clouds in the California sky that summer day. Peter was so enthralled by her beauty; he was lucky he could speak. Steph should have said, "Are you crazy? It's summertime in Southern California." Instead, she said, "Could be," and a beautiful romance began. They eventually discovered an old sixties song by the Holly's called "Bus Stop," and that became their anthem. Now they were married with a young child. Funny how life works.

As the family and the detectives approached the entrance to the church, two male parish council members acting as greeters approached. Greetings, hugs, and the traditional Christian kiss of love on the cheek were exchanged by all. Clint, a few steps behind the detectives, slipped quickly into the church virtually unnoticed. He had attached a scraggly beard, and with his brown contacts and bushy eyebrows, he was once more another face in the crowd. Dressed in a loose-fitting, faded, brown suit with an open-collar shirt, his attire blended in as well.

Clint entered the narthex of the church, which is a small room, sort of a preentrance to the main seating area of the church. There were assorted candles for sale and a circular structure with sand to insert the candles. The idea was to light the candle, implant it into the sand, and say a silent prayer. Clint bought a small thin candle, donating a dollar for it. He lit it from another burning candle then placed it into the sand. He had bought the candle to follow the church custom and avoid attention. A prayer was out of the question, but Stacy, his unattainable waitress, came to mind; somehow her memory seemed appropriate. He then approached the two giant wood doors that led to the main pew area of the cathedral where an usher stood by, temporarily preventing people from entering while waiting for an appropriate moment in the liturgy that would not disturb the solemnity.

As he stood there waiting to enter, the Kalos family came in with the detectives surrounding them. It seemed like people came out of the woodwork to greet them. At least five people surrounded them, and again the greetings and kissing started. This put the detectives on high alert, but they handled the situation deftly, scrutinizing the parishioners quickly and ruling out possible danger. Clint was surprised by all the kissing. It was obvious the affection the congregation had for Peter and his family. They bought and lit their candles, then proceeded to a nearby icon that Steph and Peter kissed, and surprisingly John kissed also. The reverence the Kalos family had for this God of theirs was truly remarkable thought Clint.

The usher finally opened the main door and Clint entered, choosing a pew near the back on the left-hand side. When Peter with his family and the detectives entered, it had been predetermined where they would sit. Their location was the last pew on the right-hand side, near the end of the pew. Richard and Jim sat on either side of the family. Sam stood guard behind the pew. The department had discussed putting a metal detector at the entrance of the church to scan all who entered, but Peter absolutely refused to accept that proposal. He felt it would have defiled the sanctity of God's house and knew he had legions of angels on guard unknown to the police force.

The church service began. The Greek Orthodox liturgy was arguably the most beautiful church service ever created. The words written by St. John Chrysostom hundreds of years ago were as relevant and uplifting that day as the day they were written. The robes worn by the priests were an artwork in themselves. Brilliant colored brocade cloth was accented by gleaming gold trim and all the different layers worn bore historical significance dating back to the time of the disciples. The eight altar boys were resplendent also, but to a lesser extent. The choir singing Byzantine hymns, the dazzling beauty of interior edifice, transported the parishioner into a supernatural realm. It was the Orthodox belief that the congregation was joined by the angelic presence of heaven and God Himself during the ceremony.

Clint had never been inside a church; what he was experiencing was complete sensory overload. He was impressed by the devoutness of the congregation and the long lines taking communion. What drove these people to believe in a force that they could not see and to worship this entity in such a unique fashion? This puzzled him.

The service eventually came to an end and Father Costa, the charismatic priest and dean of the cathedral, climbed the steps to the elevated podium. He began his homily, "Christ is in our midst," and was joined by the rest of the congregation when he followed with the words "He is and always shall be … The gospel reading today is the parable of the prodigal son: Luke 16:11. It's a story that takes place during biblical times. That's when gas was about thirty cents a gallon." Father Costa's comment elicited laughter from the congregation.

He continued. "This passage is truly profound and one of my favorites, because in this one parable the whole message of the Bible is revealed … A father had two sons; his youngest son requested his inheritance ahead of time. You can imagine how the conversation went. 'Dad, I like the farm and everything, but I'm bored, and I know if you gave me my inheritance now, I could double it in the city.' I'm sure the father thought, *The kid can't balance his bank account, and now he wants me to give him a small fortune. Grrrrrreat.*

"Fathers are a unique breed though. Do you put a damper on the optimism of youth? Do you tell your son you don't believe in his hopes and dreams? The father gave his son the money. The son went to the big city and was bombarded by its sights and sounds. A sign on a tavern catches his eye. 'Babylonian table dancers—no cover charge.' He decides to go in, just to see the sort of girls he should stay away from. He buys a round of drinks for some new acquaintances, and so begins the downward spiral of riotous living.

"Before he knows it, he's broke and has to hire out as a servant to a pig farmer. A famine hits the area, and his food ration is cut to the point where the husks he's feeding the pigs start to look like a vegan delight. He is struck with the realization that the servants at his father's farm not only eat well but have food to spare, and here he is starving to death. The son decides to return home and admit to his father his mistakes and ask if he will hire him on as a servant. The boy heads for home.

"When he's a few miles from the farm, his father recognizes his son's distinctive stride and runs toward him, arms open wide, tears streaming down his cheeks. He finally reaches the boy and gives his son a big hug and kisses him. To quote the parable, the son says, 'I have sinned against heaven, and in thy sight, and am no more worthy to be called thy son.' The father tells the servants to bring his son the best robe and he put that on him, along with a ring for his hand and shoes for his feet. He told his kitchen staff to kill a fatted calf and to prepare it for a feast. A joyous celebration ensued.

"Later that day, the oldest son came in from the fields. He asked one of the servants what all the fuss was about. The servant answered, 'Your brothers come home safe and sound, so your father has killed the fatted calf and has thrown a party for him.' The older brother became angry and refused to go in and join the festivities. The father heard about this and went after him. He found his eldest and said, 'Why aren't you coming to the party so we can celebrate your brother's return?' The son answered, 'All these years I've done everything you asked me to and never said no to you, but you never killed a calf for me so I could celebrate with my friends. Junior there takes your money, leaves town, blows it on prostitutes and you throw him a party. Maybe it's just me, but that seems way unfair.'

"The father replied, 'Yes, you've been the good son and you'll always be in my heart, and all I have is yours, but it's good that we celebrate your brother's return.' Quoting again, 'For this thy brother was dead, and is alive again; and was lost, and is found.'

"This simple parable, with a few of my embellishments, expresses the vastness and immensity of God's love for us like no other in the Bible. The Father in the story represents God and the younger son represents us, and the son's actions, our sinful nature. God wants to embrace us all in His outstretched arms and for us to join Him in His heavenly kingdom for eternity. He doesn't want to lose a single soul. When one of us who has rejected Him returns, realizing his or her transgressions and acknowledges them, God is quick to forgive and opens his arms wide like the father did in the parable. He will hug and kiss us, welcome us home, and love us forever.

It's the lost souls that the Lord cherishes most on their return. Like a father who has lost his son and then sees him returning in the distance and orders a celebration. So it will be with us as God and the entire heavenly host celebrates our return. Amen."

Father Costa did the sign of the cross. The rest of the congregation followed his lead, also giving the sign of the cross.

Clint thought, *If I had blown my father's money on prostitutes, he would have whipped my ass from one side of the state to the other.* That father in the story wasn't anybody he had ever known. What he did find very interesting though was that they had "table dancers" in biblical times, the strip bar had no cover charge, and he would have liked to top off his gas tank back then. He smiled to himself.

# CHAPTER 6

PETER WAS GUARDED BY NICK AND DARREL DURING THE DAY AT THE hospital. It was Stephanie and John who needed to be protected while Peter was out of the house. The department thought a team made up of two women might prove appealing to Steph. The responsibility fell to Cathy Murdock and Brenda Foresight, two veteran officers. They had been partners for eight years. Cathy was the older of the two at thirty-nine, with brown curly hair, attractive natural features, and tall at five foot, nine inches. Brenda, thirty-three years old, had a more petite frame weighing 105 pounds, standing five foot five inches tall. She had long, straight, blonde hair, sparkling blue eyes, and was appealing in her own right. Cathy was more down to earth and pragmatic while Brenda had a lighthearted spirit and reacted on the spur of the moment.

It was Monday and Cathy had a case of the blues. She had her long, curly, brown hair cut short over the weekend. The beautician had convinced her to cut it, saying, "It will be easy to take care of and make you look younger." Well, it didn't make her look younger; it made her look fatter. She had put on ten pounds in the last six months that for some reason she just couldn't lose. (Of course, her addiction to ice cream didn't help.) She always gained weight in her stomach. Thank God she had big boobs because at least they made her look proportional. With her long, cascading, curly locks, she had not noticed the extra weight showing on her face; however, now with the shorter cut she felt a strong resemblance to a chipmunk. She was not looking forward to the comments she would get at the department.

At the other end of the mood spectrum was Brenda, who was just getting back from a four-day fun spree in Colorado. The Sundance Film Festival was in full swing, and Brenda was able to attend screenings and a party. She couldn't wait to get to the office and tell everyone about it.

Darrel Nick, Cathy, and Brenda were in the department simultaneously that morning before they went to relieve the night shift at the Kalos residence. Beside Nick and Darrel, there were five other male officers in the area as Brenda and Cathy entered.

Nick was the first to speak. "If it isn't the PMS squad gracing us with their presence."

"Warsinski, with your double-digit IQ, I'm sure the fact that a squad is made up of more than two people never entered your mind."

"I'm sorry. The PMS duo!"

Captain Slater, a hard-nosed disciplinarian, was in earshot of the conversation and yelled out, "Warsinski, get in here!"

Nick walked into the captain's office. "Yes, sir?"

Slater purposely left the door to his office open so everyone could hear. "Warsinski, you know better than to refer to your fellow officers as the PMS squad. It's sexist, demeaning, borders on hate speech, and far below the standards we set here in the department."

"Do you know what PMS means, sir?" Nick retorted.

"Aw … a … something to do with menstrual, hell, I don't know," said the captain flustered.

"This is what it means to me, sir, when I use those initials: *providing meaningful service.* I'm complimenting these fine officers, but heck, if a guy can't say something nice, forget it."

"Warsinski, enough of your bullshit. Get out of my office."

There were chuckles and smiles from the male officers as Nick exited the office.

"You're not bringing me down, Nick. Guys, I went to the Sundance

Film Festival when I was in Colorado. Guess who I saw. Matt Damon, and I got his autograph. See," said an elated Brenda as she passed the napkin with the autograph.

The guys, unenthused, passed the napkin around quickly.

"Was Pamela Anderson there?" Nick asked.

"No, this wasn't a Playmate reunion," said Brenda.

"Don't mind them. This is cool," interjected Cathy, who was now holding the napkin.

"I just noticed your hair. It's so cute. Sorry I didn't say something earlier," replied Brenda.

"Do you really like it? It's easy to take care of," said Cathy.

"The long hair was sexy … You know, Tom Brady has hair that's easy to take care of too," added Nick.

"It's … it's good," said another male officer.

"You guys are all alike. You'll lie through your teeth to get into some girls' panties, but you can't say something nice to save your soul. It's a new look for me," stated Cathy.

"Yes, it is," said Nick, ending the conversation.

Darrel was in the driver's seat, Nick and Peter in back as the three headed home. It had been a busy day at the hospital, and it felt good to get off his feet, reflected Peter. The detectives had been unusually quiet; the twelve-hour shifts were taking their toll.

They stopped for a traffic light at an intersection that was about a mile from the house. The signal turned green, and Darrel proceeded forward slowly, entering the intersection. Suddenly, there was a thundering crash, and the deafening sound of twisting metal could be heard. Nick instinctively grabbed Peter, flinging him over his lap, his seat belt almost pulling out from its anchors. Peter's Volvo was hit broadside and pushed sideways thirty feet. Miraculously the car didn't flip before coming to a stop. Time came to a standstill.

Eventually there was movement inside the Volvo. Darrel was first out of the car with gun drawn. He unlocked the back passenger seat doors and scoured the landscape for a possible attack. Nick and Peter were stirring. After some maneuvering, Nick was able to unlock Peter's safety belt, and Darrel was able to pull him out of the car with his free hand. Nick glanced to his right where Peter had been seated. Twelve inches from his face was a large steel plate filling the space Peter had previously occupied. Nick slowly disentangled himself from his seat belt and exited the car. The bulletproof glass window had not shattered but was dislodged from the impact and gotten sheared on one side, causing tiny glass shards to explode off the edge into the air, cutting Nick's face and hands. Peter had fared much better. Most of the flying glass had landed on his back with a few small chards ending up in his hair.

"Stay crouched down behind the door. How are you guys feeling?" asked Darrel, his gun zeroed in on the car that had struck them.

"I feel like I got hit by a car," said Nick with a smile.

"I feel fine," Peter added.

"Nick, can you cover me? I'm going to check out the other car," stated Darrel.

Nick drew his gun. "I've got your back, bud. Go easy."

Peter was huddled behind the back fender of the car. Nick was standing, his revolver resting on the hood of the Volvo. Darrel, with both hands on his automatic, slowly approached the offending car. He moved toward the driver's side window, which was open. He heard groaning from inside the car and finally got close enough to see the perpetrator. The man was elderly, probably in his late seventies. The distinctive smell of gin pervaded the air. Blood trickled from a cut near his scalp, but otherwise he seemed fine. Darrel opened the driver side door and quickly frisked the senior.

"It's OK, guys. Drunk driver!" yelled Darrel.

People had started to congregate near the accident site.

"I'm going to keep Peter over here near the car. There's too many people gathering around," remarked Nick.

"Yeah, stay there. I'll call it in," said Darrel.

Clint had viewed the complete accident on his monitor. The minicamera and mike had caught image and sound. "That was gnarly," said Clint to himself. The crash sounds and the camera showing the scenery moving sideways for thirty feet was awesome. It was cutting-edge cinematography, and the camera and mike were still functioning fine. He could see the steel plate jetting up from Peter's seat and realized that Nick, by pulling Peter over his lap, had saved his life. Damn, that drunken fart had almost done the job for him. Nothing goes that easy in his line of work, but the idea of using an unknowing participant to do the kill intrigued him.

—◊—

Steph was in the kitchen cooking lasagna; Cathy and Brenda were keeping her company. Brenda sat next to John at the kitchen table, helping him color in animal figures with crayons. Cathy was jotting down directions and ingredients to Stephanie's lasagna recipe. The detectives both agreed this assignment ranked as their number one favorite. They both adored Stephanie. John was an added pleasure. They were like sisters when they were together. They talked about men, dating, diets, family, world affairs; almost any topic was open for discussion, and Steph was knowledgeable on most everything. She also brought a mother's perspective to an issue, which was an added bonus. With John the detectives could enjoy the presence of a child, without long-term responsibility. It was a perfect arrangement. Another unexpected bonus was that Steph would eventually improve on Cathy's short haircut. By using two barrettes and pulling back the hair on the sides, Steph was able to narrow the look of Cathy's face, which enabled her to finally accept the short hair and even like it.

Cathy's department cell phone rang, and she answered. "Officer Murdock speaking ... Yes ... Yes, I understand. I'll communicate that message. Thanks, goodbye."

"Is anything wrong?" asked a worried-looking Stephanie.

"There was a ... car accident, but everyone's fine. No one got hurt. Understand?"

"Peter's OK? You're sure?"

"He's fine, they're just going to be running a little late," Cathy responded.

Tears welled up in Stephanie's eyes and ran down her cheeks. Brenda went over to her and gave her a hug. "It's going to be all right, Steph."

—⁂—

The boys entered through the kitchen doorway. Stephanie, John, Cathy, and Brenda were all seated at the kitchen table. Peter and Darrel didn't have a scratch on them, but Nick's face and hands showed the seriousness of what had happened. Nick had two Band-Aids on either cheek, but there were numerous small red marks indicative of fresh wounds all over his face. He also had Band-Aids and small cuts on his hands. When tearstained Steph saw Nick, she leaped from her seat into Peter's arms. John, taking her example, slipped out of his seat and ran to his father, wrapping his arms around his right leg. "Daddy! Daddy!"

Steph blurted out, "I'll go into a witness protection program … I'll live in a cave … I'll do anything that will keep you safe, as long as I'm with you." Then she began kissing his cheek and neck. This was a personal intimate family moment. Darrel motioned with a hand gesture to the other detectives to adjourn to the living room. They exited silently. All had been emotionally touched by Steph's reaction and realized the enormity of their mission to protect this family.

Once they were out of earshot of the kitchen, Nick was the first to speak. "Cath, you know last week I was just teasing. You bust the chops of the people you care about. You could shave your head and still be sexier than 90 percent of the woman in California."

"Just when I truly thought you had reached Neanderthal status, you go and say something like that … You're a lovable jerk. You know that?" replied Cathy.

"Thanks … I think," Nick responded with a smile.

Clint was watching this *Andy Griffith* moment and said to himself, "Let's all sing 'Kumbaya.' Give me a break."

What was truly troubling was Stephanie's remark about the witness protection program. If the Kalos family went immediately into the program, he was screwed. There was no setup time for a natural kill, and a conventional hit was not what had been paid for.

Peter held Stephanie without speaking. He dropped one hand down, massaging the hair of his son. He realized he would never tell Stephanie that Nick had saved his life that day. He whispered, "I love you, sweetheart. It's going to be OK. God is watching over us."

—⚏—

Darrel walked up the steps to his mother's house. The house was a small cottage-style home, cream colored with white shutters, and had a white metal front door. He had the key but didn't want to scare her with his surprise presence. Darrel rang the doorbell and his mother, Marcy, came. Marcy was fifty-three years old, charming, and attractive. Opening the door, she said, "Darrel, I'm so glad you came."

"What's up, Mom?"

"It's your brother. He's out of control."

Darrel entered the house, closing the door behind him.

"Is he here?"

"No, he left about an hour ago. Said he'd be back around nine."

"What's been going on?"

Marcy sat on the sofa in the living room. Darrel settled into an easy chair across from her.

"Darrel you wouldn't believe the language he uses. He swears at me, says terrible things. He put a lock on his bedroom door. He's not going to school. Two days ago, Jeff fell asleep on the sofa here. He slept for twenty hours … twenty hours!"

"Relax, Mom. I'm here … I'll take care of it."

"It seems like it all went downhill after your father died."

"I know, Mom. I'm going to check out Jeff's room."

"His room's locked."

"I'm a detective. I'll get in."

"Would you like a cup of coffee?"

"That would be great."

Marcy departed for the kitchen. Darrel headed for Jeff's bedroom. Darrel tried the doorknob, and it was locked. The locking doorknob that his twelve-year-old brother had installed was inexpensive and not even installed correctly, fitting loosely inside its encasement. Darrel was able slip past the lock using a credit card.

Darrel felt sorry for his brother. His mother had given birth to Jeff when she was forty, which made him twelve years older. Jeff was never at an age where they could truly hang out together as brothers. He had always assumed a parental role in his life. Darrel had taught him to swim, play baseball and basketball, and ride a bike, the experiences a father provided. His father had died of a heart attack at age forty-seven. Jeff had just turned five. Darrel had tried to be a replacement, but he was busy working his way up the ranks in the police department. There's a lot to be said for a father's love. He had felt it with Bill, his father. Bill was a patrol officer, a sergeant, who was not afraid to tell his children he loved them. He was always there with kind words and praise for his sons. Psychologists say the foundation of a child is set by the age of five. That wasn't the case for Jeff. He reacted to his father's death with anger and tantrums. He was basically a great kid with a winning smile and natural athleticism. His choice of friends was questionable, and he had not been drawn to God and the church like Darrel. Jesus Christ and the church were the backbone and the driving force in Darrel's life. He had peace of mind and direction. Darrel prayed for his brother continually, but he needed to do more.

He stepped into Jeff's room and was immediately hit with the funky odor of unwashed clothes. The room was a mess. Clothes were strewn everywhere. The bed was unmade. Dresser drawers half-open with garments hanging out. Fast-food cups and bags were scattered about. He wasn't sure where to start. He had to think like a twelve-year-old. Under the mattress or under the bed is where Jeff would store his contraband. He checked first under the mattress and found nothing. Checking under the bed, he found sports equipment, CDs, schoolbooks, and a lunch box-size metal box. The container was locked.

Using the screwdriver attachment from his Swiss Army knife, he was able to pry the box open. Inside was a large plastic bag of pills; from their shape and color, Darrel surmised they were ecstasy. What he found more disturbing was the smaller bag of white powder and a miniature pipe with a metal bowl. Darrel had spent three weeks in narcotics, and they taught him to decipher the major drugs by taste. He put his pinky finger to his tongue then into the bag and tasted the powder. "He couldn't be!" said Darrel to himself. He had hoped it was coke, but this was worse. Jeff was smoking heroin! A veil of despair engulfed Darrel. Why hadn't he seen this coming? The huge bag full of ecstasy alluded to the fact that Jeff was dealing. That was bad enough, but the heroin and the pipe meant he was freebasing. Was he already an addict? This was Darrel's watch; how had he missed this? He was only twelve. God help us.

Enough of the self-recrimination. He needed to act! A clear vision, direction, a plan—that was what he needed. The Doc could give him some medical insight into the addiction aspect of this. Peter had known what to do with Nick's mom. Maybe he would have some answers for Jeff. Darrel took the bag of ecstasy and the heroin for evidence, shoving them into his sport coat pockets, then replaced the empty metal box to its original location.

Marcy was near hysteric when he told her that Jeff was doing drugs. His mother didn't ask for specifics as to the kind, thank God. He assured her that he would find a solution to this insanity, but he needed to go and would return before nine to deal with Jeff. Darrel got on his cell phone to Nick explaining briefly what had happened and asked Nick to join him at the Kalos home.

—m—

Darrel arrived at Peter's house around six o'clock that evening. Steph was in the living room reading to John when Darrel entered. He made his greetings then joined Nick, Peter, Cathy, and Brenda, who were at the kitchen table discussing what little information Nick had provided about Jeff's situation. Darrel joined them at the table and filled them in on the details.

"Let's get the drugs you found down to the lab and make a positive ID. I'll get one of the guys in the truck to take it over," said Cathy.

"That's makes sense. Here …" Darrel handed the contraband to Cathy. He continued. "I just can't believe my twelve-year-old brother is using heroin!"

"As surprising as this might sound, the success rate for overcoming heroin is far greater than overcoming an addiction to crack cocaine," stated Peter.

"Get out," said Darrel incredulously.

"Methadone therapy is still effective, and they have new drugs now like Naltrexone that blocks the receptors in the brain, preventing the user from getting high off the heroin. If we get your brother into a treatment program with competent supervision, there's a very good chance for success."

"Doc's the best," said Nick, beaming.

"You are a godsend," agreed Darrel.

"What needs to be done next?" interjected Brenda.

"There's a place called Dawn's Light. It's a federally funded program that is highly regarded, but we'll need to do an intervention, and Cathy's correct. We need to confirm the nature of the drugs," added Peter.

"Doc, will you help us do an intervention?" said Darrel with pleading eyes.

"Of course," replied Peter.

"Thanks. I appreciate it," added Darrel.

Peter's in-depth knowledge of drug-related problems was garnered from his four-year residency in the navy. As part of his rotation, he had tutored under one of the founding fathers of addiction medicine, Commander Preston Hall. The service may seem a strange place to find drug addiction, but really no one, no group, is immune from its far-reaching tentacles. His background experience in addictions acquired in the navy had been invaluable to him in his own practice. Drugs are an equal-opportunity destroyer, and what Jeff was going through was a vivid reminder of its power.

Clint had observed the kitchen strategy meeting and found it hard to fathom that so many were concerned about this twelve-year-old boy. If he had been discovered at twelve doing heroin, his father would have beat him senseless and then stolen his stash. The concern and camaraderie between the detectives and Peter were unreal. Their first instinct was not to beat the hell out of the kid but help him get past the obstacle. In all his past jobs and all the endless hours he had spent in surveillance on past kills, he had never come across a man like Peter. With his previous hits, there had always been a major character flaw, an Achilles' heel, but when it came to Peter, he could find none. It was still early in the game though; he would find a crack in the facade. There was always a fatal weakness, and he would find it and use it.

—◊—

Darrel, Peter, and Nick confronted Jeff that night. Surprisingly Jeff did not explode in rage but quietly acquiesced to the demands of the group and even admitted to his involvement as a dealer. After some legal arrangements and psychiatric counseling, Jeff was accepted into the Dawn's Light program.

—◊—

It was a Saturday night and the first date for Nick and Loretta. Nick had agonized over where to take her. A movie would mean two hours of silence, which seemed ridiculous when a guy was trying to find out all he can about the girl he was with. He was an excellent pool player, but a pool hall seemed tacky, especially for a first date. Giuseppe's provided the perfect solution. It was his favorite restaurant, and the Italian cuisine was excellent. It was a sad state of affairs that he could rank almost every well-known restaurant in the valley. The reality was he never cooked. Cooking seemed like a lot of energy for a product he could purchase elsewhere with no cleanup. His landlord at his apartment complex, knowing his culinary lifestyle, almost took the stove out of his unit to put into another but found it was too wide. It was true he didn't cook, but to take somebody's stove away because of that was brutal.

There were four restaurants where they knew him by name. It was like being Norm and walking into Cheers. He would keep that fact low-key when talking to Loretta. The words "chow hound" were not the first two cognitive thoughts he wanted her to imagine when she pictured him. "Big dick" was what he was hoping for, but that was not an option so he would probably have to settle for "nice guy" or, the worst-case scenario, "great personality." At the very least, he just hoped she liked him because he thought Loretta was hot.

That fact became evident when she answered the door to her condo. Loretta was wearing a cream-colored, turtleneck, cotton sweater with brown, leather, low-rise denim pants. The way her body filled out the sweater and jeans started to arouse him, but it was the cream-colored beret that she wore jauntily askew that drove him up the wall. Loretta was by far the most attractive woman he ever dated. He had always believed that the "Lorettas" of the world were out of his class, but here he was with this dream girl. He had purchased a new sport coat specifically for the occasion. It was a dark, rust, microsuede, two-button model. Even he had to admit it looked great on his stocky body. He was going to wear the coat with tan khakis and a tan shirt, but the salesman had wisely pressured him into buying a black shirt and corresponding black slacks. Admittedly he was clueless when it came to fashion, but even he knew his outfit was chic.

"I like your jacket. Is that suede?" she said as her hand caressed the sleeve of his coat. Her first words were a compliment. Yes, this woman definitely had class.

"It's microsuede. Thanks for noticing. You look great yourself. I especially like the beret," Nick remarked. So far so good; he hadn't stuck his foot in his mouth yet.

"You're sweet. I'm a bit of a nut when it comes to hats. I love them."

"If the beret is any indication, I can see why."

Their conversation turned toward decorating with Nick complimenting Loretta on her sense of style. She then proceeded to give Nick the nickel tour of the place. He was impressed by how easy it was to talk to her. Since she met Sally, they talked about their mothers and family relationships. Besides being beautiful, Loretta was bright, caring, and witty.

They eventually made it to Giuseppe's, where they had a great meal and continued to talk about everything from sports to art. The date was going better than he had hoped, but she told him little about her past relationships. It had been a long while since he had been on a date, so Nick wrote it off as par for the course.

The two and half hours they spent at the restaurant flew by. Nick felt himself falling hard for Loretta. Her beautiful golden-brown eyes enthralled him, but it was the smile that touched his heart. The ultimate highlight of the evening, however, was that this woman seemed to genuinely like him.

The overriding thought on Nick's mind on the drive home was the good-night kiss. He had been careful to grab a mint at the restaurant. Garlic breath could kill the perfect moment, and he wanted their first intimate encounter to go well. They were within two blocks of her residence and Loretta was making a point about the breadsticks at Giuseppe's, saying they needed to be added to the government's list of addictive substances when her complete mood changed.

"You can let me out here," she said hurriedly.

"We're a block away from the entrance to your condo. What kind of guy would I be if I didn't at least walk you to the door?" replied Nick.

"Oh … all right."

*There goes the romantic good-night kiss,* Nick reflected. He pulled up to the front of her building and accompanied her to the door. She gave him a quick kiss on the cheek. "Thanks, Nick. I had a great time." She looked up and off into the distance then turned toward the front entrance.

"Loretta, is something wrong?" Nick asked.

Tears welled up in her eyes. "Can you come in?"

"Sure."

The two entered the living room, where Loretta fell into his arms, her body quivering.

"Hold me, Nick. Just hold me."

"What's going on, babe?" Nick said softly.

Loretta gave a big sigh. "My ex-boyfriend was waiting outside in his car tonight." Nick turned his body toward the door ready to leave and confront the jerk. "I'll kick the bastard's ass then have him tossed in jail for stalking."

"He's gone. I saw him drive away."

"Has he hurt you or threatened to hurt you?"

"Yes."

"Do you have a restraining order on him?"

"Not yet. I was hoping I wouldn't have to."

"It's time. I'll help you with that."

"You're sweet." She looked up into his eyes, her head moving slowly toward his; they kissed. Nick slipped his tongue between her moist lips, and he could feel the passion that *fire down below* ignited. He was going to take his shot. "Would you like me to stay?" he said tenderly.

"Yes, I'd like that. If you don't mind sleeping on the sofa … I like you Nick, but it is our first date."

The old "I like you Nick, but you're sleeping on the couch line." It was a classic, but then he never liked the classics.

"I understand. That's fine," he said, lying through his teeth, to quote Cathy.

She prepared the sofa for sleeping with clean sheets, a cover, and a pillow. They said their good-nights, another kiss, less romantic, was exchanged, and Loretta exited for her bedroom. Nick stripped down to his boxers, folding his sport coat, pants, and shirt neatly on an ottoman nearby.

In the dark, his arms folded behind his head, Nick stared at the ceiling that was highlighted by the glow coming from the streetlights outside. All in all, it had been a great first date, and the thought of sex at a future time was OK. He wanted this to be a relationship that lasted.

The light in the hall went on and Loretta appeared wearing black satin pajamas. She walked over and stood by the side of the sofa.

"Nick, are you awake?" she asked.

"Oh yeah."

"If you wouldn't mind just snuggling, and I mean *just snuggling*, you can sleep in my bed.

"You like the right or the left side?"

She took his hand and led him into the subdued light of the bedroom. Loretta's beautiful body was bursting out of those satin pajamas, and the throbbing sword inside his under shorts was trying to burst out as well. Loretta couldn't help but notice. "You're going to have to do something about that," she said, smiling as she pointed to his organ that was bulging inside his trunks.

"Down, Willy, down!" he yelled. They laughed simultaneously.

"Gives new meaning to the words 'Free Willy," Loretta said with a smile.

The two eventually got under the covers with Loretta resting her head on Nick's barrel chest. His arms engulfed her in a cocoonlike embrace. Nick could feel her quivering fear subside as she found safety and comfort in his arms. She fell into a deep sleep and began to snore. It was the cutest little feminine snore, and he knew at that moment he would protect her with his life if it came to that. He wasn't much of a praying man, except when in extreme danger, but he said a little prayer, a thank-you prayer for this gift from heaven.

—⁂—

Stephanie's parents had arrived Saturday morning from Michigan and Steph was thrilled to see them. Richard and Jim, part of the weekend contingent, accompanied Steph and John to the airport to pick them up. Grant, her father, was a distinguished yet rugged-looking man with thick, silver hair, a close-cropped beard, and a Hemingway air about him. He was two years retired from his foreman's position at a steel plant in Detroit. Her mother, Gayle, a former teacher, radiated a loving spirit and had an elegant beauty about her. Steph's parents had been apprised of the current state of affairs before their arrival.

Gayle and Steph were in the living room with John, who was trying on clothes that Gayle had brought from Michigan. The toddler clothes were purchased for the California lifestyle and climate. There were three Hawaiian shirts with matching shorts and sandals. For headwear, John could choose from casual baseball caps to short-brim cotton hats. The little boy was in his element being a young "clothes horse" in the making.

"I like this one, Grandma, with the fishies," said John as he pointed to one of the porpoises on his shirt.

"I'm happy to hear that, sweetheart. You look so handsome," stated Gayle with a proud smile.

"Mom, it's hard to believe you found all these great Hawaiian outfits in Michigan of all places," Steph commented.

"Honey, we're up north, but it's not Alaska. We do get warm weather," replied a grinning Gayle.

Grant and Peter were in the backyard barbecuing. The detectives Sam and Richard were on guard duty patrolling the wall perimeter. Both had binoculars and only allowed Peter and Grant in the backyard when they were sure that there was not a high point location with a clear shot. Peter was standing next to a barbecue grill and cooking steaks. Grant was at his side, with a beer in hand.

"It seems strange to be out here with guards only a few feet away. Have you gotten used to all the security?" Grant asked.

"It's part of what you accept if you're going to put a guy like Darso away … And actually we've become close friends with the detectives who work the day shift during the week. So there have been some pluses."

"Do you think the police can truly protect you if this guy really tries to hurt you?"

"You know, Dad, I believe there are heavenly powers working around the clock too, so we're covered."

"What do you mean heavenly powers?"

"I believe angels are looking out for our safety."

"Peter, I know you're a religious man and I respect that about you, but this is the safety of the family that's at stake."

"I've prayed on it, and if you don't believe the Lord can protect you, then what's the use of believing in an all-powerful God?"

"I wish I had your faith, son." Grant put his hand on Peter's shoulder. "Peter, I've never told you this, but I couldn't have asked for a better son-in-law than you. You're an excellent father, loving husband, good provider, and man of principle and character. Your strong belief in God leaves me in awe."

"I love you too, Dad."

"See ... that kind of stuff. You're not afraid to say, 'I love you.' I like that."

"I better not burn your steak then, or I could really blow it here," Peter said with a smile.

"And a decent sense of humor. Not great, but decent."

*"Easy!"*

They both chuckled.

Clint had been privy to this scene with the use of one of the outdoor minicameras and accompanying sound hookup. *So he has angels watching over him. That's a first,* Clint thought. Should he be listening for a harp solo or the flutter of wings? This was a little much, though they did have a decent baseball team this year. *Butta boom, butta bing.*

*Where is the kink in this guy's armor?* There was one thing he said that did make sense. If you're going to believe in a God that is all-powerful, then by definition, he should be able to do anything. Even prevent him from accomplishing his natural kill, but then Clint didn't believe in a God so *bring it on. Bring it on.*

—⚏—

Phil Darso was seated at his elegantly styled desk in the study or "library room" as he liked to call it. The walls were covered in mahogany with the shelves made of the same wood. Every book was hard covered and leather bound with twenty-four-karat gold leafing. All the classics were there, from *Oliver Twist* to Shakespeare. Phil had never actually read any of them, but they sure did look good. Well, he had gotten halfway through *Moby Dick*. That had to count for something.

He had earned his master's degree in the streets, from the schools of hard knocks. His Machiavellian philosophy toward life with a little Darwinism thrown in for good measure had suited him well. He was a multimillionaire from the drug trade alone. That didn't include his real estate holdings. He didn't believe in the stock market. He invested in things that were tangible. He bought in Santa Monica and Westwood before they were hip places to go. Phil had also invested in property along the Strand in Manhattan Beach when houses were going for the unbelievable sum of $500,000. He was a shrewd businessman and was admired by the investment elite. Phil had a natural aptitude for numbers that held him in good stead with his drug empire. He kept all the figures in his head and was so astute he could remember transactions from the previous year. Phil kept daily tabs on all aspects of his drug dealings; in a cash and carry business like drugs, that's what it took to stay on top.

Caesar entered the study for their morning meeting. Ten o'clock was the appointed hour for the daily rundown. Caesar held in his hand what looked like a grocery list. It was in actuality a list of the dealers and the money they had garnered for the day. For example, bananas represented the Compton dealer, tomatoes signified the East LA contingent, and so on. Phil scoured the list, nodding his head in approval at the figures.

"I don't see Blueberries on the list. What's going on with the Inglewood kid?" said Phil.

"There was a problem. The kids' brother turned out to be a detective in the force. He found his stash and turned him in. They already put the runt into a recovery program," stated Caesar.

"Damn it … Didn't anyone know about this kid's brother?"

"You know how it is, boss; we don't exactly get resumes on these kids."

"Yeah, yeah, I know."

"When he gets out of the program and is back on the street, do you want the guys to rough him up?"

"I don't want this kid's brother, the detective, to get the cops riled and start a vendetta against us."

"Then what do you want done?"

Darso contemplated his predicament. "When you get lemons, you make lemonade. When this kid gets out of the program, we'll threaten him, scare the shit out of him. Tell him if he doesn't give up some names from the recovery group, he's dead meat. From that, we'll have a list of kids we already know are addicted. Use one of them as his replacement, dealing the drugs, and the rest are new clients … win, win."

"That's brilliant, boss!"

"It's just good business. I could go for some raw sex. Get some hookers over here. You know, the regulars. Make it three if you want one."

"Sure, boss, will do."

Caesar turned and left the room. He would call and get the girls, but only the two for Darso. Since Jimmy's death, his desire for sex had waned. The fact that he did not intervene to help, and that life had continued on like nothing happened, bothered him. His role as a glorified lackey had not changed, and his gratuitous behavior toward Phil was starting to grate on him internally. He felt emasculated and could feel the anger boiling up inside, but he had a call to make. Phil did not like to be kept waiting.

—◆◆◆—

The pool hall was upscale with forest green and black plaid carpeting, dark, wood-toned walls, and state-of-the-art pool tables. It was Nick and Loretta's fourth official date. Nick had helped Loretta get the restraining order on her ex-boyfriend Dale. It had been served two weeks earlier. There had been some hang up calls and one threatening "I'm going to get you" message. All the calls had originated from untraceable cell phones, so it was difficult to pin it directly to Dale. Nick was sleeping at Loretta's condo on a regular basis, but there was no intimate sex; a lot of kissing though and she was a great kisser. Their relationship had truly blossomed, growing from a friendship to a profound, heartfelt union.

Loretta filled in the backstory on Dale. They had met at the fitness club she frequented. He fancied himself a bodybuilder and had a better than average physique. Dale was charming when he wanted to be, but that charm veiled his true nature as a controlling, self-centered egotist. In the three weeks they had dated, she had never had sexual relations with him. Once Loretta had a glimpse of the "real" Dale, she refused to see him. On their last date, she spurned his sexual advances and he had gotten physically abusive, painfully twisting her arm almost to the breaking point. She only avoided further abuse because they were outside and onlookers were present. Dale apologized profusely about the incident, swearing it would never happen again, but Loretta, undeterred, quit answering his calls. At that point, he went into stalking mode.

Nick tried to act as if everything was copasetic that night, but his senses were on high alert. He was sure they had been followed to the pool hall. Part of him hoped that Dale would come out of the shadows and confront him. Nick wanted this stalking issue settled. He was concerned about Loretta and the profile that she provided in regard to Dale made him believe a restraining order would not stop him.

It was Loretta's turn at the pool table. They were playing stripes and solids. Nick had sunk three of her solid balls before missing his fourth shot. On her turn, Loretta with careful precision proceeded to clear the table sinking what seemed impossible shots.

Nick was the first to speak. "Please tell me your father was a pool player and you had a table in the rec room."

"Read 'em and weep!" was her reply as she raised her fist in victory.

"Since 'read 'em and weep' is a card term, that would be a no."

"I'm a natural."

"Naturally lucky … or the end of the world as we know it is here."

"You can't stand that you were spanked by a woman."

"That's not true. I would actually like to be spanked by a woman. It's the losing at pool I hate."

"Watch it!"

"I am watching it, and what I see, I like," Nick said with a smile.

"Enough of that! Want another game?"

"Rack 'em. I'll get us some more beers."

Nick walked over to the bar at the other end of the room. There was a huge mirror spanning the wall above the bar. Nick ordered two beers, one regular and one light beer. Or as he liked to say, "one leaded and one unleaded." The bartender walked away to fetch the beers when Nick looked back at Loretta in the reflection of the mirror. A tall muscular man approached her, grabbing her arm. Nick swiveled his body around and headed back toward her.

"If you don't want to be carried out of here, you better let go of the lady!" Nick yelled as he moved forward.

"You think you're tough." Dale grabbed a pool stick that was leaning against the table and began waving it. "I'll shove this up your ass."

"Now you shouldn't have gone and said that," Nick replied as he continued walking forward. He passed by a pool table and grabbed three balls.

"You know what they say … One." Nick threw the first pool ball, hitting Dale square on the forehead. Dale dropped the stick and fell to his knees in pain, grabbing his forehead. "Ahhh!" Dale screamed in pain.

"Ouch! Now that's going to leave mark," Nick said. Then he threw another pool ball at Dale while blurting out the word "Two."

There were four men in close proximity to Nick who grinned and chuckled at his "leave a mark" line.

His pitch hit Dale on the right shoulder, forcing him backward to the floor. Dale whimpered loudly, "Ow!" Dale clenched his shoulder with his free hand and moved his body into a prenatal position, still with one hand on his forehead.

Nick was only a few yards away by this time when he yelled, *"Three strikes you're out in the old ball game." His throw blasted Dale on his leg, in the calf area.

"Please stop. I'm sorry … Please," Dale pleaded.

"Dang, you must not have done enough crunches at the gym today," Nick chided.

Nick had been a pitcher in Little League and learned early on if you hit two or three players with fastballs at the beginning of the game, few batters were willing to hover over the plate. He had won more than a few games using that strategy. Though he didn't have a great knack for pitching strikes, he was sure good at connecting with the batters. Ah yes, the lessons of Little League.

Loretta was all over Nick hugging and kissing him. A half hour after calling the department, Dale was hauled away for violating the restraining order that had been placed on him.

Nick became a hero in the pool hall. Witnesses congratulated him and asked about his pitching prowess. Nick was happy to regale them with stories from his Little League days. By the end of the evening, however, the word going around the joint was that Nick was an ex-pitcher from the majors. No one was sure how that rumor got started. Little League, major league, hey they were both leagues, weren't they? Free drinks were provided courtesy of the management. The four men, who had stood close by, after praising Nick, joined the couple playing pool. The incident with Dale turned what was shaping up to be a sleepy night at the pool hall into exciting water cooler fodder for the patrons, and a good time was had by all, except for Dale of course.

—⁜—

They took a Lyft car back to the condo. Nick set a limit of two beers whenever he was driving, and he had far exceeded that number. Loretta had tipped a few more than was typical for her, but the relief of knowing Dale was put away was cause for celebration. The euphoria from the evening and the alcohol left the couple feeling a warm yearning for each other.

Loretta typically went into her master bathroom to undress and change into her pajamas, but this night was different. She walked into the bedroom with Nick following close behind and turned on a small lamp located on the dresser that bathed the room in a soft golden hue. Loretta then turned to face Nick, smiled coyly, and began to unbutton her blouse. This was done with a lingering sensuality; it was a slow striptease. After the blouse fell to the floor, the bra, her pants, and her thong underwear followed. Nick loved thong panties, or "butt floss undies" as he liked to refer to them. Loretta stood nude before him. Her body was glorious.

He quickly unbuttoned his shirt and threw it to the floor. He pulled Loretta toward him, her warm breasts pressed against his chest. He could feel the surge of passion running through his body as he kissed her.

—⧟—

Nick and Loretta were lying in bed enwrapped in each other's arms, covered by a sheet from the waist down. Their bodies glistened with sweat.

"Nick, that was incredible," whispered Loretta.

"For me too," said Nick, winded.

He wanted to tell her more, to tell her that he loved her, but was it too soon? Was he just reacting to the euphoria of the moment? Would she respond in kind? No, he wasn't going to tell Loretta that he loved her, at least not yet. What he did say was "Loretta, I'm so glad I met you." Talk about corny! Why did he open his big mouth?

"I'm glad I met you too. You're such a sweetheart." She then kissed him on the cheek.

*Well, sometimes corny is OK,* he thought. Nick could feel the veil of sleep engulf him and did not fight the urge.

—⧟—

*Dawn's Light lived up to its reputation,* Darrel thought as he walked down the hallway toward Jeff's room. The facility was clean, the staff friendly and the recovering occupants respectful. He approached Jeff's cubical with trepidation. Would his brother be angry and combative once he had time to reflect on the circumstances that brought him here? Would he focus on the fact that Darrel had turned him in? Darrel prayed, "Please, Lord, soften his heart toward me." He reached room 232, took a deep breath, and released his pent-up fears with a great exhale. He knocked on the door.

The door opened and Jeff greeted him with a smile. "Hey bro, how's it going?

Darrel smiled back. "Great. How about you?" They exchanged the casual handshake of the hood.

"Just hangin' … Sit down." Jeff motioned to a chair across from the bed. Darrel eased into the seat. Jeff sat on the bed.

"Are you doing OK here?" Darrel asked.

"Yeah, they give you stuff for the withdrawals. It hasn't been that bad, and we get a lot of counseling."

"To be honest with you, bro, I thought you were going to be pissed at me for turnin' you in."

"I was for a while, but in therapy I found out that a lot of my anger was because of Dad … his dying so young and all. The psych guy said I have abandonment issues."

"You know he loved you."

"Yeah, I remember him telling me."

"That was the great thing about Pop. He wasn't afraid to tell you he cared."

"I know. I talked to Mom yesterday and apologized for all the crap I put her through."

"She was happy to hear from you, huh?"

"Yeah, she was cool, but I really messed up this time, didn't I?"

"We all go through our valleys, bro."

Almost instantly tears began to flow down Jeff's face. "You don't think I disappointed Dad too much, do you?"

Darrel got up from his chair, sat next to his brother, and put his arm around his shoulder. "Bro, Dad's love was unconditional." Jeff turned and hugged Darrel tightly.

"I'm sorry," he said while sobbing. "I'm sorry."

Darrel's eyes welled up with tears. "I know. I know," Darrel soothed.

"Thanks for being there when Pop died."

"You're my brother. I love you. That's what brothers do."

Darrel released his grip on Jeff.

"I love you too, bro. We're like a couple of schoolgirls here, bawlin' our eyes out," Jeff responded.

"That's all right. It feels good to let it out."

It did feel good. Darrel could almost feel his father's presence smiling down from heaven on the two brothers, his sons. He relished the moment.

# CHAPTER 7

As much as Clint enjoyed the research aspect of his job, he was becoming stir-crazy watching the Kalos family. It was way too much reality TV. He was feeling horny and thought of going to his favorite gentleman's club, but instead he went to the restaurant where Stacy worked. What prompted him to go there puzzled him. Clint wasn't sure she'd even be working. However, when he arrived an hour before closing, there she was filling saltshakers for the next day's clientele.

His favorite booth was open, and he gravitated to it. The restaurant was nearly empty. Beside him there were only two other patrons, which meant she would be able to talk to him for more than just a few minutes. Stacy smiled when she saw him come in, but it was not the glowing kind of smile he was usually graced with. It never ceased to amaze Clint how one woman could be so truly beautiful. He had dated and been with, in the biblical sense, many truly attractive women, but they always seemed to fall short of being that elusive "ten." He dated strippers, so they were pretty, and their bodies were usually on the "high side" of a ten-point scale, but there was toughness, a cold, calculating aspect to these women that robbed them of true beauty. Stacy was the kind of girl that a guy dreamed about. Her smile was special and seemed to rip through his very being. Clint hated feeling vulnerable, but he truly yearned for this woman.

Stacy came over to his table. "Hi there," she said with a forced smile. "Good seeing you again."

"You too," she said in a lackluster, low-key manner.

"Stacy, I don't mean to pry, but you don't seem to be your upbeat self."

"I guess I'm not good at hiding my feelings. Just some personal problems I'm dealing with. What can I get you?"

"Cup of coffee and a piece of apple pie, if you have it?"

"Yes, we still have some apple. Be right back."

Stacy returned with the pie and coffee, placing the food on the table.

"Thanks. I have a pretty broad shoulder if you feel like venting," said Clint.

She gave him a discerning look and then sat on the cushioned bench across from him. "I found out my boyfriend was cheating on me today … with a stripper of all things!"

Clint took a hard gulp. The good news was that he had a lot of experience in that area and could give her insight into that lifestyle. The bad news was he might know (in the biblical sense) the girl personally. He opted for a neutral stance.

"Man, that's cold!"

"I feel so stupid. I really thought he was the one … that we'd be married someday."

"Don't blame yourself. We can all be deceived. No one's above it. We all get hurt."

Stacy sighed. "I suppose you're right." She began to cry. "He said he loved me and wanted to spend the rest of his life with me. Why would he cheat on me?"

What Clint said next was completely out of character and totally against his nature. "I don't know why he would do that, but if you had sworn your love to me, I would cherish that love till the day I died."

Her teary eyes stared into his eyes, momentarily confused, and then she smiled a smile that could light up the darkest corner of a man's heart. "That's very sweet, Rod."

Her using the name Rod sent a chill through his body. It seemed his whole life was based on a lie and now the woman he cared for most knew him by a false label. Clint didn't care; he would take any tidbit of attention this woman gave him and savor it.

"I hope I wasn't being too bold; I just think you're an extraordinary person and your ex-boyfriend is a fool."

"You keep that up, I'm going to get a swell head," Stacy replied with a smile. She wiped her eyes and stood.

"Would you like to go out for a drink after you get off?"

"I don't drink, but I'd like to talk with you some more so that would be fine," she said with a slight grin, and then she turned for the kitchen.

—⁂—

Clint was seated in a comfortable easy chair in his monitor-filled office area. The monitors were off; the only light in the room was coming from a small office lamp on the desk situated near one of the screens. It shed a soothing light on the room. The music he had played was a smooth jazz sax solo. He was lost in reverie, reflecting on his evening with Stacy. Clint's comment to her about sworn love and commitment was so totally against his pragmatic philosophy of life. Maybe it was her piercing blue eyes that had a way of looking right through you that had thrown him off. Then there was her smile and the way her shimmering white teeth gave her just the slightest overbite that he found irresistible. Clint had to admit he was smitten.

They had gone to a grill/lounge for drinks. She ordered club soda with lime he a Diet Coke. They talked about life, gliding into the subject of religion. Stacy was a Christian and proud of her faith. Clint had lied and said he was also but as an aside mentioned he didn't attend church as much as he should. Deception was a major aspect of his business. From the makeup to the wardrobe and the dialects, he had taken deceit to new highs. With Stacy though, it didn't seem right, but she was so thrilled when he told her he was a Christian. Her response was "I thought you might be. There's gentleness about you, a certain honesty that comes through."

*Would someone please remove the dagger from my heart?* he thought.

"What's your favorite passage from the Bible?" was her follow-up question.

"The story of the prodigal son, because in that one story the whole message of the Bible is revealed," Clint responded.

Stacy was off the hook impressed by the answer.

He went on to regale her with the story, telling about the "Babylonian table dancers" and some of the other humorous anecdotes that the priest had mentioned. Stacy actually belly-laughed at some points in his narration. Even that was cute. Damn! Plagiarism *smajorism.* So he ripped off the whole sermon. It was a compliment to the priest's masterfully delivered, insightful homily. However, he would send a rather generous donation to St. Sophia Cathedral. The points he garnered by the rebroadcast of that sermon were priceless.

Stacy really opened up after that and was even candid about the fact she was a virgin. Clint kept silent on that subject, one of his few moments of lucidity. He felt sorry for her poor schmuck of a boyfriend; the stripper he knew had been just a sexual release from frustration for the guy. No man in his right mind would purposely sabotage a relationship with this woman. She was bright, funny, and had a wonderful quality of making the person she was talking to feel special, significant. While stressing a point, she had touched his hand. He immediately felt a pang of desire shoot through his body. That emotion was quickly extinguished when the subject of occupation surfaced. He stated he owned his own business working out of his home. Clint confessed to being somewhat of a computer geek, saying he created web sites. He did have the expertise and the technical skills to do that, so it was more of a white lie than a flat-out fib. Stacy was computer literate, but just barely. She used her computer more as a glorified typewriter than a business tool.

They talked for over two hours. He told her wonderful stories of Rod's make-believe family, and she regaled him with tales of her youth, focusing on the relationship she had with her parents and sister. Ella, her sister, was her only sibling. He was impressed by the obvious love she had for her relations. Clint felt like telling her the truth about his family. He sensed that there was a vastness to her understanding and that she might even give him words of comfort to heal the wounds that had scared his life for so long.

Who was this girl? What was happening to him? Why now, at this point in his life? In the final analysis, he realized the answers didn't matter. He was falling in love.

# CHAPTER 8

Night had fallen as an unmarked police car pulled up in front of Loretta's condo. Darrel was seated in the driver's seat, Nick riding shotgun next to him. Their shift had ended at the Kalos residence.

"Well, bro, I'll see you in the morning. Tell Loretta I said hi," commented Darrel.

"I will. Thanks for the ride, Bud. Take care," replied Nick as he exited the car. Nick quickly walked toward Loretta's front door.

Loretta had been good for Nick, Darrel thought. He had dropped about ten pounds and there was a spring in his step as he rushed to see her. There was also a sort of peacefulness about him. He was still crazy, but a more relaxed kind of crazy. Inward calm, tranquility—those were good words to describe the subtle changes that Loretta's presence had elicited in his life.

Nick had always been an upbeat optimistic guy, but with this new romance, he was downright joyful. Darrel was happy for his friend, to the point that he hoped he could find that same kind of joy for himself. Find a woman who would fill that lonely valley in his heart. He had fought the good fight, staying away from women who could have surely filled his physical needs but didn't have the heart, the soul, he was searching for. Church was the arena he hoped would provide the girl who could combine both the spiritual and the physical traits he desired in a woman. There were a lot of females at church who were interested in him. However, none of the potential candidates were attractive enough, or they were looking for men in the parish who made big bucks. In the final analysis, Darrel had decided to leave it up to God. He had worked a miracle with his brother John, and if he would only be patient, God would provide for his needs as well.

While driving, a beam of illumination from a streetlight reflected off a small object lying on the floorboard below the dash. It attracted Darrel's attention. He reached down and grabbed the object in question, which turned out to be a cell phone. Immediately he realized it was Nick's. The question became: should he go back and give it to him now, or should he just wait until tomorrow morning? Darrel knew there was a real possibility that if he turned back, by the time he reached the condo, he might interrupt Nick and Loretta in the throes of passion. Would he even need the phone tonight? No, he wouldn't. Darrel continued toward home.

Back at Loretta's condo, Nick had put his key in the lock to open the door and was surprised when he found the door unsecured. He would have to remind her that she had to be more careful. He stepped inside and was about to close and lock the door when he heard the words.

"Stand perfectly still, or I'll blow your ass away." There standing in front of him was Dale, holding a shotgun aimed at his chest. Loretta was seated on the floor farther back in the room, her mouth, wrists, and ankles covered in duct tape. Dale, walking backward, demanded, "Now walk slowly into the room, and I mean slowly." Nick crept, snaillike, past the alcove wall into the living room. His mind was racing. He had not shut the front door completely; it remained slightly ajar. That was a plus.

"Now I want you to raise your left hand and with your right hand very slowly and carefully open the jacket and remove your gun with your fingertips," instructed Dale.

Nick followed his instructions carefully, laying his automatic on the floor.

"With that same hand, pull up your pant leg and take your ankle piece and put it on the floor, again with your fingertips," said Dale. Nick did as he was told. His reflexes were fast, but he knew any quick move would be countered with a shotgun blast.

"Now back up a few steps," Dale continued.

Nick moved back as requested. Dale stepped forward and kicked the guns across the room.

"You're not the bad ass now, are you?" screamed Dale.

"You can't kill us and get away with it," said Nick as loudly as he could. He knew that most of the people who lived in the condos were home from work by now and the walls were thin. Someone would call the police.

"Watch me," smiled Dale.

"You'll spend the rest of your life in prison. Do you want that?"

"I want to see you beg for your life, but first strip down. We're going to have some fun."

"No, I'm not stripping down, you sick fuck. If you're going to kill me, then pull the trigger."

"I said strip!" Dale was screaming again with a drug-crazed look on his face.

"Fuck off!" Nick yelled in defiance.

Dale started walking toward him when an object went flying across the floor, capturing the attention of both men. The projectile settled a few feet from Dale's feet. Nick recognized his cell phone and immediately dove for the floor. Three gunshots were fired! The first bullet penetrated Dale's forehead. The second hit him in the neck, shattering his Adam's apple. The third bullet entered his chest, piercing his heart. Dale fell to the floor dead.

Darrel stood from his kneeling position next to the alcove wall. "You all right, bro?"

"I never thought your raspy ass voice could sound so good," said Nick with a smile. He was already next to Loretta, removing the duct tape carefully from her mouth.

"Nick, are you all right?" said Loretta tearfully.

"I'm fine, sweetheart. Did he harm you?" said Nick as he continued to remove the tape from her legs and hands.

"No, he surprised me when I came in. He broke a window in the kitchen door and got in that way, then taped me up, waited for you."

"He's dead," said Darrel after examining Dale's body. He then walked over and stood next to Loretta and Nick.

"Bro, I'm so glad that you knew to hit the ground when I slid the phone across the floor. It's the only thing I could think of, to get you out of the line of fire," continued Darrel.

Nick went over to Darrel and gave him an emotional embrace. Darrel could feel his body trembling. Nick would never tell anyone his true feelings about that night. There was no doubt in his mind that Dale would have pulled that trigger if Darrel hadn't intervened, especially after he had egged him on with words like "you sick fuck." His hope was that the shotgun blast would be so loud that neighbors would call the police and they would arrive in time to save Loretta. However, Nick harbored the likelihood that Dale would have killed Loretta and then turned the shotgun on himself. He had actually started praying as Dale stepped forward, just seconds before Darrel's shots rang out. Nick knew anything he said to Darrel in regard to saving his life would seem trite. What he wanted to say was how much he loved his partner and that he was the brother he never had, but that wasn't the manly thing to do.

Instead, Nick said, "Thanks, Bud. I owe you big time."

"Na-a-a, just glad I could be there for you," responded Darrel.

Loretta got up from the floor, went over to Darrel, and gave him a hug.

"Darrel, I can't thank you enough for making this nightmare come to an end and for saving this big lug here," said Loretta as she pointed to Nick.

"He's not much to look at, but he's fun to have around," Darrel responded with a grin.

"Hey, watch it!" replied Nick, smiling.

"Bro, what made you come back to return the phone? You could have given it to me in the morning," Nick continued.

"That's what I was going to do, and then I remembered your mother calls you on your cell, so I came back."

"You're a good guy," said Nick.

———※———

It was a picture-postcard kind of day in Santa Barbara: blue sky, sunshine, and a temperature of seventy-two degrees. Clint (or Rod) was walking hand in hand with Stacy up State Street. She was dressed in faded, form-fitting jeans, a white tank top with a matching white baseball cap. There was something about a woman wearing a baseball cap that Clint found extremely sexy; it gave Stacy a sort of reckless, jaunty persona. This was their first official date, and he was in high spirits. They found a small bistro with outdoor seating and settled at an exterior table. Stacy ordered fish, and when the entrée arrived, she picked at the salmon with indifference. Clint was puzzled by her behavior. "Is everything all right? You seem distracted," he asked.

"It's that obvious ... I'm sorry ... My sister is going through a tough time, and I'm worried about her," said Stacy.

"Feel like talking about it?"

"She met Walt at the supermarket over the meat counter. I know it doesn't sound very romantic. They both reached for the same package of pork chops. I know, but it's true. Walt's a cement contractor and makes a good living at it. He's got that rough kind of good looks and is well-built. My older sister is a looker in own right; anyway, it was love at first sight. They dated for three months and then got married. He's not a Christian, but Ella thought if she led by example, he might be swayed to embrace Christ. That didn't happen. He wouldn't let her work. He was jealous and controlling. She has to call him whenever she leaves the house, and recently, he has started beating her. He uses his open hand so as not to leave a mark. Ella broke down and told me all this last night."

"That's terrible. I had some cement work done recently at my house. Walt rings a bell. What's his last name?"

"Waneright. Do you think you know him?"

"What's the name of his company?"

"Cement to Be."

Clint smiled, "No, I would have remembered that."

"Rod what am I going to do?"

"I don't know what to tell you." It was true he couldn't tell her, but Clint did know what to do. Stacy had given him enough information to track the A-hole down. From there he would handle it. This was something he could do for her that was right up his alley.

"Will you pray for Ella?"

"Sure."

"Prayer is so powerful. It's like Philippians says: 'We can do all things through Christ which strengthens us.'"

"Yes, we can." He didn't know how the Philippians would have handled the situation, but with a little help from the Black Stallion, it would be dealt with. Hey, cement to be.

—⁘—

Attention to detail had always been a hallmark of Clint's nature. This endeavor was no different. He took a break from the Kalos assignment and tailed Walt for five days. It turned out Walt was laying more than cement. He had a girl on the side that he would drop in on after work. He would sojourn at her apartment for an hour or so, long enough to have a few drinks, dip his wick then leave. It was getting dark early, which would give Clint the cover of darkness when he confronted Walt outside the girl's apartment. The girlfriend resided in a flat located at the end of the complex near a stand of trees. This was fortunate for Clint because he could immobilize Walt in an inconspicuous area that was close by.

He would use his demon makeup for this exercise. The demon persona was his favorite. It was a three-hour makeup job using over thirty prosthetic pieces he had manufactured himself. The final result was a being that looked like a combination of the devil and Freddy Krueger. He used scarlet-colored, animal-like contacts that made his eyes glow red. Combined with the pointed canine teeth and claw-like gloves he utilized, this was a creature right out of a horror flick. He turned the outside of a hooded poncho into leafy camouflage and created pants, the legs of which looked like tree stumps. Clint's boots were turned into clumps of grass. This wasn't Halloween, but it was sure as hell going to be devil's night.

The next evening, he placed himself next to the wall near the door to the girlfriend's apartment. In the shadows with the hood of the camouflaged poncho over his face, he looked unmistakably like a small tree. Thirty minutes passed when the occupant of the apartment above Walt's girlfriend approached. He was a small-framed, bespectacled, thirtysomething nerd. He immediately spotted the small tree, Clint, and walked over to it.

"It's about time they put some shrubbery around here … a little mangy looking though, could use a trim," said the bespectacled geek.

Clint thought, *What's this tree-hugging, save-the-tuna, Johnny Appleseed going to do now?*

The geek pulled a leaf from the camouflaged poncho to examine it closer in the light.

Clint immediately yelled out, "Oww!"

The geek's face contorted in stark fear. "I'm sorry … I'm sorry." Then he jammed the leaf between a few others and fled up the stairs. It took every molecule of self-control Clint possessed to stop him from breaking up in laughter. It was good that he had kept his composure because Walt exited the building at that moment.

It took less than two seconds for Clint to sneak up behind him and execute a sleeper choke hold that caused Walt to pass out. Clint quickly dragged him into the miniforest area next to the apartment complex. There was just enough light from the buildings security lamps to highlight the grotesque features of his face as he pulled off the leaf-covered hood. Walt was bigger than he had anticipated and strong. He put up a decent struggle, but Clint's years in special forces made his efforts futile. Slowly Walt came to senses. Immediately Clint gave him a punishing blow to the solar plexus, causing him to gasp for breath. Then with his opened, clawed hand, he smacked him hard on either side of his face.

Walt eventually focused on Clint's masked face. A look of complete terror enveloped him.

"I'm God's avenging angel here to take you straight to hell. Your harsh words toward your wife, the physical violence you have inflicted on Ella, and your adultery have been observed. You have been judged, found lacking, and are convicted," said Clint in an eerie deep-pitched voice.

"I can change. I will change. I'll never lay a finger on Ella again. I'll love her and cherish her. I'll stop the adultery, I swear. I promise. Please, I beg of you. Give me another chance," pleaded sobbing, devastated Walt.

"You don't believe in God. You give no glory to Him. Why should He pardon your transgressions?"

"I do believe. I promise I'll go to church. I'll do whatever it takes. Please give me another chance."

"Your plea has been heard, and your desire granted, but if you should ever default on your promise, I will return with a consuming fire and go 'medieval' on your ass." Damn! Clint realized he was stealing lines from *Pulp Fiction*. It was so good until then.

"I promise. I promise. Thank you. Thank you!"

"Keep your vow or I shall return!" yelled Clint, then he quickly disappeared into the miniforest.

Walt took a huge sigh of relief as he stood and dusted himself off. He thought, *At least you can reason with God's avenging angels, but talk about ugly!*

—⬯—

Stacy opened the door to her apartment and greeted Clint with a smile.

"Welcome to my humble abode. I have so much to tell you," said Stacy.

Clint's eyes roamed the room. "Your place is nice," stated Clint.

He spoke the truth. The living room was painted a light cream, except for two raspberry-colored accent walls. The art as well as the furniture had a modern feel, and although the abode had a minimalist look, it was still elegant and cheery.

"Interior decorating has always been an interest of mine."

"It shows. Martha Stewart has nothing on you, girl."

Stacy smiled proudly. She had put a lot of effort and creative energy into her apartment and relished the compliment.

"Thanks. I try." After showing Clint the kitchen, her bedroom, and the bathroom, which were equally impressive, she returned to the living room. Stacy led him over to her sofa, where they both sat down.

"Rod, I've got such great news. Our prayers have been answered. Walt has turned his life around completely. He apologized for his violent behavior and verbal abuse and swore he would never say a harsh word to her again. He's even going to church with Ella!"

"Praise God," responded Clint.

"I want to thank you … for your prayers. Proverbs says that God hears the prayers of a righteous man." Stacy's well-meaning words always cut Clint to the quick. Calling him by his fake name was bad enough, but to say he was righteous, geez!

"I'm not righteous."

"I know we're all sinners, but somehow I feel you made a difference with my sister and Walt."

"Maybe a little. Only God knows for sure," Clint said with a smile.

"Do you think Walt has changed for good?"

"Yeah, my gut tells me he's had a permanent attitude adjustment."

Stacy made dinner at her apartment that night for Clint. Nothing fancy—spaghetti and meatballs with some French bread on the side—but it was the first time she had cooked for him so that made the simple meal unforgettable. After dinner the two adjourned to the living room, reclined on the sofa, and engaged in an old-fashioned make-out session. Her soft moist lips melted into his as their tongues engaged in a liquid ballet. Stacy had a way of running her fingers through the hair on the nap of Clint's neck that sent surges of passion through his body. The ears were the major erogenous zone for Stacy, prompting goose bumps to appear on her upper body at the slightest nibble. Clint did not allow his hands to wander. He longed to touch her breasts but was willing to wait. He knew Stacy wanted to go slow.

Something inside Clint had changed. He truly cared for this woman, and where the relationship would lead he was not sure, but he would follow the road to the end. What he did know for sure was that he was living a lie, and it was starting to nag at him.

—∞—

The white plastic basket was full of recently dried clothes. Steph had carried it in from the laundry room and dumped the contents on the kitchen table. Cathy and Brenda were on duty that morning. Cathy joined Steph at the table and assisted her in folding the garments. Holding up a small, hooded sweatshirt, Cathy remarked, "Children's clothes are so cute."

"I know … You should see the darling little jackets they have out, and John loves wearing it all," replied Stephanie.

"It must be fun buying for him."

"Yes, I enjoy it."

John, who had been on the floor nearby playing with a small toy truck, walked up to Steph and said, "Mommy, I tink I pooped my pants."

Cathy smiled as she finished folding the sweatshirt and stacked it neatly on a stack of similar garb. Brenda, who had been in the backyard smoking a cigarette, came in, locking the door behind her. "What's up?" Brenda asked. Steph with John in hand was heading toward the bedroom. "I've got to change my little Winnie the Pooh here."

"I not Winnie the Pooh," protested John.

"A look at your diaper will tell us differently I think," said a smiling Stephanie.

"Steph that's bad, don't leave your day job for a stand-up act in Vegas," remarked Cathy with a grin.

Steph smirked, then exited with John into the hallway.

Brenda sat down next to Cathy and began folding clothes. She stopped temporarily to rub her neck.

"Are you all right?" Cathy asked.

"Yeah, I guess … My neck hurts and my left arm is sore. I think I overdid it in the gym yesterday … And remind me the next time to stay away from the sausage-and-egg special at Hank's. I'd kill for an antacid," replied Brenda.

"I'm sure Steph's got something. Go ask her."

"You're right. I'll be back." Brenda stood and exited for the bedroom.

Moments later John and Steph entered the kitchen. Cathy looked up from where she was seated and asked, "Did you have something for Brenda?"

"This is a doctor's house. We've got everything … But she doesn't look well."

"Where is she now?"

"In the bathroom."

A look of concern registered on Cathy's face. John went to his toy box, opened it, and pulled two miniature cars out. Then he wandered out of the room into the hallway, stopping in front of the bathroom door where Brenda was cloistered. *Benda,* come out and play," pleaded John. "Benda play with me, please," begged John again.

Stephanie joined him at the door.

"Sweetheart, Brenda will be out soon, she needs some private time, OK?"

"OK."

"Brenda, are you all right?" There was no response. Steph knocked on the door.

"Brenda!" Once again there was no response. Stephanie tried turning the doorknob, but it was locked firm. Stephanie quickly scooped up John and ran into the kitchen. Cathy was on her feet as soon as they entered.

"What's wrong?" Cathy blurted out.

"Brenda's not answering from inside the bathroom," said Steph as she retrieved a key from inside a cupboard. Pressing the key into Cathy's hand, she said, "Here's the key." Cathy grabbed it and ran to the restroom door.

Yelling, "Brenda! Brenda!" Cathy unlocked the door and found Brenda seated on the commode, hunched over motionless.

Clint was seated in front of the monitor, observing as the events transpired.

—⁓—

The lighting in the hospital room was subdued. Brenda lay still in her bed with an oxygen mask covering her face and assorted tubes extending from her arms. Cathy was seated next to the bed, holding Brenda's hand.

"You're going to be all right. Just keep on fighting," said Cathy, teary-eyed.

Peter had quietly slipped into the room and gently tapped Cathy on the shoulder.

"Could I speak to you outside for a few minutes?" Peter asked.

The two slipped outside where they were greeted by Darrel, Nick, and Stephanie, who was cradling John asleep in her arms. The group was eager to hear what Peter had to say. Brenda's swift collapse and consequent hospitalization had left them starving for answers.

Peter began haltingly, "We believe … that Brenda suffered a massive heart attack that induced her coma."

"But how—how could that happen?" asked Cathy.

"She had blockage in the arteries to the heart and her smoking further constricted those arteries initiating the attack," said Peter.

"She can come out the coma, right?" interjected Steph.

"All things are possible, but she's in grave danger. I suggest we all pray for her," replied Peter, grim faced.

The news hit like a wrecking ball. Brenda was thirty-three and until now seemed to be in perfect health. A look of impending doom registered on the faces of the group. Cathy, who was standing next to Nick, began to sob. Nick instinctively turned toward her and engulfed her in his arms as she wept. He had only a week before faced death manifested in the muzzle of a loaded shotgun. In an ominous way, Nick could identify with Brenda as she hovered near the border of the great unknown. Darrel put his hand on Cathy's back as her tears soaked Nick's shirt.

"Brenda's strong, Cath. She can overcome this … Let's not lose faith," cajoled Darrel.

"He's right. Prayer can work miracles. Peter has told me of patients that he was sure would not make it through the night and today are alive and well." Steph turned to Peter. "Isn't that true?"

"Yes, I've seen miraculous recoveries, and I know firsthand the power of prayer. Truly, anything is possible," replied Peter.

Clint, in his "Pano the Filipino" orderly disguise, was standing nearby, next to a cart of linens he had rolled in. From his vantage point, he had witnessed and heard all of the conversation. His only contact with Brenda had been from a distance, her video image on his monitor. He had thought she was pretty and had a sweet personality. She seemed out of place as a detective. There was no hard edge to be found in her.

John had stolen her heart. She lit up every time the little boy entered the room, and the feeling was mutual. The two spent hours together. The activities included everything from playing children's games to Brenda reading stories to him. Clint was by no means in a position to judge family dynamics, but he had to admit Brenda would make a great mother. In his line of work, he could not afford the luxury of tenderhearted feelings, but deep down, he hoped she would pull through.

—ᴍ—

Steph, Darrel, Nick, and Peter prayed when time permitted at her bedside. Mostly they were silent prayers, but occasionally in anguish they would speak aloud. Brenda's parents arrived from Montana and the heartbreak continued. The look of agony on the faces of these kind, dear people at the sight of their unconscious daughter was brutal to witness.

Brenda's prognosis continued on a downhill spiral. Her initial heart attack had cut oxygen to the brain, which was bad enough, but a smaller follow-up attack was devastating, taking her condition from guarded to extremely critical. Three days after arriving at the hospital, her EEG showed no brain activity and Brenda was breathing solely by means of a ventilator. There were no miracles to be had for this young woman. Her seemingly bright future had come to an end.

Funeral plans were made. Brenda would have a full-on department funeral with an honor guard and the haunting sound of "Amazing Grace" being played on the bagpipes. This was of little consolation to Brenda's parents. It was the ultimate cruelty for a mother or father to witness the death of their child. Such a fate bespoke of an unjust universe, an unloving God.

—∞—

Peter, Steph, and John were not allowed to attend the funeral; the department considered such a public venue too much of a security risk. Maybe it was for the best, Peter thought. Brenda would be remembered in their hearts as the loving friend who bonded with their son and whose cheerful demeanor brought a smile to many faces. They explained her death to John as best they could. They told him that it was Brenda's time to go and be with Jesus. He replied, "She be happy … Jesus got good toys."

Cathy and Steph were not so easily pacified. Surprisingly Steph had a harder time coping with Brenda's death than Cathy. Death was part of the job in Cathy's world. Thankfully it was not a common occurrence. However, Cath had lost friends before, but no one as significant and dear as Brenda. Steph, on the other hand, had never lost anyone who was truly close to her, and more troubling was that her prayer as well as the prayer of all the others had not been answered. She confronted Peter on the issue during a shift change, in the presence of the guys, Cathy, and the new replacement, Cecelia. Brenda's successor was in her early forties with jet-black hair, pleasant facial features, and a lean body. Cecelia was low-key given the circumstances; however, she was capable and had a pleasing personality that would be revealed in time.

Steph purposely brought up the topic while in the company of the detectives to get feedback on the inner conflict she felt. She directed her first question to Peter. "Why did she have to die? We all prayed for her, and God is all-powerful so why didn't he save her?"

Peter replied, "First of all, I don't have all the answers. There is a certain divine mystery that surrounds God that is unexplainable by us, his creation. What I do know is that if prayer could have saved Brenda, she would be with us now. We all prayed sincere heartfelt prayers; the Lord listened and responded no. He would not save her. Why? I can only guess. Had she reached some spiritual plateau? Steph, you said that Brenda told you by reading John his Sunday school books she had actually gotten insights into her own faith. One example was using an apple to describe the elements of the Trinity. It has one form with three parts: the skin, the interior substance, and the seeds. Simplistic, but you said it helped her understand the Trinity. The Bible says you have to see God with childlike eyes. Had she reached a point in her spiritual journey where her faith was so intense, simple, and pure that she had found the divine answer to the meaning of her life here on earth and now it was her time to move on? Or was it as simple as God just wanting to experience her radiant presence up close and personal, in His realm? I don't know, but what I do believe is that Brenda is in a place where there is no pain or suffering, where she is reunited with loved ones in a celestial home experiencing ultimate peace, joy, and love."

"Doc, I like it when you talk about God … You got a way with words," said Nick, smiling.

"That all sounds like a nice sound bite, but what about the 200,000 people who lost their lives in that tsunami a while back? They said a third of those were children. How can a loving, caring God allow that to happen if He values us so much?" added Cathy.

"He cared enough to allow His Son to be tortured and then be crucified on a cross for us. I'd say he understands the depth of human loss and suffering. The Bible talks about children in heaven. There are no mistakes when it comes to God. We just don't understand His divine plan," said Peter.

"I miss her so much," lamented Cathy.

"That's where the sadness comes in. We miss her essence, her smile, her fullness of heart, her spirit, but we're here only for a short time compared to eternity and we'll see her again sooner than we might imagine," continued Peter.

"You're right on, Doc. It's all about the resurrection, never-ending life with God. Sure gives a person peace of mind, doesn't it?" was Darrel's response.

"Yes, it does," stated Peter.

"It is a comforting thought; you have so much faith," said Cathy, perplexed.

"Yes, he does. That's what I love about him," blurted Steph.

"All right, all right, enough of that. Let's get on with the job of living," said Peter.

The camera zoomed in for a close-up on the monitor. Clint wanted to look into Peter's eyes. How could he be so sure? Where did he get his faith in a God he could not see? *This guy is too good to be true,* thought Clint once again.

# CHAPTER 9

IT WAS A BALMY SUMMER NIGHT AND STILL LIGHT OUT WHEN CLINT SET out for the cafe to pick up Stacy. He was driving his motorcycle, a Harley-Davidson Softail Deluxe, he had bought just a few months ago. This was a man's ride, he thought. It was big, black, with contrasting silver accents, chromed out to the max. The wide whitewall tires, gleaming spoke wheels, long-barreled shotgun pipes, tombstone taillight, and low seat mirrored motorcycles of a bygone era. The guttural pure rumbling that emanated from the bike was hereditary and classic Harley. He had seen a photo a few years back that showed Clark Gable with two of his buddies on motorcycles similar to his as they tooled around Hollywood. The motorcycle oozed testosterone, and he loved the feel of the bike between his legs as he devoured the open road.

Inside the restaurant, Stacy was seated at an empty table near a window. She had never seen the bike before and was slightly taken back by the sight of her boyfriend on a motorcycle. She thought how intriguing Clint was. He was a study in contradictions. Here was this mild-mannered Christian computer geek with a rock-hard body and bad-boy looks who could quote scripture and rode a Harley. Yes, even Stacy knew a Harley-Davidson when she saw it. She would never admit this to anyone, especially her Christian girlfriends, but deep down in her feminine psyche, she loved that he drove a motorcycle. It was dangerous, sure, but she thought of princes and knights in shining armor when she saw Clint drive up on his mechanized black steed. She exited the restaurant and joined him out front.

Clint took off his black helmet and smiled when he saw Stacy approach. She locked his image, at that moment, into the recesses of her heart. His hair was longish and tussled, and he was wearing a snug, bright-blue, open collared shirt with short sleeves rolled up above his bulging biceps. He was also adorned in his favorite, faded, Levi's jeans, the ones that looked like they were sprayed on that highlighted his perfectly shaped butt. To round out the outfit, he sported a pair of aged, black, leather, cowboy boots. His presence at that moment reminded her of James Dean.

Clint handed her the extra helmet that he had attached near the rear of the bike.

"Hop on."

"I can't. I'm wearing a dress," protested Stacy.

"Cut the crap. It's either the bike or you walk."

Stacy feigned anger, but secretly she loved it when Clint was forceful with her. "My dress is going to be up to my neck when I get on this thing!"

Clint smiled smugly. "Gee, that would be terrible."

Stacy grimaced, shook her head in defeat, put on the helmet, hiked up her uniform skirt as discreetly as she could, and threw her leg over the bike. It was not very discreet, given that she flashed her pink panties to Clint's ever observant eyes. The sight of seeing between Stacy's gorgeous legs made him hard. He wanted this woman.

Once securely stationed on the back of the motorcycle, Stacy wrapped her arms tightly around Clint's waist. He could feel her firm breasts against his back. They were headed to his house, and he wondered what the events of that evening would bring. Whatever was to transpire, at least the ride over would be a kick!

—m—

They reached Clint's suburban home just as the sun was setting. The exterior of his abode was a statement of form and function bonding in structural simplicity. It was medium in size and had a definite oriental feel, displaying a stylistic pagoda roof and wooden-plank shell covering. The outside wood was stained in three shades of brown from light to dark that came together in a complementary union. Large picture windows on either side of the entrance door revealed the interior sliding wood and rice paper like partitions called shoji screens. Giant bamboo stalks along with other manicured Asian-inspired foliage comprised the landscaping of the house. Clint wasn't sure why he was so drawn to oriental-inspired structures, but his many years training in the martial arts with Asian masters could be the source.

Clint drove the bike up the black asphalt driveway, activated the electric operated garage door, and parked his obsession next to his Viper. The car was also black, with a black ragtop. He had modifications done on the car to further increase the already mega horsepower. It was a rocket on wheels. He had spent over $90,000 on the car, including the mechanical upgrades. For that kind of money, he could have bought a top-of-the-line Porsche or a Jag, but he liked to buy American. Yes, it sounded corny, but his military stints in foreign countries where anti-American sentiments were at times high had tainted him. Yes, he was a killer, but he was true to the red, white, and blue when it came to loyalties.

Clint enjoyed his toys. Material things were important to him. A nice home, the car, the bike—they were cherished elements of his life, but there were times he missed the personal relationships other men enjoyed. He had no friends. Besides the superficial congenialities doled out to the cashier at the supermarket or the girl who managed the cleaners, he was isolated, living in his own world of intrigue. He missed the interpersonal relationships that he viewed on his monitor as he watched the Kalos family engage in the business of life. Getting his rocks off with a busty stripper helped, but he still felt alone, as if searching for the light switch in a darkened room. He did not want to admit to himself that deep in the harbor of his soul he yearned for love. Stacy had become his shining beacon of hope, an answer to childhood dreams lost.

The garage was pristine, with not a single oil spot on the floor. Stacy was impressed with the garage and its cleanliness, but more importantly with the hot car! Of course, her interest was purely from a Christian perspective. It was comforting to see a truly righteous Christian man receive the overflowing blessings of God, or something like that. Whatever, the car was hot. She extricated herself from the bike and entered Clint's home.

The oriental theme of the exterior was carried on into the interior of the house as well. The off-white walls were contrasted by black lacquered and rattan furniture. The sea of white was broken by one jade green wall that anchored the room. Black onyx statues of Samurai soldiers and Japanese landscape prints were the catalyst for the art in the space. A five-foot-high, dark, aged, wood sword rack holding three Samurai swords was the focal point of the living area. It stood as a silent reminder of Clint's vocation. Stunning in its masculine elegance, the interior of the house was a visual testimony to his admiration for the Far East.

Stacy was stirred by the sumptuous interior of the home. "Your place is awesome. You're into feng shui, aren't you?"

"I'm actually into a by-product of that philosophy; it's called *fun way*. Same furniture you just use it differently," Clint said with a smile.

"That's bad."

"Along with learning martial arts as a kid, I also studied Asian languages. Most people don't even know what the words *feng shui* mean."

"It has something to do with balance, right?"

"The literal translation for that term is 'My dog has herpes.'"

Stacy laughed. "Who knew? And I bet you aced those Asian language courses."

"Ohh yeah," said Clint with a grin.

"Well after looking at your place, I'd assume we're having sushi or Chinese for dinner."

"Sushi, that's fish bait and I'm not a big fan of Chinese … It's Greek cuisine tonight."

"Go figure … That makes me two for two."

Clint engulfed her in his arms. "You don't need to keep score with me. I hit it out of the ballpark when I met you," he said before kissing her.

Looking up into his eyes and shaking her head, she murmured, "You're a sweetie pie."

"That's me, Mr. Sweetie Pie," Clint said with a smile, as he thought, *That's a stretch. The Black Stallion, a.k.a. Mr. Sweetie Pie. Ah, to look at life through innocent eyes.*

Clint took Stacy on a tour of the house, even showing her his office with the monitors. He figured if he kept the room off limits, it would only pique her curiosity. All the monitors were disconnected prior to her arrival as a precaution. The presence of so many viewing screens intrigued Stacy. "Why do you have so many television sets?" she asked.

"An electronics store was going out of business and had them marked down so low, I couldn't resist. I'm a big sports fan and this way I can watch four or five different games at the same time."

"That's cool."

Clint was pleased that she bought the explanation. He did not want to dwell on facets that related to his profession. He showed her his Asian-inspired bedroom done all in rattan and the bathrooms, one of which had a deep, extralarge stone and tile tub. She was enthralled with the expansive bathing area.

"It's more like a minipool than a bathtub," commented Stacy.

Clint thought, *Wouldn't it be nice to take a skinny dip with her before dinner?* But it was too soon to go there. He left the washroom commenting on the tub, "Yes, it's very relaxing after a long day."

The last leg of the tour was the kitchen, a magnificent, black, stainless steel and wood creation. Black countertops, sleek metal appliances, and wood the color of sand completed the culinary arena. In an alcove off the kitchen was a small, black, lacquered table with four chairs. Clint pulled out a chair for Stacy and she settled into it. After placing two bamboo place mats down and two empty wine glasses on the table, he went over to the refrigerator and pulled out a foil-covered ceramic pan then placed the dish into a preheated oven.

"You already cooked before I came here. *Is there anything you don't do?*" exclaimed Stacy.

"Actually, that would be cook. I went to this great Greek restaurant near here, of all things called the Athenian Owl, and got takeout."

"You're so honest."

"Now don't start calling me Honest Abe. I thought I had a lock on Sweetie Pie."

"I'm finally starting to see a little bit of your computer geek side come out … It's interesting."

"Man, that's a quick ride down from Sweetie Pie to interesting computer geek … Well at least we're having Geek food," said Clint with a chuckle.

"That's so bad it hurts," replied an amused Stacy.

"Hurts so good … What'll it be: green tea, bottled water, or low-cal lemonade?"

"Green tea sounds good."

Clint retrieved the green tea from the refrigerator and poured it for two. Soon after, the Greek food was ready and served. It was a sumptuous meal embracing a combination of diverse delicacies. There was a spinach pie made with cooked spinach and feta cheese folded inside a strudel-type topping called spanakopita. Next was a lasagna-style dish, pastitsio, made with layered hamburger and elbow noodles, covered with a cheesy soufflé topping. The classic stuffed rice and meat, grape leaves, called *dolmathes*, were also in evidence. The final ingredient in this Greek smorgasbord was a small rack of lamb smothered in an herb tomato sauce.

It had been a long day at work for Stacy and she was hungry, but the way she devoured the Mediterranean food surprised her. The meal went beyond being just delicious; it was spectacular. The conversation was impressive as well. She was surprised at the wealth of information that Rod possessed on so many diverse subjects.

It seemed like they talked for hours before withdrawing to the living room. The song list for the background music featured some classic artists like Frank Sinatra, Nat King Cole, and Ray Charles and current singers, such as Ed Sheeran and John Legend. The two ended up reclining on the long sleek sofa across from the sword rack. Clint stared at Stacy with adoration.

"You have the most beautiful eyes," Clint remarked.

"Thank you," said Stacy as she smiled back at him.

Clint began nibbling on her neck, causing goose bumps to appear. Stacy could feel the sexual desire welling up in her inner being. While using his tongue to massage her inner ear, he began to unbutton her dress. Stacy softly groaned with lustful anticipation. With the front of her dress now open, he moved his hand over her bra and began massaging her breast. Her entire body began to tremble.

Clint longed to be inside her. It was his belief that sex was the one area of life where the act was as good if not better than the hype. So much of life was a disappointment, but having intercourse was brilliant, so base in nature yet exhilarating in its tactile sensations and smells. The one facet of the act that he found most enthralling was the look on a woman's face when in the throes of an orgasm. It seemed even the homeliest of women, at that moment in time, became transformed into a beauty. All facial lines, crow's feet, skin ailments, and any perceived human defects disappeared in a sea of radiant splendor. There was divinity intrinsic in the act, and maybe that was the reason God's name came up so many times during its culmination. He yearned to see Stacy's face in the throes of ecstasy. She was gorgeous to begin with. What would he see when she reached her zenith of pleasure? He felt sure that it would be an unexplainable, celestial quality that inspired Greek sculptors and artists from every epoch of history, but he needed to get back to the business at hand, so to speak.

With one hand still massaging the exterior of the bra, above her breast, he slid his other hand beneath her back and with a pinch of his fingers unhooked her bra. In an instant, he could feel her body tense up and Stacy sat upright, pulling her bra over her breasts. "Will you tell me one thing?" she yelled.

Needless to say, this was not the reaction Clint was hoping for at this point in his sexual exploits. "Yeeeaaah, if I can."

"How come when you ask a guy to hook the back of a necklace for you, he fumbles with it for an hour, but somehow with one hand, while you're lying flat on your back, he's able to unhook your bra in a millisecond with the dexterity of a heart surgeon?"

He realized in an instant this was not your typical *Jeopardy* question. So he didn't say, "Do you want my answer in the form of a question?"

"The tension of the elastic is equal to the force of the hand divided by the distance between the index finger and the thumb to the fortieth power" was Clint's bullshit answer. He wasn't gonna reveal the ultimate male secret that has confounded woman for ages, unless there was a chance of getting laid. Stacy flashed him a look that said, "You're not getting any tonight so come clean."

"It all has to do with heredity. The male has a genetic predisposition to excel in conditions that will cause successful procreation of the species," said Clint. *Damn that sounded good,* he thought.

"I'd like that in layman's terms, please."

"When a guy's horny, he can pretty much do anything to get nooky."

"Thank you" was her simple response as she broke into laughter.

"I went a little too far tonight, huh?"

"Yes, you did." Stacy hooked her bra and buttoned up her dress.

"Stace, in the final analysis, I'm a man tempted by the most beautiful woman I've ever met. I hope this …"

She put her hand over his lips and with compassion reflecting from her sky-blue eyes said, "I know. I want you too, but there's a time for everything. God has a purpose … a plan for us. It's gonna be all right." She leaned over and kissed him on the cheek.

Clint waxed philosophical. The old kiss on the cheek. So much for seeing her face in the throes of ecstasy. There was always tomorrow.

It was a rainy Monday morning when Clint stepped out his front door to retrieve the newspaper. He removed the plastic bag that covered the paper and scanned the headlines on the front page. The lead headline read, "Darso Murder Trial Looming." The write-up went on to describe the alleged child abuse and mentioned Peter by name as the primary witness. This was the first time he had been given any details in the case. Clint had heard bits and pieces at the hospital, but he had no idea how gruesome the boy's demise had truly been. The article described the welts, the horribly swollen face, and the child's traumatic death. District Attorney Vince Darelli was on the move, shaping popular opinion any way he could. He wanted nothing less than a public outcry, and he was achieving his goal. Even Clint felt a twinge of sympathy for the kid.

However, the most startling aspect of the piece was the fact the trial was to start in two months. Time was no longer his friend. Clint knew that Darso would want Peter dead before the month was over. His clients did not like to cut it close when it came to their own wellbeing. *Damn it.* Clint could feel the anger welling up inside. As much as he hated to admit it, he admired Peter and was fond of Stephanie and their son, John, as well. Here was a family that had achieved the ideal loving relationship, and now the time had come for him to destroy it. He had done forty professional hits in his lifetime and, barring a few exceptions, monitored the victims' lives with the same intensity as he had done with the Kalos family. Most of the others had come up short. Whether male or female, they all had major character flaws. He had ended the lives of child molesters, thieves, pimps, murderers, and drug pushers and could loosely say he had held the moral high ground. Sure, there were some exceptions. The one that came to mind was Wendy. She was the only child from a wealthy family (the steel business) who had married her car mechanic boyfriend. What she had perceived as true love turned out to be an attraction to a physically abusive, woman-chasing asshole. Clint would have preferred to kill him. Instead, Wendy died of poisoning from bad tuna he had made accessible to her, and the mechanic inherited a not so small fortune. Clint was paid double his going rate, but it still didn't feel right. Hell, we all know life isn't fair, yet he had to acknowledge because of his unique line of work he literally controlled people's destinies. Clint hadn't tasted tuna since the day of Wendy's demise. Hey, paybacks were a bitch.

Peter was different. There was no major flaw. He was a loving husband, father, and friend to all who knew him. Damn, he even had a sense of humor. Clint needed to come to grips with his reality. This was a job, a vocation; he did not have the luxury of picking and choosing his marks, but still, he wanted to think this through. He had never refused an assignment before, and there were no rules in his line of work. There was always a first time for everything.

—⚬⚬—

It was another busy day at the hospital. Nick and Darrel were on duty shadowing Peter as usual. The flu season had brought people in by the drove. Peter couldn't remember when he had been this busy. An attractive twentysomething blonde pushed a wheelchair into the room with a handsome, rugged-looking man seated in it. The man was wearing a short-sleeved shirt and cargo shorts. Peter immediately noticed his artificial legs, but it took a few seconds to register that the man had artificial arms and hands as well. His arm and hand prostheses were the best he'd ever seen. Clint, sporting his Pano the orderly disguise, was in close proximity under the auspices of organizing the hospital linen cart. He was close enough to Peter and the rest of the group to see and hear everything that was going on.

Eve, the attractive blonde, was the first to speak. "Hi. I'm Eve Wilson, and this is Jack my husband." She extended her hand as she spoke. Peter shook her hand. "I'm Dr. Peter Kalos. It's a pleasure to meet you." He then extended his hand to her husband. "And you, Jack." After glancing down at his artificial hands then up again at Peter, Jack flashed him a venomous stare as if to say, "Hey slick, can't you see my hands are fake?" Peter took it all in stride. Continuing to look at Jack he asked, "What brought you into the emergency room today?" Eve intercepted the statement, saying, "He's had a high fever … feels achy all over and has been getting the chills." Peter found it interesting that Eve had become Jack's spokesperson. It was then that Peter discerned the tattoo on the right arm of Jack, just above where his prosthetic arm ended. The Marine Corps's signature eagle, anchor, and globe symbol was unmistakable.

"I noticed your tattoo … You're a marine," said Peter.

"Yeah, so what about it?" responded Jack.

Peter continued. "My uncle and cousin were in the Marine Corps."

"Jack fought in Afghanistan," interjected Eve.

Jack flashed a harsh look that screamed, "Too much information!"

"I did my residency in the navy, and as one military man to another, I want to personally thank you for your sacrifice. You put your life on the line so that others can be free. There's something divine in that," said Peter haltingly. His words were laced with feeling.

"Cut the crap, Doc. Save it for someone who cares" was Jack's reply.

Peter paused a moment to take a good look at Jack. Sitting before him was a man who had the natural good looks to be on a US Marine Corps recruitment poster. He had a young Tom Selleck's features. Dark wavy hair and a strong jawline combined with expressive brown eyes provided Jack with an almost movie star appeal, but here was a man who had given up on life. The fact that he had a bad case of the chills, the temperature outside was in the low sixties, and Jack was wearing a short-sleeved shirt and shorts was not lost on Peter. Jack was playing the role of the martyr, and the artificial limbs were his sacrificial offerings to the world.

"You say you're a marine, but you're not like any marine I've ever met … You're a coward," said Peter.

Nick and Darrel, both wide-eyed by the statement, did an immediate double take at each other, floored by Peter's words. Clint, "Mr. Always in Charge," fumbled the sheets he was holding, almost dropping them to the floor. Eve, mouth open, had a "deer caught in the headlights" look on her face.

Jack's face reddened and his brows arched in anger as he pressed his lips together in steely resolve. His expression had turned from callous disregard to one of pent-up fury. Slowly searching for power lost somewhere in the far reaches of his soul, Jack moved his artificial arms and placed his hands on the side rails of the wheelchair. Using what appeared to be superhuman strength, he pushed himself up to a standing position. Then the miraculous occurred. Jack began to move his artificial fingers. Haltingly at first then with more speed, kicking in every computer chip housed in his state-of-the-art limbs, he forced the appendages on his hand into a fist. This was all accomplished as he glared at Peter with an unquenched hatred he had kept at bay—hatred reserved for the enemies he had confronted in battle. With raised arms, hands clenched in fists, Jack moved his right leg forward and then his left. His forward movement was stiff and awkward, reminiscent of Frankenstein on a good day, but he was walking.

As he approached Peter, he began throwing wide haymaker punches. Peter astutely stepped back out of range of each of the punches. Jack, seemingly possessed, continued moving forward, forcing Peter across the room as he wildly threw his fists. Peter finally became backed up to the wall at the far end of the room. Jack, determined to hit his mark, took one last ferocious punch. Peter stepped inside his throw, coming face-to-face with Jack. It was only then that Jack noticed the expression on Peter's face. He saw the reassuring smile and the tears that had pooled in Peter's eyes, a face that resonated with love. He had seen the look before, in his mother's and father's eyes, in the eyes of his wife, Eve, and in the eyes of his comrades, his brothers in arms. It was only then that he realized what he had done and fell on Peter exhausted. His arms landed on Peter's shoulders, wrapping around him for support. With his cheek next to Peter's, Jack whispered, "Thanks."

Nick and Darrel quickly rushed over and lifted Jack off Peter helping him back to his wheelchair. Eve, ecstatic, ran over and threw her arms around Jack. "Sweetheart, do you realize what you just did? You moved your arms, your fingers, and you walked. I knew you could do it. You're amazing," she said, giving him a big kiss on the cheek.

"Yeah, yeah, yeah" was Jack's modest reply, but he was lovin' it.

Peter looked at the couple before him and the words of a friend came to mind. They were the words to a poem written by Judy Taylor, a reflection born of her reality as a quadriplegic whose body had been ravaged by polio. Only words from a stanza, but they spoke to the heart. "Now I can see the beauty in my sadness."

Clint, still standing at his vantage point next to the linen cart, was astounded by what he had witnessed. His respect for Peter was growing, and he knew he would have to make the life-or-death decision soon as to his future.

Eve and Jack left the hospital that afternoon and returned to their two-bedroom ranch home in Toluca Lake. It had been an exhilarating day for both of them. Jack had been in such a foul mood since his return from Afghanistan that to see him upbeat was epic. The last eight months had been a kind of slow torture for Eve. She played her role as loving wife, but Jack's daily gruff, caustic demands were more than she could take. The war and his injuries had changed him. The once affable, take-on-any-challenge soldier she had met six years before had become a complaining tyrant. She so longed to have him back, but now, she had grown to resent him. The doctors had predicted that Jack would be able to move his prosthetic arm and fingers as well as walk if he only put some effort into it. The best cutting-edge technology was employed in his prosthetics and the doctors were more than just a little annoyed that Jack refused to even attempt to use them.

Eve's only respite from Jack's constant badgering was her mornings. Jack was a late sleeper, another aspect of his life that had changed since his return. She would wake at about six, read the paper, have a light breakfast, and drink her coffee. That was her sanity break, and she relished those moments away from his presence. To add to the misery, their sex life was nonexistent. Not that Jack made her feel particularly amorous, but she missed the intimacy. Even a hug with prosthetic arms would have filled the void. Fortunately, nothing was missing in regard to his genitalia. God had mercifully spared the family jewels, but they might as well have been blown off. When Jack lost his arms and legs, he felt emasculated. It was castration by default. The truth was their marriage was on the rocks, and Jack was oblivious to the fact.

That Tuesday was like no other. Jack came home invigorated; his flu symptoms vanished. He had stood up and fought, and in the process, he had found his courage—the courage he had left on a desert road in a biblical land on the other side of the world. He felt like he could accomplish anything now. He flashed Eve an unmistakable lustful stare. She shook her head in disbelief and smiled. Jack gave her a lingering kiss and slowly began to undress her. Yes, he was awkward and slow. Eve pretty much undressed herself, but that only added to their building sexual desire. Jack knew how to drive Eve into orgasmic ecstasy. That day was no exception. Eve reflected on her marriage and the beauty of two people knowing each other so intimately that they fulfilled each other's innermost sexual needs: two individuals bonding together as one. With some clumsy maneuvering they were able to position themselves and consummate intercourse. Jack was on sexual fire and seemed to last forever. Finally, they climaxed, together. The sheer joy and comfort Jack experienced from this release blanketed his inner being with a peace he had never known. It was a peace so profound and powerful that it defied explanation. He was finally able to accept his role as a soldier fighting in defense of a people he did not know or truly comprehend. The animosity he felt toward the Afghan people as a result of his injuries melted away in a sea of forgiveness and understanding. They had suffered also. Their history was a testament to suffering.

He had rediscovered his manhood. He could stand up and fight again even if it was on artificial legs using prosthetic arms and fingers. Jack felt he had been given a second chance by God. He would accept life as it was not as he wished it could be. He apologized to Eve for being such a "butthead" in the past and told her how much he loved her. Then suddenly a marvelous event occurred that reassured Eve no matter what obstacles they faced in the future, their marriage would endure. It happened immediately after Jack made his admission of love to Eve. He let out a loud fart. After a long-strained silence, when the two of them could hold it in no longer, they laughed a gut-wrenching laugh that brought tears to their eyes. Eventually their laughter subsided, and Eve laid her head on Jack's chest. He ran his artificial fingers through her hair and told her how beautiful she was, and she affirmed her love for him.

Eve contemplated the events of the day and thought how strange life was. That one human being could so profoundly change the course of two people's lives, but that was exactly what Peter Kalos had done and she had not thanked him.

# CHAPTER 10

CLINT WAS SEATED IN HIS VIPER, INCHING THROUGH TRAFFIC. UNFINISHED road work had brought travel to an almost standstill. He was to pick up Stacy from work and was already running ten minutes late. The call to her on his mobile phone had gone unanswered. Unknown to him, she had forgotten to charge her cell phone. He was about to call information and contact the restaurant when traffic broke free. A left turn put him two blocks from the diner. Stacy had impatiently stepped outside to see if she could spot him. As luck would have it, the car in front of him was commandeered by an elderly woman in a beige 1982 Dodge going about fifteen miles an hour below the speed limit. (Isn't that always the way when you're running late?) He tried tailgating her while revving his engine, but she was oblivious to his actions. Even when he blared his horn at her, there was no response. In between his badgering of the senior, he kept his eyes on Stacy.

He was still about a block and a half away when he saw the nightmare unfold. A large, late-model, maroon van stopped directly in front of Stacy. Three men exited through the back doors of the vehicle; working quickly they grabbed her, and as she struggled, they forced her into the back of the van then sped away.

Clint could feel his senses ignite, the adrenaline pumping through his veins. He pressed on the accelerator and turned the steering wheel to his right; he jumped the curb, which landed him on the sidewalk. Once on the sidewalk, he slammed on the gas pedal. The Viper rocketed forward, hitting sixty miles an hour in seconds. A family consisting of a mother, a father, and a young son was all on bikes fifty feet ahead of him, blocking the sidewalk. Quickly he turned to the left and went over the curb, which straddled the car half on the road and half on the embankment. This avoided the family on bikes but put him side by side with a Ford truck and on a collision course with a parked car. Once again, he pressed on the gas. He barely shot through the gap between the Ford and the parked car, hitting a patch of clear road. He gunned it. The van had made progress though, just making the light at a nearby intersection. Clint laid on the horn as he ran the red light. A garbage truck had just entered the intersection. The driver hit the brakes simultaneously as Clint swerved to avoid it. Miraculously the vehicles missed each other by inches.

Clint knew his way around a racetrack, another key aspect of his profession. He realized, even with taking every precaution and researching a natural kill situation thoroughly, that unexpected events happen and have to be factored in. Being able to escape a plan gone awry was crucial. He was naturally mechanically inclined, a boon when it came to souping up engines used in various trade trucks. He was so adept at driving that stunt coordinators had noticed his talent while at the track and he was on the short list for chase scenes or when a difficult car maneuver was called for. He even belonged to their union, known to them as Chet Bolton.

Caught up in the frenzy of the chase, Clint had to force himself to think. How would he stop the van? The truck was nearly 5,000 pounds heavier than the Viper. Stacy was a concern also. If the van came to a crashing stop, she might be thrown forward and hurt. Clint figured if he used his car as a battering ram and hit the front of the truck at the right angle and at the right speed, he could force its wheels against the curb and literally sheer them off the axle and bring it to a grinding halt. It was a shot he had to take. He floored his car, jettisoning it forward at over seventy miles an hour as he struck the van. The sound from the collision was ear-shattering, the grating noise of metal scraping against cement adding to the decibel level.

The Viper forced the van to a crushing stop, demolishing the front wheels in the process. Clint's plan had worked but had taken a devastating toll on his car. The Viper was completely crushed in and twisted on the passenger side, the frame literally forced into a U shape. He had to exit his vehicle via the driver's side window, then immediately approached the truck.

The swarthy motorist of the van, with his bandana clad head, recovered quickly from the crash and pushed a large caliber gun through his open window. Clint was prepared for that contingency. He ducked out of the range of fire and rushed to the driver's side door grabbing the hand holding the pistol. He pulled forward on the hand until the motorist's arm was at full extension. Clint, using his forearm and elbow, broke the arm of the driver, forced it backward toward his head, and then with his other hand pulled the trigger on the gun. The pointblank gunshot from the magnum pistol pretty much blew the scumbag's head off.

Clint wrenched the van door open, pulled the dead body out of the truck, and entered the vehicle. Once inside he spotted Stacy on the floor near the back of the vehicle, but before he could approach her, another thug rushed toward him with a large knife in hand. Using a martial arts move, he used the forward motion of the assailant and an arm hold to wrench the knife from his attacker. Then Clint grabbed the knife and drove it through the chest of his opponent. Clint, judging the depth of the knife, knew he had penetrated his heart.

He then headed for Stacy, but before he could reach her, out of a dark corner of the van another punk advanced, throwing a chain around his neck in an attempt to choke him. Clint threw back his elbow, catching the guy in the solar plexus. His attacker bent over in pain from the hit. Clint grabbed him by the collar and threw him against the side of the van, then grabbing his throat with one hand, he crushed his windpipe. The back van doors suddenly flew open, and the final dirtbag jumped out and ran like hell.

Clint rushed to Stacy's side, kneeling next to her. "Are you all right?"

A tearful Stacy replied, "Yes."

Clint leaped from the van and ran after the final attacker. The guy had a good half-block lead as the chase began. The daily Spartan workout routine Clint pursued came in to play here. He believed wind sprints to be a must in any training regime, and his diligence to that mantra paid off. He began to gain on his prey (and this was a guy running for his life). Clint got within three feet of his victim then dove, his arms catching him around the legs. The tackle sent the dirtbag to the ground with a thud. The thug, dazed by the fall, had his arms outstretched, with his head resting on the cement. Clint climbed onto his back. His left hand clutched the back of the neck of the escapee and pushed it against the cement, locking it against the ground, and then with his right hand, he threw a devastating punch directly to the temple. Clint could feel and hear the skull crushing beneath the force of his blow. The man died instantly, but that wasn't enough for Clint. He grabbed his head with both hands and twisted, breaking his neck. Only now would Clint's vengeance be quenched.

He ran back to the van, where a small crowd had gathered.

An elderly man, dressed casually, had emerged from the crowd and was peeking inside the back door. "Is there anybody in there?"

Clint grabbed the man's shoulder. "I've got it handled from here."

Clint stepped into the van. There was just enough light coming from the front window of the van to discern Stacy on the floor. She was holding what was left of her panties, a shredded piece of silky cloth. Stacy wanted to put them on but cognitively couldn't fathom they were destroyed far beyond use. Clint stared at her, moved by her helplessness. He asked the question that was paramount in his thoughts, "Did they …?" Tears streamed down Stacy's cheeks, as she shook her head no. He ripped open his button front shirt, the buttons flying in all directions. Pulling the shirt from his bare upper body, he knelt next to Stacy, wrapping the shirt around her hips and legs, covering her dress so that no one would get a glimpse of her private parts. He then lifted her up in his arms and carried her from the van. Once outside he spotted a cement bench near a bus stop. Working his way through a stunned group of bystanders, he took her over to the bench and sat, cradling Stacy in his arms.

Once settled on the bench, she looked up at him and asked, "Did you get the one that ran? Are they all dead?"

Clint looked over at the crippled van and said, "Yes, they're dead, all of them. There's nothing to fear now."

Stacy lifted up her hand and brushed back a few strands of Clint's hair that had fallen across his brow. Almost in a whisper, she said, "Thank you." Stacy closed her eyes and rested her head against Clint's bare chest as they heard police sirens approaching.

—⁂—

Clint was seated in Chief Freeman's office. Stacy was in another room talking with female staff officers knowledgeable in molestation, part of the city's rape task force. Although she had not been physically penetrated during the attack, there were psychological scars that needed to be addressed. For Stacy, the knowledge that all her attackers were dead was a major comfort to her. There was no conflict with her Christian beliefs in this regard. Stacy knew that evil existed in the world and that as a Christian she was called on to be ever vigilant and to fight Satan's influence whenever possible. In her mind, Clint had acted as an avenging angel. She had no doubt that the young men in that van had succumbed to the dark side (to coin a *Star Wars* term). Stacy would overcome the trauma of the day's events the way she always had, by trusting in God. He had used Clint to spare her the horror of being raped, and he would be there in the future to protect and guide her.

This was nearly a worst-case scenario for Clint. Sitting in the office of the police chief, now on the radar of law enforcement, was not a good thing. He was prepared as always. There was a Velcro-sealed compartment in his wallet that held his Ranger military identification with an accompanying license. He was now Buddy Wilson, ex-Ranger. Clint had thought for an instant to walk away from the scene, but he could not leave Stacy alone to handle the repercussions of the assault and he could be identified. Hell, his car was there—what was left of it. So he would face this head-on.

Chief Freeman entered the room. The chief extended his hand. "I'm Police Chief Max Freeman."

Clint extended his hand, shaking Max's. "Buddy, Buddy Wilson. How are you, sir?"

Max could see the military training come through; being referred to as "sir" was a hallmark of anyone who had recently been in the service.

"I'm doing all right; what about you? That was some confrontation you had out there."

"I'm fine, sir."

"You killed four people today."

"I know."

"Typically, we would hold you while we determine whether charges will be filed against you. However, let me give you some background on the men you killed. These guys were out of El Salvador. They were wanted there for armed robbery, murder charges, and extortion. When they infiltrated this country, they changed their MO. They went from robbing banks to home invasion robberies. Once inside the home, they not only robbed the victims but would rape the women. If confronted with any resistance, they would simply shoot all the victims. We suspect them of over twenty home invasions, fifteen rapes, and four known murders. These guys were some pretty bad hombres. We could never get a line on them because they never followed any kind of pattern. They picked upscale neighborhoods anywhere from San Francisco to San Diego. This was a first though, grabbing a girl off the street. If the rape had been successful, we believe they would have attempted it again. We found evidence from one of the home invasions in the van so we know we have the right bunch. Basically, the district attorney sees your actions as self-defense; you were protecting your girlfriend. No charges will be filed. Personally, you have my thanks for getting these guys and the thanks of the Los Angeles police department for your valor. There is, however, the matter of the reward—$25,000 to be exact.

"A $25,000 reward? You must be kidding!"

Max smiled. "No joke, and District Attorney Darelli wants to present the check to you in a ceremony with a plaque from the city."

"Thanks, but I would prefer to be anonymous on this. I killed those guys because they kidnapped my girl and were going to rape her. I don't want a reward for that. Isn't there some sort of fund for families of officers killed on duty?"

"Yes, of course there is."

"Why don't you split the money between that and some sort of victims of violent crime foundation?"

Max shook his head in disbelief. "Are you sure you want to do that?"

"Absolutely, and I really don't want any publicity on this. Being an ex-Ranger and these guys being from a foreign country, the media might take this and blow it out of proportion."

"I see your point … I'll take care of it. I can allude to the press that you were part of an undercover unit working with the department. I'll square it with Darelli."

"Thank you, sir. I really appreciate it."

"Thank you, for the contribution and for getting those guys … They broke the mold with you, son. God bless."

Max stood and shook Clint's hand.

Clint walked out of the office followed by the chief. Stacy was seated on a bench directly across from Max's quarters. Both men noticed her presence.

"I see your girl's waiting for you. Thanks again, Buddy. Take care," said Max.

Stacy overheard the chief's farewell words and thought how truly special Rod was. People tended to feel close to him after only knowing him for a short while. Here was the chief of police calling him buddy, a term of endearment between friends. Only Rod could elicit that kind of Christian love from a previously complete stranger.

Stacy stood and smiled as Clint approached. "Would you mind if I spent the night with you at your house?" she said.

With a grin, Clint said, "I think I can arrange that."

—∞—

It was late when Stacy and Clint arrived at the house. They were both physically spent and headed directly to the bedroom. The question arose of what Stacy was to wear for sleep attire. Clint offered up a worn, thin, ribbed tank top and old boxer shorts. Stacy took one look at the tank top and said, "I might as well be wearing a wet T-shirt. Look how thin the fabric is."

Clint replied slyly, "Gee, I didn't even notice that."

"Yeah, right" was Stacy's reply.

"All my body armor is being refurbished at the metal shop."

"No one likes a smartass," said Stacy with a smile.

"Smart ass … That's not a very Christian thing to say."

"How about no one likes a stinking Philistine who's lying through his loincloth?"

Clint laughed. "You're good."

"That's right, so find me a sweatshirt to wear as a top."

Clint relented and produced an old Jaguar football sweatshirt. He was initially drawn to the team by their name. He had actually thought of using Jaguar as his assassin moniker but settled on the Black Stallion because it seemed to capture the essence of his natural kill philosophy. The initial success of the team had got him hooked and he was now a diehard fan.

The two finally settled into Clint's bed. Clint was clothed only in his boxers. They got under the covers. They said their good-nights and kissed tenderly. Clint wrapped his arm around her; Stacy laid her head on his bare chest.

As tired as they both were, sleep did not come easy. The events of the day hung in the air like fog on a dark night. No words were spoken as the two graciously kept silent so as to allow the other to find the healing tranquility of sleep.

Ten minutes elapsed, when Stacy moved her head from Clint's chest into the nape of his arm so as to look up and see his face. Although the room was dark, she could see his features clearly, illuminated by the light of the moon emanating through the Japanese paper shade. His eyes were open as he stared into the darkness trying to make sense of the momentous occurrences that day. Stacy spoke softly but clearly. "I want to spend my life with you." He was overwhelmed by her words. As hard as he tried, he could not stop the tears that flowed from his eyes. He clutched her shoulder drawing her close. Clint kissed Stacy passionately, long, and hard.

Stacy, breathless, was the first to speak. "Let's …" Clint was sure the next words out of her mouth would be "make love," but to his surprise she said the word "pray."

"Ah … OK" was his response.

Stacy got out of bed and knelt, clutching her hands in prayer as her elbows rested on the mattress for support. Clint followed suit; however, he intertwined her arm in his, the way he had seen Peter and Stephanie do. Stacy liked that, pulling him close to her.

"Dear Lord, thank You for Your many blessings to us. Thank You for bringing me through this day unharmed and for this man I love kneeling beside me. We kneel before You in awe and thanksgiving knowing it is impossible to truly comprehend Your nature and the immense love You have for us. May we always have a place under Your wings, and may Your angels guard over us forever. I love You, Father, Son, and Holy Spirit … my God" were her words.

Clint was impressed by her simple prayer and exhilarated that she was in love with him. He was intrigued that she would share the news with God before she had told him, but that was Stacy, always the Christian.

Stacy twisted her head to look at Clint. "It's your turn."

Clint was blindsided; he wasn't sure what to say. "I … I like to pray in private."

Stacy gave him a compassionate smile and responded, "Sweetheart, it's me."

There was no getting out of it. "Lord, it's been a hell of a day (maybe not the best opening for a prayer). As You know, I've never truly been afraid for myself, but when Stace got kidnapped, I've never known fear like that. There's no one on earth I care for more. Amen."

Clint surprised himself. He had not meant to share that information with anyone, especially Stacy. It showed weakness, but it was the truth.

There was a cathartic feeling that enveloped him as the words passed from his mouth. Stacy's statement about not truly comprehending God had struck a chord. Could there really be a God? He had lived his life completely in his own self-absorbed world, a professed Darwinist; he had taken survival of the fittest to a new level. He was screwed big time if he was wrong. There was a part of him that yearned to believe. He had always been "the bad boy," and he liked that aura, but with Stacy, he wanted to be more. He wanted the divine serenity that he saw in Stacy, the inner beauty she possessed, but he had long ago chosen his path and there was no going back.

Stacy was surprised by Rod's prayer. He was so articulate and knowledgeable when it came to the Bible, yet his prayer was so simple and basic. She was moved by his candor in regard to her safety, but she had witnessed firsthand the brutality he possessed, his vengeful side. It was curious to her that he did not thank God in his prayer, but the love he felt for her was evident. She worried about his safety too, but he was a computer geek albeit a gorgeous one. How much trouble could he get into?

—⚌—

The Bookmark was under twenty-four-hour surveillance and Clint reviewed the video daily. Any movement within the store was detected immediately, especially near the sight of *The Art of War* book. It was a Tuesday and Clint was at the hospital keeping tabs on Peter when Phil Darso entered the bookstore and left a note for Clint inside the infamous volume. The three-by-five note card read, "My antagonist is supposed to die of natural causes not of old age. We need to talk." It was signed only with the letter P.

Once Clint retrieved the message, he set about arranging a meeting place with Darso. He followed his routine for a week and found a perfect rendezvous point. Phil had a habit of washing his top-of-the-line black E-Series Mercedes on Thursdays at a nearby car wash and Clint decided that it would be there that they would meet. He was going to return the money and walk away from the hit. It would be a first for him; he truly admired Peter and did not want to see his demise. He would tell Darso extenuating circumstances prevented him from completing the hit. He knew it meant trouble. Darso had paid up front in cash and a refusal even with the money returned would not placate a man like Darso. His meeting with Phil was two days away and Clint was on edge about it. It was unusual for him to feel uneasy about any situation. He was a man that was always in control, but Darso was a formidable figure and Clint needed to be at the top of his game when they met.

—⚡—

Peter was in the car with Nick and Darrel being transported to work. It was another beautiful day in Southern California. Darrel was seated in the back seat next to Peter. A large billboard that was in prominent view had just changed its advertisement. The previous ad for an upscale restaurant had been replaced by one advertising a gentleman's club, the Peppermint Walrus. There was a photo, from the neck up, of a beautiful blonde-haired girl, presumably a dancer from the club. The car came to a halt waiting for the red light. Peter was mesmerized by the billboard to the point that Darrel noticed his rapt attention. Darrel commented, "Beautiful girl. It's a shame she's wasting her life at a strip club."

"Yeah," Peter responded, coming out of his stupor.

Clint was at his desk monitoring the videos that morning and caught the scene. He thought it odd that Peter of all people would be captivated by a billboard of a stripper. *He's human after all,* Clint thought, *just checking out the menu.*

—⚡—

It was one o'clock at night when Clint's video computer monitoring system set off a sound alarm indicating movement outside the Kalos residence. Clint was inside the bathroom adjacent to his office brushing his teeth, getting ready to retire for the night, when he heard the siren. With toothbrush still in his mouth, he walked into the office area to view the monitor. The video cameras scanned the area, but nothing seemed amiss. Suddenly the satellite tracking system began to beep. Peter was on the move!

Clint, while inside the Kalos home inserting the video and sound equipment, had also inserted a dime-sized tracing device inside Peter's jackets. The appliance was disguised with the words "inspected by #13" and attached with an adhesive backing to interior pocket of the coat. Peter, wearing one of his jackets, had slithered out the master bathroom window undetected and thrown a baseball against a tree near the back wall, activating the video camera that swept that area. When the camera turned toward the noise, Peter jumped over the wall and ran toward a waiting Uber car parked on a side street near his home. Peter escaped observation by the police contingent monitoring his house from the van nearby.

It took Clint only a minute to grab his satchel of high-tech surveillance gadgets, and soon he was tracing Peter's advance from a location monitor in his newly acquired Corvette. Peter was headed for the city. Clint was intrigued. What could possibly draw Peter from the safety of his home to the city in the middle of the night?

—⋘—

A half hour had elapsed when the signal on the monitor ceased movement. Following the video map, he tailed the halted beacon to a parking lot where he saw the Uber sedan at a standstill and Peter next to it pacing back and forth. Above the doorway adjacent to the lot was a large sign that read, "The Peppermint Walrus." Go figure! This all seemed so out of character for Peter.

Clint parked his car a discreet distance away. He opened his satchel and retrieved binoculars and a small saucer-shaped device used for deciphering dialogue at long distances. He rolled down the windows in the car, inserted the Q-tip-size hearing mechanisms into each ear, and readied the listening dish for use. With binoculars in hand, it wasn't long before he saw the back door to the club open and a huge mesomorph of a man exit. He was obviously the bouncer. He held the door open as a parade of attractive, shapely women departed the club. As the last girl went through the door, the bouncer said, "Take care. Drive ..." Clint picked up static instead of the bouncer's last word. Damn it! He hated it when his equipment malfunctioned. It was only a week ago that he had tested the piece of crap. Of course, it worked fine then. He assumed the last word the bouncer said was "safe," but any kind equipment failure wasn't acceptable. He would just have to deal with it.

Then he saw her, the girl featured on the billboard. She was more striking in person. Her long, blonde, curly hair accented a picture-perfect model's face, and her curvaceous body seemed like it wanted to bust out of her T-shirt and tight jeans. Clint could feel the sexual desire rising in his loins. She was a stunner. Peter spotted her immediately and rushed over. The girl recognized Peter, but her expression was not one of elation but of disdain. The bouncer immediately noticed Peter's presence and yelled, "Chelsea ... *OK?*" The static had once again blocked out a word, in this case the word "you."

"Yeah Cal, I'm fine! I ... deal with this guy!" she yelled in response. The word "can" was being blocked out in her reply. Clint's aggravation with the equipment was starting to build. The back of Peter's head was the view through the binoculars so reading his lips was out of the question.

Then Peter spoke. "You know that I love you and want you ..." Peter then extended his arms in an attempt to hug Chelsea. His action infuriated her, and she responded by pushing him back. She shouted, "Get out of here! Go back to your wife and kid." There was no mistaking that line. It came through loud and clear for Clint.

The bouncer was now on the move headed directly toward Peter. Following the adage "discretion is the better part of valor," Peter went back to the waiting car, entered the vehicle, and departed the scene.

Clint was stunned by what he had just witnessed. The one man he truly admired had totally disappointed him. Peter had obviously had a relationship with Chelsea at some point in his past, but his marriage was rock-solid; why would he risk losing it all for this bimbo? Sure, she was fine, but Steph was no slouch in the looks department, and she adored him. With Stacy in his life, he knew firsthand what it meant to be loved. Yes, he found Chelsea sexually arousing, but he wouldn't put his relationship with Stacy at risk and he wasn't even having sex with her.

Disappointment was quickly turning to anger for Clint. What an asshole: saint by day, lecher by night. It takes all kinds. He was beginning to buy into the whole Christian thing too. Could he trust anyone? Could Stacy turn on him, find someone new? *Life is shit.*

Clint turned the ignition key to the Vette, put the car in gear, and sped away.

# CHAPTER 11

It was Thursday, the day Clint was to meet with Darso. After a sleepless night, Clint had decided to go ahead with the kill. He had concluded that Peter didn't deserve the adulation his friends and family bestowed on him. He was living a lie. His life was a fabrication. All his seemingly altruistic actions were premeditated, done to impress the people around him. Hell's avenging angel would give him his payback in this life, and his name was Clint. The Black Stallion would gallop into his life, exacting retribution.

Phil arrived at the Suds Car Wash late in the afternoon, later than Clint expected. A wiry Hispanic kid, sporting an aged baseball cap worn askew, dressed in a grimy Suds T-shirt and equally gritty jeans, had taken over the final detailing of his black Mercedes. He had just finished putting the liquid shine dressing on the tires when he walked over and stood next to Phil. "Mucho beautiful car, senor," said the ruddy-faced Hispanic as he smiled, revealing a prominent gold tooth. Phil saw the gold tooth and thought, *He's probably got more money in that gold tooth than he made in a half a year working at the car wash.* Darso shook his head and thought, *It must be a cultural thing.* He was about to hand the kid a dollar tip when the boy continued speaking. "Amigo, she fine car, look like a black stallion." Phil knew instantly who he was talking to. He grabbed Clint's arm just below the shoulder, and as he squeezed, he said, "You haven't finished the job ... The interior needs to be cleaned up now. You know I paid for it!

"Let go, amigo, or you not use that arm again," replied Clint, staring defiantly into Darso's eyes. Phil stared back into Clint's eyes and saw there was no fear. He loosened his viselike grip.

Clint continued. "I do the job, but it not natural." Phil knew that he was speaking about the natural kill.

"I don't care if it's natural or not. I want that interior cleaned up ... in two days." Phil stuck the dollar back in his pocket and turned to look at his brilliantly detailed car. He swiveled around, taking one last look at Clint, smiled, and said, "Killer job ... Hasta la vista."

Even in car wash speak, Clint knew he had two days to kill Peter. The irony was he could make it look like a natural kill, but it would mean killing Stephanie and John as well as the detectives on duty. While inserting the video and sound equipment in the house, he had attached a divergent gas hose from the main line to the stove into the crawl space beneath the house. He could divert the gas from the main hose to the crawl space by using a cell phone connection and ignite the gas using the same technology. The hose as well as the mechanical ignition device were made of completely combustible materials not detectable by arson investigators. It was his failsafe plan. He always had one.

Yes, Clint was an assassin, but he was not a mass murderer. He would take out Peter, but he would spare the family.

—✠—

Stacy opened the door to her apartment and greeted Clint with a smile and a kiss.

"Running a little late, huh?" said Stacy.

"Is there a problem?" replied Clint curtly.

"No. I'm just happy you're here. I'm making stir-fry. It'll only take a few minutes to cook. Come join me in the kitchen."

Clint followed her into the kitchen. Stacy went back to her food preparation dicing a few more vegetables for the wok. She then began sautéing the chicken.

"How was your day?" continued Stacy.

"Got the car washed. It took forever to get out of there. Didn't we have stir-fry on Tuesday? Isn't it kind of overkill to have it again on Thursday?"

Stacy turned and glared at him. "From the moment you walked in, here you've been a real *skutch*."

"Skutch! I take it that doesn't mean a breath of fresh air," said Clint with a smile.

She was not in the mood to be placated by humor. "No, it doesn't have to do with fresh air. It's an Italian expression; it means you're a pain in the rear. So what's up? This is not like you. What's going on?"

"Have you ever questioned your faith in God?"

Stacy looked into his eyes puzzled. "I don't know if I've ever questioned His existence. God is God. His divine essence is impossible to totally understand. I know I've questioned some of the plans He's had for me. What's happened?"

"Someone who I respected even admired turned out to be a fake. He was supposedly this ideal Christian and then turned out to be a total hypocrite." As Clint finished his last sentence, it struck him that the statement actually was a perfect description of himself.

Stacy delicately stroked his cheek with her hand. "Rod (ouch!), people are going to disappoint you. We're all faulted. We're all sinners. It's not the religion that's wrong. Christ's words are as true today as they were 2,000 years ago. Try to find it in your heart to look past this man's sinful actions as you would look past your own weaknesses."

Clint's expression turned deadly serious. His eyes zeroed in on hers. Stacy steadied herself as she waited for Rod's response. *"I've got weaknesses?"*

"Rod, you're incorrigible," Stacy said with a smile.

"Just call me the Skutch Meister."

Clint used humor to dodge the topic under discussion. Stacy's forgive and forget policy bothered him. He believed in absolutes. Life was black and white; there was no room for shades of gray. Stacy was good and he was, well, not so good. He wondered if there was any hope for their relationship; so much of their history was based on lies, right down to the name she called him. He had never desired a woman more than he yearned for Stacy. He wanted to touch her, explore every nuance, every crevice of her body. He wanted to see the look of euphoria on her face as they climaxed together in sexual bliss. Yet there was a part of his inner being that wanted to leave her undefiled if he wasn't going to be there for her over the long haul. Maybe there was a molecule of goodness inside him. He knew how to ignite her passion and could probably seduce her, but the aftermath for her would be self-recrimination. The thought that she would disparage herself because of his actions was more than Clint wanted to deal with. Stacy was the kind of girl you married. There's a sentence he never thought he'd express. Marriage was a reality that was hard to comprehend for him. Hell, he was an assassin, a little aspect of his character he had failed to divulge to Stacy. Given all that, there was still in the recesses of his heart a longing to be with her in a union that kept them intimately together on a daily basis. He was crazy about her. Stacy seemed to be perpetually on his mind. There was a part of him that wanted to come clean. Tell her the truth about his dark past. Would she still love him? Clint could not take the chance of being rejected. It was better to live a lie than to risk living without her.

Tuesday would be the last day of Peter Kalos's life. Clint would take him out in Ranger fashion, a bullet to the skull. He was an accomplished sharpshooter and had medals for it from the service, but this would still be difficult for him. He had gotten to know Peter, and as much as he hated him now, they had a history. It benefited Clint that there had been some freeway shots from an anonymous deranged shooter two days previous that injured a commuter. California had a history of snipers surfacing periodically, and although no one who was familiar with Peter's circumstances would believe this was a random shooting, it might be misconstrued by those unaware of Peter's case as the work of the freeway triggerman. It would not be a natural kill but might be considered by some to have the semblance of an unscripted slaying.

October was ending and in a week daylight savings time kicked in so it was dark by seven o'clock in the evening. Peter worked a ten-hour shift, finishing at eight. Nick and Darrel had gotten into the habit when departing the hospital of placing Peter in a location thirty feet from the glass doors when one of them retrieved the car. They believed incorrectly that he was far enough back to be out of view from a potential shooter. Only someone who worked in the hospital and knew the routine would realize there was feasibility for a hit; an angle from the roof above the generator room could achieve a fatal shot. The location was two hundred yards away, but Clint had taken his scope to the roof and confirmed he had Peter in his sights.

Darkness encompassed the hospital and its surroundings. Clint was dressed in hospital maintenance coveralls with a toolbox in hand as he ascended the fixed metal ladder to the roof. He carefully unpacked the pieces to his sniper rifle and methodically assembled the weapon. Sprawled out with his stomach to the asphalt, Clint assumed the sniper kill position.

Within twenty minutes Darrel, Nick, and Peter entered his field of vision as expected. Nick went to get the car as Darrel stayed back to protect Peter. Clint zeroed in, centering his telescopic sights on Peter, who was in the midst of a conversation with Darrel. Peter was smiling as he spoke, so typical of his demeanor. He was a man who seemingly was continuously upbeat and genuinely cared about others. Scenes from Clint's many weeks of surveillance flashed before him such as Peter's loving, playful interactions with his son and Stephanie. There was the flashback of John, Stephanie, and Peter dancing to sixties music. Then there was evening prayer time and the happy banter and laughter that emanated from the interaction of his family and the detectives. These were all mental pictures that flooded Clint's mind. Of course, that was all an act. Peter was a cheating son of bitch, a lying sack of shit. Clint needed to concentrate on the task at hand. He took a breath then released the air from his lungs and gently began to pull on the trigger. This would be the culmination of Peter's existence, his being. With one bullet, Clint would send Peter into the abyss from which no man returned.

Then the impossible happened; Clint froze. He could not pull the trigger. It was a first. He had always been able to complete a hit. What was happening to him? Was he getting soft? Stacy's words haunted him. "Try to find it in your heart to look past this man's sinful actions as you would look past your own weaknesses." He knew he could never cheat on Stacy. How could Peter cheat on Stephanie? He was putting everything he valued at stake. His family, friends, and even God would reject his actions. Although Clint would never screw around on Stacy, he was no paragon of virtue either. He was living a life of deception and the small fact that he killed people made it kind of hard to judge. Clint began to disassemble the rifle as he mulled over his troubling thoughts.

After packing the weapon into the toolbox, Clint crawled to a nearby wall and sat resting his back against the physical barrier. He saw Nick pull up with the car and Darrel quickly shuttle Peter into the back seat. Clint shook his head in disbelief as the car sped off. He realized his inaction would prompt a whole new series of events. Darso would not stand idly by as the trial quickly approached.

—◊◊◊—

This would be the last day of work for Pano at the hospital. There was no further need to keep the charade up. Clint was not going to kill Peter so there was no reason for the surveillance at the hospital. He could have just never shown up for work again, but Clint liked to tie up loose ends. He found it paid off in the long run. Dressed in his hospital work clothes, Clint was walking down the hall heading toward the personnel department to give his one-day notice. In his peripheral, he caught sight of a mop of curly, blonde hair attached to a female figure that had all the right curves. She seemed lost as she stood looking around in the middle of the intersection of four hallways. When she finally turned and faced Pano, he was shocked to behold Chelsea, the stripper. Pano was the only individual in her field of vision, so she approached him.

"Do you know where I might find Dr. Peter Kalos?" she asked.

"Me ... me know Dr. Kalos," said a flustered Pano.

"Do you know where he is?"

Pano had seen Peter in the lunchroom five minutes earlier, but did he want to give him up? There might be another scene similar to the parking lot incident. Peter would be humiliated in front of his coworkers and friends. *Gee wouldn't that be terrible?*

"I know. I will show you," said Clint with the slightest grin. Yes, it was a shitty thing to do, but Peter deserved to face the music. Pano guided Chelsea toward the lunch area.

Peter was seated at a long, rectangular table flanked by Nick and Darrel when the two entered. Darrel was closest in proximity to Chelsea when she spoke.

"Peter!"

"Chelsea," responded Peter, startled.

Darrel recognized her immediately from the billboard. All three men stood simultaneously. However, only Darrel was agile enough to knock over his chair as they stood. Peter rushed over to her. Chelsea had tears streaming from her eyes as she buried her head in Peter's chest. "I'm sorry ... I'm so sorry. Forgive me?" she blubbered.

"It's OK; it's going to be all right," consoled Peter. He then turned to the men around him. Clint thought, *How is he going to get out of this one?*

"Guys, this is my sister Chelsea," said Peter. Then he motioned with his hand toward Clint. "This is Pano, part of our cherished staff, and Darrel and Nick, members of LA's finest."

Chelsea wiped the tears from her face with her hand. "Hi," she said meekly.

Looking at Nick and Darrel, Peter pointed to a secluded area of the lunchroom and said, "I'm going to go over there and catch up."

"Yeah sure," said Darrel.

"That's cool," responded Nick. The two walked out of earshot and sat at a small table.

Clint thought back to the parking lot of the Peppermint Walrus and attempted to reconstruct the sentence that had been so incriminating. "You know I love you and want you." Could there have been more words to that conversation that had been cut off? Maybe that sentence finished with four words like "back in the family." Clint's assumption was correct.

After sitting for a moment in silence, Chelsea regaled Peter with her somber story of a cocaine addiction and the journey that led her to reject the family and ultimately drove her into the exotic dance industry. Peter's presence in the parking lot that night had been a wake-up call. She had been drug free for a week but still had the yearnings. Peter reassured her that he would get her into a program immediately. She would be in Dawn's Light recovery program by the next morning.

Chelsea then asked about John and Stephanie. Peter brought her up to speed on all the family news, including the impending court case, which came as a shock. They talked for almost an hour. After the two exchanged addresses and phone information, they walked arm and arm out into the hallway. He reassured her of his love and gave her a hug and kiss. Chelsea left revived. She received more than love from her brother that day; she had her family back.

# CHAPTER 12

CLINT'S FOREKNOWLEDGE OF STRIPPERS GAVE HIM A STRONG INKLING of what Chelsea would tell Peter about her past. He figured drugs had played some role in her life. More than once in his engagements with exotic dancers he'd been asked to score drugs. He never did. They were usually cross addicted when it came to substance abuse and the purchase of an alcoholic beverage in some way shape or form satisfied their initial cravings. Many times, there was a traumatic event that culminated in their decision to pursue an exotic dance career. One girl he had dated for a short period in his past had been raped. During her time on stage, she used her nude body to taunt her male onlookers as a sort of sexual payback. For other dancers, the drugs alone loosened any moral inhibitions they had against performing unclothed. Then there was the money. Top performers could garner an immense amount of cash for just a few hours of work. This was an incentive few girls could say no to. Peter's surprise appearance had obviously spurred some deep desire in Chelsea to reform. He figured that Peter would get her into a recovery program as soon as possible.

All said, there was a lot to digest after Chelsea's visit to the hospital. It rattled him that he had come so close to killing Peter based on a misconception. Peter was a class act. Even the way he had introduced Pano as "part of our cherished staff" was a testament to his personal integrity.

The whole "Christianity thing" needed to be reexamined. Peter had put himself in danger by leaving police protection behind in an effort to reestablish contact with his sister. For Peter it was all about others. That fact that he was putting his life on the line to testify was evidence of his depth of character and commitment to justice. He truly had a love for humanity. Clint yearned for part of that ethereal essence the Greeks call agape love, the unconditional brotherly love for another. His youth had been so full of rejection and pain; could he shed the hard exterior he had created as a protection against the hurt? Stacy was the one individual who had opened the door to the possibility of being better. There was a purity that resonated from her inner being. Her love for God was indisputable, and his response to her intrinsic divinity was to deceive and distort the truth about himself. Clint was never one to beat himself up, but the lies were getting to him. He had monumental decisions to make.

Peter would be his first consideration. The threat to his life had increased dramatically with the passing of Darso's two-day deadline. He would return the money to Darso, but he had no doubts that there would be another hire to take his place. Clint would stay on at the hospital as Pano the orderly as another set of eyes to avert danger from Peter's path. The weapon arsenal he stored at the house would be transferred to a hidden compartment in the Vette. He would no longer be the hunter but a protector for the hunted.

—◊◊—

Darrel had arrived early at Dawn's Light recovery house. This was the last of his brother Jeff's thirty-day recovery program. When Darrel reached Jeff's room, the door was open, his brother's packed duffel bags were organized neatly on his bed, and Jeff was pacing back and forth in anticipation of his arrival. On seeing his brother, Darrel was impressed by his neat appearance and healthy glow.

"How's it going, bro?" said Darrel.

"I'm cool. Good to see you," replied Jeff with a smile. The two brothers hugged.

"Looking forward to goin' home," continued Jeff.

"Mom's got some fried chicken and sweet potato pie waiting on you."

"I hear that," said Jeff, beaming.

Darrel scooped up two duffle bags and Jeff grabbed the third.

"I'm out of here!" shouted Jeff as he looked around his room for one last time. The two brothers left the room and headed down the hallway. At the end of the hall, they walked into a vestibule that had been turned into an office. After completing sign-out forms, they headed for the front door. As Darrel and Jeff exited the building, they came face-to-face with Chelsea, who was coming up the stairs.

Darrel was first to speak. "It's Chelsea, right? You're Dr. Kalos's sister."

"Yes, that's me. You're Detective …?"

"Darrel, Darrel Washington," he said with a smile as he extended his hand to shake hers. Turning toward Jeff, he continued. "This is my brother Jeff."

"Hi, Jeff. It seems that good looks run in the family … It's a pleasure," responded Chelsea with a smile as she grasped Jeff's hand in acknowledgment.

Darrel was struck by Chelsea's beauty and poise. *Did she really think he was good-looking?* On their previous encounter she had worn heavy makeup that smeared when her eyes drenched her cheeks with tears. Today she looked different, natural. She had applied makeup, but just a light cover with lipstick that had only a hint of red. Her clothing was different too. The clingy blouse she had worn when he first saw her was replaced with a looser-fitting, pinpoint, oxford blouse. It was a more proper Brooks Brothers look. This by no means hid her natural attributes; her ominous figure was still evident.

"It's good seeing you again, Darrel, and meeting you Jeff." She looked at the entrance. "I've got to go in here or I'll be late."

"Good seeing you too," Darrel responded.

"Pleasure to meet you," added Jeff.

Chelsea quickly traversed the steps into the building. Darrel turned his head toward his brother. "Hang here for a sec."

He dropped the two bags he was holding and swiftly navigated the steps following Chelsea. Darrel caught up to her a few feet from the makeshift office.

"Chelsea."

She turned to him.

"I don't mean to bother you again, but I figure if you're Dr. Kalos's sister you've got to be special, and I'd like to get to know you better. I realize that you might be in here a while, but maybe after that we could go out for a cup of coffee or lunch," said a very nervous Darrel.

Chelsea was taken back. She truly did not see this coming. She knew that most guys found her desirable because of her looks, but no one had ever called her special and especially not in regard to family lineage. She smiled.

"Yes, I'd like that. I wasn't able to get into the live-in program. I'm in here on an outpatient basis."

"Great … I mean … a … Could I get your number then?"

"Sure," said Chelsea with a slight grin.

The two exchanged numbers. Then Darrel floated out of the building and down the steps to his brother, who was anxiously waiting for him.

"Did you get her number?" asked Jeff.

Darrel shook his head yes. "I got game."

"You got no game. I was the one she thought was good-looking. She just said yes to you to get to me."

*"Are you still on drugs?"* Darrel said, grinning.

"That's raw, bro, especially me walkin' out of here clean," responded Jeff with a smile.

"She is sweet," replied Darrel lost in fantasy.

"That girl be packin'!"

"Be respectful." However, Darrel couldn't help pondering his brother's statement. Not only was Chelsea beautiful, but she did have a knockout figure.

Darrel followed up, after seeing Chelsea, with a phone call two days later. He arranged a lunch date at a popular Hollywood hangout called Roscoe's Chicken and Waffles. The menu wasn't all that varied, but the food was outstanding. He wanted to be upfront with Peter so he told him about his impending rendezvous. Peter was concerned, not so much because Darrel was going out with her but because recovery programs frown on relationships developing during a rehabilitation period. His final words on the subject were "I trust you, Darrel. I know no matter what the circumstances, you'll act like a gentleman." Darrel was a Christian and wouldn't have premarital sex with her on account of his own moral standards, but Darrel respected Peter's concern.

The day he was to take her out, he scheduled himself off. It worked out better that way with Peter needing round-the-clock protection. He dressed casually in a light blue, long-sleeve, merino wool polo sweater that accentuated his muscular physique. His dark navy pants were made of tropical weight wool. Navy socks and a pair of casual black Italian loafers rounded out his ensemble. When he picked her up from her upscale apartment complex, he found Chelsea dressed in a winter-white, cotton, knit, V-neck sweater and black, form-fitting, boot-cut dress pants. The five-inch heels of her black leather boots accented her already sumptuous body. There are women who can work a sweater such as Marilyn Monroe, then there's Chelsea. Something about the white sweater against her large breasts had Darrel forcing himself to stare at her face, and her face was beautiful!

When the two walked into the restaurant that was a known hangout for many celebrities, it seemed like every patron in the establishment turned to look and ponder what movie or television series they had seen them in. They were a striking couple, both magnificent specimens of male and female beauty.

After getting settled at their table, Darrel was the first to get the conversation rolling. He told her about his job and in particular his mission of guarding Peter, playing down the grave danger he was in. "It's routine to assign officers in these cases just as a precautionary measure" was his less than candid summation of his duties. He described in detail Peter's acts of charity, love of family, and compassion for those around him. Chelsea was particularly moved by the story of the new leather coat being given to the shivering destitute man. She commented, "He was like that as a kid."

Chelsea did not relate much about her past until they returned to her abode, where they shared a pitcher of iced tea. There was a quality about Darrel that broke down the barriers that engulfed her heart. He cared, was not judgmental, and was a great listener. In the privacy of her surroundings, she revealed the startling truth of her past. There were only two children born to the Kalos family. Peter was the first conceived, followed by her birth four years later. Both her parents were of Greek descent, second generation, born in the United States. Her father was the quintessential loving Greek parent, and her mother the caring nurturing counterpart.

Early on, Chelsea's father invested in the restaurant business, creating two highly successful eating establishments. Peter was always the obedient loving son who could do nothing wrong. He was a straight A student, captain of the track and tennis teams, handsome, gregarious, and from an early age possessed a kind and loving disposition.

Chelsea loved her brother for all those reasons and more but was not cut out of the same mold. She was what her father lovingly called "a piece of work." Confrontational seemingly from birth, she rebelled against everything. Her mother said she even refused to breastfeed. She would get A's in English and science and D's in math and history. She fought with the girls in her class and belittled the principal when being disciplined. Having developed early, boys would comment on her blossoming womanhood, but not in exactly those terms. The aftermath of which was a slew of bloody noses and deviated septa. There were tender moments in her youth when she would snuggle with her father and hug and kiss her mother, telling her how much she loved her, but those moments were few and far between. Chelsea knew she was loved; her parents told her on a daily basis even after disciplining her for some infraction. Maybe that's why she felt confident in her life of disobedience. She could always go home. The Kaloses were a faithful family attending church on a weekly basis, but even that was a struggle. Chelsea refused to attend church with the family and threw tantrums when forced to. She did, however, believe in God.

This confrontational behavior continued into her late teens and culminated in a major battle regarding a high school graduation road trip to New Orleans with four friends. Her parents did not believe she was mature or responsible enough to take part, given there was no appropriate chaperone. There was screaming and harsh words, and Chelsea said some things she shouldn't have. A few hours later on a trip back from the grocery store, both parents died in a head-on car crash precipitated by a teenage drunk driver.

"I never got to tell them I was sorry for what I said or tell them how much I loved them," said Chelsea, holding back the tears.

"They knew," responded Darrel, his voice cracking with emotion.

"I blamed God, and after graduation I took my inheritance and hit the road, and I guess I've been running ever since. Along the way I got involved with drugs and made some choices I regret. I kept track of Peter and the family through a cousin."

"Time for a fresh start?"

"Yes, it is."

The two had talked for three hours in the confines of Chelsea's apartment. Darrel made some parting remarks and rose to leave; Chelsea stood as well. She extended her hand in a farewell gesture. Darrel gently took her right hand by the wrist and with his other hand tenderly grasped her left hand; he then turned both of her hands, palms up, and gently kissed them. Almost as if he were kissing the hurt away from a child's cut hand. It was an immensely tender gesture.

He looked up into her tear-filled eyes. "God hasn't given up on you. Don't give up on him" were his last words before departing.

It was the first day back at school for Jeff, having completed the substance abuse program at Dawn's Light. He had kept up with his bookwork while in the program, but it was still a bit of a struggle acclimating to his previous junior high school routine. Besides focusing on his courses, he was actively attempting to dodge his former cohorts in crime Dog and Banger. By two thirty, it seemed that Jeff had eluded the duo. He stopped in the restroom to relieve himself before heading home. The urinals in the men's room reached to the floor. He leaned his body against the smooth white surface of the receptacle, pulled out his male organ, and began to relieve himself.

Seemingly out of nowhere, Dog and Banger appeared and took positions on either side of him. At thirteen Dog was one of those adolescents who developed early possessing, the stature and musculature of NFL linebacker. (How does God do that?) However, he was not the brightest bulb in the candelabra. Banger on the other hand was small for his age and lean, but he had the intellect. It was as if God had taken a chapter out of *Of Mice and Men* when he brought these two boys together. Dog immediately grabbed Jeff by neck and shoved him forward, jamming one side of Jeff's face against the wall and pinning his body against the urinal. Jeff was left defenseless, holding his dick in his hand.

"It's good to have you back. Got yourself all cleaned up. That works for us! By tomorrow mornin', I want a list of four names of guys from your little recovery group and their phone numbers," said Banger, sneering.

"How am I supposed to do that?" pleaded Jeff.

"You know the sayin'. Just do it! Keep your brother out of this, if you want to keep holdin' on to that little baby maker of yours. Meet ya here at eight, and you best have those names and numbers," decreed Banger.

It was at this moment that Dog, using every brain cell in his oversized cranium, came up with a comment so introspective that it rivaled that of a Mensa scholar. "Yeah, do it" were his words of wisdom. Socrates got nothin' on you, Dog.

Dog and Banger left as quickly as they had appeared.

—⁓—

Ten o'clock Monday morning was the time that Phil Darso had decreed for review of each week's drug trade activities. Caesar and Phil met in the mansion's library/office. Seated at the mahogany desk was Phil as Caesar entered the room.

"Good, you're here on time," said Phil.

"Boss, I'm always here on time."

"True. I say that to keep you on your toes. How are the figures for last week?

"They're up 20 percent from the week before."

"That's what I like to hear," responded Phil, smiling. "Didn't we have a kid that went into a recovery program about a month ago? Blueberries, right? He should be out by now."

"Boss, how do you do it? I was just going to tell you about that."

"I'm not just a pretty face. I have brains too." Phil grinned.

The pretty face line elicited a smile from Caesar. "You're right. The kid, Blueberries, just got out of a drug program. Our plan was to get some names and phone numbers from him of other druggies trying to recover."

"I know. How did it go?"

"Couple of our guys put heat on him and the kid came up with the numbers."

"Great!"

"No, it's not so great. The four names and cell numbers matched those of four LAPD detectives."

Phil produced a wide toothy grin. "The kid's got gonads. I would have liked to have been there when those calls were made."

"What do we do now? Rough the kid up?"

"Na. If the kid comes home hurt, there could be negative repercussions we don't need. He's the one whose brother's on the force, right?"

"Yeah."

"Let's fold our cards on this one."

"OK … What's going on with the witness, that doctor guy?"

Phil's expression changed instantly. He scowled and blurted out, "That

Black Stallion son of a bitch sent the money back with a note saying extenuating circumstances prevented him from completing the mission."

"What an asshole," responded Caesar. Secretly, however, Caesar was pleased. He was rooting for the doctor even though he knew the repercussions of attempting to testify would end his life.

"I've got it handled. He'll be taken care of."

Phil's words sounded so confident. It sent a chill through Caesar. What had Darso planned for the Black Stallion?

Darrel and Chelsea had just returned to her apartment after having spent the evening at the Alhambra Dinner Theater. Darrel wasn't a huge theater patron, but they were doing a favorite of his, *The Sound of Music.* He had seen the movie on television when he was eight and the music and lyrics had impressed him so much that he pressured his mother into buying the tape. Darrel proceeded to memorize the melodies and all the words to the songs then would serenade the family with his renditions. His parents found it enjoyable, but extremely weird.

Chelsea was hanging up Darrel's leather jacket in the closet when she said, "I liked the play … You know all the lyrics to the songs, huh?"

"I wasn't singing along too loudly, was I?"

"Most of the songs sounded like a duet, but that was OK."

"Come on … No one around us said anything."

"Who in their right mind is going to tap a six, four, muscle-bound, black guy on the shoulder and tell him to put a cork in it because he's singing "Edelweiss" too loudly?"

"Get real. I wasn't that bad."

"And then when the Mother Superior went into her rendition of 'Climb Every Mountain,' why did you yell out, 'You go, girl'?"

Chelsea walked over and sat on the easy chair across from Darrel.

"That's a great song … Guess I got carried away," replied Darrel with repentant smile.

"Hey, whatever works for you. It was cool with me," said Chelsea playfully.

A loud pounding on the door interrupted their conversation. From behind the door came the words "Chelsea, it's Ben. I scored some great shit!" There was more pounding on the door. "Let me in. I know you're in there. I can hear you talking."

Ben's presence at the door put an immediate damper on Chelsea's upbeat demeanor.

"What is he doing here? I've told him before I quit," said a melancholy Chelsea.

"I got it," replied Darrel as he stood and walked to the door, pulling his wallet out of his back pocket.

Darrel opened the door where he greeted Ben, a strung-out, gaunt, red-eyed shell of a man. His eyes grew as wide as saucers on seeing Darrel.

"I'm Detective Washington with the LAPD. How may I help you?" said Darrel as he flashed his badge.

"Ahh, I got to bounce out of here. Later," said Ben as he quickly turned around and scurried off.

Darrel shut the door and walked back to the sofa.

"Thanks," murmured Chelsea.

"It's going to be all right. For some people, it takes longer to get the message."

"I just don't want you to lose respect for me."

"That ain't going to happen."

"It might when I tell you how … how I made my living." Timidly she continued. "I was a stripper. I don't do that now, but not too long ago that's what I did."

Darrel did not show a shocked response as he said, "OK."

"You knew?"

"There's that huge billboard on Lankerchiem with your face on it. Kind of hard to miss. In fact, that's how your brother knew where to find you."

"I was pretty heavy into drugs when I agreed to do that. Not the greatest move if I wanted to stay incognito. They gave me $3,000 to use the picture."

"That's a lot of money."

"I made a lot of money stripping. I never did lap dances though.

"That's … good."

"Even with the drugs, I saved a lot of it. Now I have a good chance of getting a job at Kerns doing makeup."

"I can see where you would be good at that."

"Darrel, I like you a lot. I just don't want you to think I'm … cheap."

"I don't. We've all had our ups and downs. Life's a journey. We grow. We change. It's my faith that's kept me grounded. I'm a Christian so for me it's all about forgiveness and renewal. You're going to beat this drug thing."

"I like talking to you. You make me feel good. You give me hope."

"It's like Roman's says. If God be for us, who can be against us?"

# CHAPTER 13

Nick, Darrel, and Peter were on their way home from the hospital in the retrofitted Saab. Darrel was driving while Nick was in the back seat next to Peter. The detectives had gotten into the habit of varying their routes each day to Peter's home as a precaution. Peter was scheduled to work until seven but was released early when it was discovered they were overstaffed on what had become a particularly slow day at the hospital. It was four o'clock and the sun was just beginning to set as the three headed for Burbank on local streets. Darrel noticed that a late-model Chevy Impala had been tailing them.

"Nick, turn around and check out that Impala. It's been following us since we left the hospital."

Nick instinctively drew his weapon as he turned to look at the car. He could make out the driver's face clearly. "I can see the guy's lips move. It looks like he's talking into a speaker that might be attached to the visor."

"This doesn't feel right. Buckle up."

After turning his torso forward, Nick reattached the seat belt he had unbuckled earlier to get a better look at their pursuer. Darrel hit the gas pedal as he took a hard right at a nearby side street. The Impala mimicked the turn, following close behind.

What Darrel didn't realize was that he was caught in an intricate web of fifteen cars (each car carrying approximately five individuals) that had been tailing him via high-tech walkie-talkies. Darso had offered the Third Street Gangtas out of East LA, drug trade acquaintances, $25,000 to kill Peter and gave them $10,000 up front for any necessary equipment to complete the job. Of all people, it was Banger who brokered the deal. There were seven cars shadowing the Saab on parallel streets to his right and left. Once he committed to the side street, the seven cars to the right formed a blockade with their cars. The barricade extended beyond just the street; the gang's cars went up on lawns to prevent Darrel from driving off the road to circumvent them. The cars that were following on the parallel street to his left then converged to block his escape route if he doubled back.

Darrel's right turn had led them into a trap. The gunfire started immediately, sounding like five-pound sledgehammers hitting the car in staccato fashion. A quick look in the rearview mirror told him the options behind him were quickly deteriorating. The thought of ramming the blockade in the juncture between cars crossed Darrel's mind. He didn't believe he could build up enough speed to succeed but said a quick prayer and pushed the gas pedal to the floor. It was their only chance of escaping.

He hit the one-foot opening between the cars at fifty miles an hour. The initial crash and screeching sound of metal hitting metal was deafening. The two cars he hit separated, but not enough to squeeze through and the impact had brought the Saab to a standstill.

Smoke was rising from under the hood as Darrel shoved the car in reverse and hit the gas pedal again. Driving backward at full speed, he could see the cars aft were already bumper to bumper, forming a jagged metal wall. It was useless to ram them so he angled the car toward a mom-and-pop grocery store. The store was L shaped with the entrance on the right protruding forward and a small parking lot filling the space to the left. Darrel hit the brakes as he positioned the car so that the L juncture of the two walls acted as barriers behind the driver's side of the car. The rain of bullets continued unrelenting during all this maneuvering.

With the two walls of the grocery store protecting them from the rear, and the Saab acting as a barrier in front the three men, they opened the doors on the driver's side of the car and crawled to the ground. The only upside to this situation was that the bulletproof glass and the steel plates that were inserted in the doors worked like charms. The glass enabled them to see their assailants without being hit by gunfire. However, the enormous firepower aimed at them was so merciless they could barely get a shot off in defense. Then the enemy began to close in.

The cars that had previously been used as a blockade began to approach. They moved within forty feet and encircled them. The Gangstas, emboldened by their overpowering ability to deliver firepower and their tactical ground advantage, began to leave their cover and walk slowly forward, firing at will to finally finish their quarry. We're talking over seventy gang members heading for the final kill. Darrel looked over at Nick, and he responded with a knowing look.

Nick yelled over the sound of pouring gunfire, "You thinking what I'm thinking? They get within ten feet—"

"I stand up on the right and you on the left and we kill as many of these assholes as we can," interrupted Darrel as he finished Nick's sentence.

"Sounds like a plan!" Nick yelled back.

"I'd like to defend myself. Does anybody have an extra gun? I'll go over the top of the car," shouted Peter.

"Here's my thirty-eight," Nick responded, taking his ankle gun and handing it to Peter. Both Nick and Darrel loaded full clips into their automatics. All three men exchanged eye contact, and although not a word was said, the admiration and love they had for each other spoke volumes. The fringes of the gang were already at ten feet when Darrel yelled, "On three ... one ... two ..."

Suddenly there was ear-splitting blast as a Gangsta car exploded in flames. Then a second explosion ripped through another car as it was destroyed in an infernal of flame and smoke. The approaching thugs stopped in their tracks, turning to see what was transpiring. Out of the smoke and flames emerged a lone figure dressed in black. He was wearing a black T-shirt, black cargo pants, black boots, side arms in black holsters strapped to his hip, black flack vest, and black sunglasses. (Johnny Cash would have been proud.) The intruder was carrying a black rifle as well and commenced firing. The Gangstas scattered, running for cover. The constant spray of bullets from the one rifle seemed to engulf the scene.

From behind the Saab, Darrel exclaimed, "Who is that guy?"

"He's my guardian angel ... sent by God," responded Peter.

Nick replied, "If he's sent by God, we need to get God to arm the LAPD. He's carrying a tricked-out Russian Saiga-12K with an autoload magazine. It's an upgrade of the old 'Street Sweeper.' He's shooting shotgun shells. In that black holster with the stock folded over, looks like he has an Israeli IMI mini Uzi, and on the other side, by the look of the grip, I'd say that holster's sporting a Heckler and Koch USP—.45, Mark 23 semiautomatic. The grenades attached to his flack vest are Arges 84s. They have a plastic shell that incases about 5,000 steel balls."

Peter turned to Darrel. "How does he know that?"

"Don't ask. He's a weapons geek. That's the one thing he knows about besides food," replied Darrel.

"The food comment, that's cold, bro. It's my hobby," said Nick.

"Nick, he's got to reload soon. Let's get ready to give him cover," stated Darrel as he aimed his gun over the car.

Clint was in his element. He didn't believe in reincarnation, but the thought that he might have been a Spartan soldier during the Peloponnesian War made him smile. He had the heart of a warrior. It was his belief that true soldiers are born, not manufactured. As a child, playing war was a passion for him. Using wood and nails he constructed toy weapons; he even whittled a pistol from a block of wood when he was ten. He loved the challenge of it all: building his physical stamina and pushing his body to the point of exhaustion to ready him for conflict brought a satisfaction that was hard to describe. The pent-up anger he felt from a family life gone bad gave him a reservoir of hate to draw from—a potent weapon in itself. He could veil his opponent in a shroud sewn from the fiber of abuse and rejection his father had woven. This was a valuable asset in his chosen vocation as a hit man. His targets lost their humanity, enabling him to become unattached when he pulled the trigger. Observing Peter's life had changed that. This was a man who he could believe in, he could trust. Stacy's presence in his life, along with Peter, confirmed that goodness actually existed. This raised the possibility that there was a caring God who was master of the universe.

The Third Street Gangtas, on the other hand, he could cloak with a blanket of disdain and contempt. They epitomized evil, and all shared the face of his father. It was as if this day had been predestined and Clint chosen as the solitary gladiator to confront the lawless horde. Every aspect of his life seemed as if it had been a tutorial in preparation for this fight. Even his recreational activities were instrumental in honing his battle prowess. He was an avid video game practitioner, especially those that were war related or dealt with armed combat. Some of his favorites were the Medal of Honor series along with the Call of Duty anthology. The titles he preferred that were not war related included *Max Payne, Grand Theft Auto,* and of course the *Hit Man* installments. The video games kept his hand-eye coordination in peak condition. Clint complemented this visual/manual union with actual confrontation in the paintball arena. There was a group of ex-servicemen that met on Wednesday and Thursday nights at the local paintball joint. This was the closest he came to having friends; however, Clint never joined the gang at the neighborhood pub afterward. He didn't drink and his background history didn't lend itself to congenial situations. When asked about his military background, he responded with two words: "covert operations." No one inquired further after seeing him in action with a paint gun. He was by far the most naturally gifted player in the group.

When Clint walked through the smoke and flames to confront the Gangstas, he was already in the zone. The adrenaline pumping through his veins produced a euphoric high that intensified all his senses. The Saiga-12K was a potent weapon. The initial magazine inserted in the rifle during the opening confrontation contained shells possessing only buckshot and the spray hit with lethal accuracy. Twenty-five gang members fell to the ground wounded; the majority were incapacitated. Clint crossed the battlefield walking tall. After finding protection among the assorted cars, the Gangstas returned fire. Clint could hear the bullets whizzing by, but there was a seeming invincibility that shielded him from their gunfire. The only time he moved for cover was to reload, and Darrel and Nick provided a sufficient volley of fire to ward off any potential threat. Peter did not use the thirty-eight to join the detectives in the cover fire. He would kill to defend himself, but his divine purpose was to save lives.

The second magazine loaded into the Russian rifle was strictly comprised of slugs. Clint stalked individual targets with this ammunition. This course of action he found reminiscent of a high-spirited game of *Grand Theft Auto*. The slugs hit their targets with the force of a freight train, with a nine out of ten-strike consistency. One unfortunate gang member used an open door for cover and was killed when the slug drove through the door into his abdomen. The laws of probability would dictate that Clint should have been struck by at least one bullet, but his attackers were not used to this sort of intense combat and when zeroed in on panicked, affecting their aim.

When he experienced a particularly strong pocket of resistance, he threw a grenade. After using two more magazines of slug ammunition, Clint strapped the rifle to his back and pulled out the mini Uzi in a mop-up effort. The Uzi was lethal in its own right, finding numerous marks with a deadly spray of fire. Finally, he drew the HK Mark 23 from its holster, targeting any final survivors.

Holding the gun with two hands, arms extended, he scanned the spectacle of devastation before him. He would take a few steps forward, halt, do a 360- or a 180-degree turn seeking any remaining quarry. A Gangsta who was lying on the ground wounded managed to reach his shotgun, raise it, and aim at Clint. He was a split second too slow as Clint pumped three shots into his chest.

The sun was setting and the shadowy figure of a man, cast from the light off the roof of the grocery store, appeared on the street before Clint. He quickly spun around and fired twice. Both shots struck the head of his opponent. After surveying the scene one last time, Clint ended up just a few feet from the damaged Saab. The two detectives and Peter were standing now, thrilled to see their deliverer in such close proximity. Clint turned, gazing through his sunglasses at the trio before him.

"You guys all right?" said Clint in a friendly tone, almost as if he was acquainted with the three men.

"Yeah," stated Nick.

"Sure," responded Darrel.

"Yes … I'm … I'm all right," stammered Peter.

Clint flashed them a slight smile and walked off as the blaring sirens quickly drew near.

A few seconds after Clint had vanished, police cars and emergency vehicles bombarded the locale. Peter quickly jumped in to assist the medical contingent in saving the lives of the remaining conscious victims.

The official description of the event read, "A gang war erupted in North Hollywood between the Third Street Gangstas and a yet undetermined rival. Dominance over drug trade was believed to be the perpetrating cause of the conflict." The story made the headlines and for a few days captured the public's interest but was soon a forgotten footnote in California's gang lore, and that was the planned outcome the police department and district attorney had anticipated. The trial was swiftly approaching, and the safety of their prime witness did not need to become fodder for the editorial page.

In regard to Clint's presence in the conflict, they could only conjecture. Was he a rogue member of their SWAT team who had gone on a vigilante hunt? Possibly, he was part of an unknown right-wing paramilitary group looking for a cause. Whatever his origin, the mysterious intruder had performed an invaluable service in saving Peter. Chief of Police Max Freeman had his own thoughts as to the identity of the unexplained visitor, which he kept to himself.

Nick and Darrel continued their guard over Peter, staying close during his lifesaving pursuits. Finally, the last medical van disappeared into the twilight. Peter was exhausted as he arched his back and walked the immediate vicinity to relieve the strain. He ended up standing directly in front of the demolished Saab. The car had over six hundred bullet holes, the front end was completely caved in, and all four tires had been blown out, leaving only the dented rims. Peter, with head bent down, stared at the car, mesmerized at the extent of the damage. Nick noticed Peter's dejected stance and forlorn look and wondered what thoughts were racing through his mind. Was he contemplating his mortality and how close he had come to death? Nick walked up to Peter, putting his hand on Peter's shoulder, and said, "Are you OK, Doc?"

"Yeah, I'm fine, but my insurance agent is going to be pissed!" countered Peter.

# CHAPTER 14

STANLEY KING HAD MANAGED THE BOOKMARK STORE FOR FIFTEEN years. At sixty-two he had taken early retirement from a machinist job because of a bum knee; when he saw the job advertisement in the local paper, he applied immediately. He loved literature and reading, was computer savvy, and had worked as a librarian for a short time in college. He had met Mr. Shockley (Clint in geezer disguise), the owner, only once in fifteen years, the day he was hired. Stanley thought Mr. Shockley seemed like he was in his late eighties when they met so long ago and often wondered how long his job would last given it was tied to the life span of the owner. He stopped being concerned after the fifth year had passed. Stanley was a widower, his wife having passed a year previous to his being hired at the Bookmark.

He could have made ends meet without the job, but the $500 every week meant he could live comfortably. A direct deposit was placed into his checking account each week. The job kept him somewhat active and gave him almost unlimited time to read, a passion of his. The establishment sold used books and Mr. Shockley's only demand was that he left the store exactly the way he found it and was never to reorganize the store or purchase books. That was fine with him. There were no heavy manuscripts to move. Given the purchase regulation, the store never accumulated new stock.

He was the lone employee and worked eight to five with an hour lunch Monday through Friday and weekends off. The store grossed almost no money. He kept a hundred in the till for change and made deposits at the local bank's drop-off box. Beside some of the strange individuals who walked into the place, who seemed like they would be more comfortable in a pool hall than a bookstore (for some reason they always ended up in the back of the store), it was a dream job. Stanley figured the shop was a write-off for Mr. Shockley so making a profit didn't matter. There was a group of retired friends who would come in periodically to chat, which gave balance to his many hours of reading. The shop had come to symbolize to Stanley what was great in all books. The Bookmark was a place to be enlightened, travel unexplored frontiers, expand the recesses of your imagination, and ultimately dream.

The bookstore was completely monitored for sound and visual activity by Clint. Any movement in *The Art of War* area was immediately flagged by the computer and would be reviewed by Clint that evening. If a three-by-five card was inserted in the book or cash deposited in the volume with the recessed slot, Clint would retrieve it at night after closing and only when in disguise as Mr. Shockley. If Stanley got ill, there was a cell phone number he could call and leave a message. Clint would conceal himself in the Shockley persona and fill in for Stanley during sick days. Fortunately, Stanley was rarely ill. The bookstore was an effectual front for Clint and the fact that books were involved in the concealment process pleased him immensely. He was an avid reader himself and believed his ability to interpret words was the most valued perception he possessed.

That Friday started like any other for Stanley and continued uneventfully until four that afternoon. It was at that time a visitor entered the establishment. He was of those individuals that Stanley liked to refer to as "those guys," the pool hall variety that had come in sporadically over the last fifteen years. His physical presence was disconcerting. The back and sides of his head were shaved. The top of his skull featured a mop of thick hair that was formed into a myriad of two-inch spikes the tips of which were dyed a bright red and at the base black. He was wearing a tight red T-shirt, presumably to match the hair, and black skintight jeans. His five-foot, ten, body was obviously in peak condition as his rippled muscles revealed themselves through the indentations on his form-fitting T-shirt. Like all the others, he worked his way to the back of the shop. Stanley had examined that area thoroughly to find out what was the attraction for the pool hall types. That section of the store dealt with weapons, war, and martial arts. These kinds of guys seemed to be attracted to violence was Stanley's conclusion after perusing the shelves; somehow that did not come as a surprise. *I guess even dim-witted thugs need to learn how to fight,* he thought.

"The vision" in red and black worked his way over to the shelf where *The Art of War* book resided. He pulled it off the shelf and inspected the volume. After flipping through the pages and finding nothing of interest, he returned the book to its original location. The next book he pulled down was the volume with the inserted slot. He stared at the square indentation inside for at least a minute. (yes, there was a hole in the book Einstein) then placed it back where he had found it.

Next he began to scan the immediate area surrounding the books, including the shelves, walls, and ceiling, looking for hidden cameras. Clint had done an amazing job camouflaging the cameras. Many of them resembled the rivets in the shelving so closely that even Clint had trouble telling them apart, and the others were hidden with equal deceptive finesse. The visitor knew they were there; he just couldn't figure out where. Frustration kicked in and he returned to the front of the store where Stanley, seated behind a low counter, was reading. He walked up to Stanley and asked, "Are you the owner?"

Looking up, Stanley said, "No I just manage the store."

The intruder then bent over the counter and grabbed Stanley by the collar, pulling him over the two-foot surface, and backhanded him across the face. Stanley's glasses went flying. "I want the owner's address!"

screamed the thug. He punctuated his remark with another slap across the face.

"I'll give you everything I've got. His phone number, PO box address. Just don't hurt me." The absolute fear that Stanley felt registered with his assailant. He threw him back, where Stanley fell to the ground.

"I want it now!" shouted the thug as his pale white face turned red with anger.

Stanley rose to his feet as quickly as was physically possible and worked his way over to his desk. He had the information in a small gray notebook. After turning to the page where the phone number and address were located, he began looking for paper and a writing implement to make a copy for the jerk. The intruder snapped up the address book from the desk and ripped out the page that contained the needed information. Then the punk swung around, facing the bookshelves in the front of the store, and screamed at the top of his lungs, "I'm coming after you, you horse's ass!"

—ᘉ—

The phone number of the message on the cell phone was that of the bookstore. Clint retrieved it immediately. It was Stanley saying that he could no longer work for him at the shop and that today would be his last day. Clint rushed into the office to access his video communications network and view the tape from the cameras inside the store. When he saw the redheaded customer enter, Clint instantly became suspicious. Once the guy entered the combat section and looked inside *The Art of War*, book he knew for sure who had sent him.

"Where does Darso find these scumbags?" said Clint to himself. He obviously got him at a discounted rate. An experienced assassin would never reveal his appearance to his target, especially when he was also a hit man. Clint magnified the image of his pursuer and realized that he had seen this dude before. He racked his mind trying to remember where. Then it came to him; it was the red hair that helped make the connection. It was an inch or two longer now, but it was him. He was a high-ranked combatant in the new ultimate fighter franchise called the Total Submission League or the TSL. Clint had actually seen this guy fight during a televised match. He was talented in all the right areas: martial arts, boxing, and wrestling. The scumbag had won his bout decisively using all three styles.

Clint continued to view the tape witnessing the assault on Stanley. Clint felt sorry for his former manager. Beating up on an old guy sucks; it's cowardly. He would send Stanley a computer-generated letter thanking him for his years of service and explain that he was closing the store permanently within the month and enclose a money order for $5,000 in appreciation for his years assisting in the shop. (Yes, he was going to close the bookstore.) Clint realized he could no longer indiscriminately take another person's life, whether they deserved it or not. He had almost killed Peter on faulty conclusions, and Stacy's influence was making itself felt. Clint wanted to come clean and tell her the truth about his past. The Bookmark had served its purpose; now it was time to move on. However, he was in a kill-or-be-killed situation with this redheaded maggot and Darso was still out there, so he couldn't hang up his guns just yet. He continued to view the store tape to its conclusion. The "horse's ass" comment produced a grin on Clint's face; he'd been called worse. The scumbag had the rudiments of a sense of humor given he was able to relate stallion with a horse's ass. He wasn't ready for the *Comedy Zone* and really needed to change that hair color, but he did have balls, even if he was one taco short of a fiesta platter.

# CHAPTER 15

THIS SATURDAY NIGHT WOULD BE LIKE NO OTHER. CLINT HAD DECIDED to tell Stacy about his past. He wasn't sure how detailed he wanted to be, but he would need to tell her about his profession as a hit man and come clean that his name was not Rod. No impending confrontation he had faced in the past could rank with the kind of anxiety he was feeling at that moment. Would she reject him? Was this the last time he would see her? Stacy brought a beauty and light into his life that he did not believe existed. Her loving presence had changed him. He enjoyed just being around her. There was a positive energy that emanated from her being that touched his soul. Clint hated to admit it, but he was hopelessly in love.

The plan was to invite her to dinner at his place and after they had eaten he would drop the bomb about his former life. Clint had the sinking feeling that there was no way he was going to spin this story to make things right between him and Stace after all was said, but he couldn't go on living this lie. He wanted her to know about his background, his true family, no matter how ugly it was. If she loved him, after all this was on the table, their love would withstand any challenge, the future held.

Stacy would arrive in an hour so Clint began preparing the meal. He would roast a chicken and do a vegetable medley as a side. She arrived on time of course; the meal and subsequent dinner conversation were pleasing.

Clint kept the discourse upbeat focusing on what was going on in Stacy's life, her work, family, and friends. They had grown so close that she had become astute in discerning his moods and he wanted the time to be right when he made his startling disclosure. The two finished eating and adjourned to the living room. Stacy was the first to sit, finding a place on the sofa. She fully expected Clint to sit next to her, but instead he pulled one of the chairs that flanked the coffee table and settled in across from her.

He began. "I have something I have to tell you."

"You're scaring me ... What's wrong?"

"I haven't been completely honest with you."

"OK ..." He could hear the apprehension in her voice.

"I'm not who I seem. I don't create web sites for a living. I'm a hit man."

She stared wide-eyed at him, but looking relieved, she responded, "I thought you were going to tell me you cheated on me and met someone else."

Clint was dumbfounded. Women: you got to love 'em. I'm a stone-cold killer, but that's OK as long as you didn't cheat on me.

"A hit man. Is that like a DJ or something?" continued Stacy.

Was she really that naive? Could her Christian background so totally shield her from reality that she didn't even know what a hit man did?

"No, a hit man is paid money to kill people."

It took a few seconds to register. She stared at him with the look of someone who had learned for the first time what went on in the Nazi concentration camps. Her delicate blonde eyebrows inched skyward as her lips pressed together in a frown. It was then that tears began to flow. At that moment, Clint realized the enormity of his past actions. He had never felt guilt or remorse, but if he could take the pain away that he saw in Stacy's eyes, he would have done anything. He looked at her angelic face and saw a child's eyes gazing back at him.

Once Stacy calmed from the initial shock, Clint continued. He touched on aspects of his work, the natural kill phenomena, his code name, disguises, video surveillance techniques, and the function the bookstore played.

"The people I killed were the dregs of society; they kind of deserved it … except for Peter." He told her about Peter and how by witnessing his daily life he had transformed his own.

"What about your family? Do they know?"

Clint told her the truth about his family, regaling her with stories of his father's alcoholic fits of rage. He told her of the countless beatings and the verbal abuse he withstood.

"How many people have you killed?"

There was a long pause before Clint answered, "Forty."

"My God!" There was a pregnant pause. "You're obviously not a Christian, are you?"

"No."

A long moment of silence ensued. Then Stacy uttered the words that cut into his very being. "I'm so disappointed in you."

Clint looked down; he could not bear to look into her eyes. It seemed like a half hour passed before Stacy spoke again.

"Do you even believe in God?"

"I want to believe."

Suddenly Stacy's calm demeanor changed, and she was once again the wounded child as she bent her head down and sobbed. Seeing her cry was more than he could handle. Leaving his chair, he knelt at her feet, putting his hands on her knees.

"I'm sorry, sweetheart … I'm sorry," Clint said, his voice cracking with emotion.

"How could you?" muttered Stacy through her tears.

"I'm sorry, sweetheart … Please forgive me," whispered Clint. Finally, he could hold it in no more; he cried. He laid his head in her lap as his arms wrapped around her waist.

"Forgive me," he pleaded through his tears.

Stacy looked down on the tortured soul before her, his head still resting in her lap, and gently ran her hand through his thick sandy-brown hair.

"I forgive you, but it's not my forgiveness you need. Only the Lord can forgive you for what you've done. You took it upon yourself to play God.

I don't care how bad you thought these people were or how much you suffered when you were young. Do you really believe that you're the only one that's had a traumatic childhood? That doesn't give you the right."

Clint was now gazing up at her. "I know, but how do I make myself straight with God? Will you help me?"

Stacy flashed him that "melt your heart" smile of hers and said, "Yes, I'll help you as best I can, my precious Rod." Both of her hands were still imbedded in his dense locks as she said these words.

He thought, *Aw geez, now I've got to tell her that it's not precious Rod; it's precious Clint. That's going to go over big.*

"Ah, concealment and disguise were a big part of what I used to do … and … ah … that went as far as names too. My real name's Clint."

*"What?"* she yelled as she pushed him back off her.

"It's Clint … I can't call you … Clint, I can't. I don't know what to call you," she said, anger dripping from every word.

"I can think of a couple names you could use, but I know you don't swear."

Stacy frowned and shook her head in disgust.

"Maybe go the opposite way, use terms of endearment like sweetheart or honey.

Stacy flashed him a look that could kill.

"I take it, from the dagger stare you're giving me, that Snuggle Buns is out of the question."

Stacy's frown turned to a smile, then to a wide grin, and finally she laughed. Clint joined in with his own laughter as he sat on the sofa next to her. Once the laughter subsided, he took her into his arms and kissed her. It was a passionate kiss, one she wouldn't forget.

# CHAPTER 16

THE SUN WAS SETTING AS CLINT'S BLACK CORVETTE PULLED INTO THE parking lot of Stacy's apartment complex. Tonight would begin his first steps in the lifelong journey of Christian discovery. Stacy had created a Bible study for him. His thoughts reflected on the evening when he had cried and asked for help. The fact that he had wept and then asked her for assistance annoyed the hell out of him. That display of emotion showed weakness and the plea for help, surrender. It was so unlike him; however, he knew that one act of submission had saved his relationship with Stacy. He didn't like being introspective. He was a take charge kind of guy and felt religion was for people who didn't trust in their own capabilities. His surveillance of Peter poked a huge hole in that assumption, but he still wasn't ready to relinquish his ego. Was Stacy worth all this?

Yes, she was worth wading through the dark waters. Just being around her lifted his spirits. He had already battled in her defense and would be her protector for life if she would have him. Stacy was unique. She had character and was decent, not unlike Peter. They both had nobility about them. In comparison Clint found himself lacking. Their loving dispositions had a magnetic effect on people. Deep down he yearned to find that loving flame within himself. He had never trusted anyone before. His family had been such a disappointment. Now he was placing his heart, his soul, his very being in Stacy's hands. He would be asked not only to trust her but to trust in a divine essence. This was uncharted territory and would be an experience like no other.

Stacy answered the door with her radiant trademark smile. Clint never ceased to be amazed at her beauty.

"You're on time. That's a good start," said Stacy.

"Would it be OK if I kissed the teacher?" added Clint with a smile.

"Clint, it's not about that tonight."

"I realize that. Let's say it's a Christian kiss of love."

"Well, all right."

Clint leaned in to kiss her on the lips and ended up getting a peck on the cheek. It was obviously not what he expected.

"So that's a Christian kiss … Can we shoot for something a little more pagan?"

"Clint!"

"Just kidding."

Stacy was all business as she walked into the dining area of her apartment. Books, some stacked, others opened, were scattered over the entire dining room table. She took a seat at the table, where Clint joined her.

"I suppose we should start at the beginning. Do you believe God created the universe?" asked Stace.

"I'm sort of a Darwinist, but I'm open to that. When I've witnessed a beautiful sunset on the ocean, it's kind of hard to believe that happened as a result of a huge explosion in space, a big bang."

"Good. The Bible says that God has implanted in our heart's knowledge of his existence. Do you believe evil exits?"

"Oh yeah. You have to meet my dad sometime."

"Then reversely you believe there's good in the world?"

"Yes, I know you."

Stacy smiled modestly. "I'm not that good, but thank you. So there's good and evil in the world … Then it stands to reason that if God's creation started a long downward spiral into sinfulness and evil, He would want to save us by sending part of Himself in human form."

Clint interrupted. "So He sent His Son. I've read parts of the Bible: the story of creation, Adam and Eve, Satan's fall from grace, God's relationship with the Jews, and segments of the New Testament ... There are so many references in literature to scripture that no one who is a serious student of the written word can avoid it, but I just can't relate personally. It all seems like a lot of made-up stories with a few historical underpinnings."

Stacy pondered his statement. "There's a couple of books here I want you to read. *Mere Christianity* by C. S. Lewis and Rick Warren's *The Purpose Driven Life*. I also have *The One Year Bible* that has daily readings for the complete year and a King James Bible for you."

"Geez, I just got here, and I already have homework ... There isn't going to be a quiz tonight, is there?"

"Oh, stop it."

Stacy went on to explain the best she could about the Trinity and her relationship with Christ, stating how she never felt alone because He was always just a prayer away and the everyday miracles in her life.

"There are no mistakes; you and I met for a reason." she continued. Stacy then left the table and returned with a DVD.

"Have you seen the movie *The Passion of Christ?*"

"No."

"Let's watch it together."

The two adjourned to the living room. Stacy put the disc into the player and joined Clint on the couch. She slipped her hand into his as the movie began. Clint was not so much moved by the film as he was by Stacy's reaction to the movie. He figured she had viewed it at least once before, so he was amazed at her emotional response. During the scene where Christ was unmercifully lashed, she squeezed his hand as each swing of the whip hit its mark and the constant stream of tears that cascaded down her cheeks touched him deeply. He would read those books. Clint wanted to know more and believe with the same intensity that Stacy felt. She had personalized her belief in a way he could never have imagined.

Beyond Stacy's reaction, the suffering that Jesus sustained struck a nerve with him. Christ was beaten and scourged with horrific brutality. At a point when it seemed He could take no more, Jesus stood, straightened his back, and assumed a posture almost in defiance of His Roman assailants as if to say, "Is that all you got? Bring it on." Clint was impressed by the undefeatable spirit, the courage, and felt driven to learn what drove this Man, this God.

It was hard to concentrate on divine matters though, when there were other pressing concerns that weighed on him. He still had to deal with the redheaded punk, and someone had to stop Darso before he ordered another hit on Peter.

—◈—

On the drive back from Stacy's, Clint mulled over his future course of action. Disclosure of his past to Stacy and her subsequent religious instruction had affected him. The part of his life symbolized by the Black Stallion was over. Stacy's condemnation of his actions ("Do you really believe you're the only one that's had a traumatic childhood? That doesn't give you the right …") pierced his armor of self-righteousness. She was right. He knew of children that were sexually abused by their fathers and they had not turned into paid assassins. Thankfully he was spared that humiliation. His chief reason for taking lives randomly had been hatred of his father. Now Clint felt that logic feeble, weak. Given all that, what was he to do with the scumbag that was after him? He could shoot him, but somehow that didn't feel right. It was one thing to mow down assailants indiscriminately to protect Peter another when it came to his own welfare.

It seemed ages since he had been in a good one on one fight, but that was what Clint intended to do. The confrontation would be a bare-fisted battle to the death, and he knew his opponent would be a worthy adversary.

—◈—

The location for the upcoming confrontation would be a fourth-floor room, an empty office space, in an abandoned building in Hollywood. The structure was completely boarded up, a relic of a bygone era. Clint had discovered it while tailing one of his targets. He would meet his nemesis in the afternoon. Daylight would provide enough illumination given he had torn off the boards on three windows inside the enclosure.

After sweeping the area for combat thoroughly, he inserted a large, circular, metal piece into the stud above the only door into the room. Over the header to that door, he also placed a narrow metal platform that he secured into nearby uprights behind the wall. Clint then doubled a three-foot stretch of black rope, attaching it to the metal loop above the door. Finally, the makeshift arena was ready for combat.

Clint figured his would-be killer would scout out the only location he had an address for, which was the vicinity of the PO box. Clint canvassed the area in disguise—another one of his favorites, "the drunken derelict." He went all out on the outfit and makeup. The brown beard with the silver accents he used was woven from real hair. The clothes, which he had purchased from a thrift store, he purposely soiled to mimic the disadvantaged who lived on the streets. Using sandpaper and a metal wire brush along with various colors of fuller's earth (dirt used by costumers in the film industry for aging) Clint was able to capture the essence and look of his derelict persona. He even went as far as soaking his tattered coat with stale beer. Part of the makeup he used was a bronzing agent that produced a dark tan that even George Hamilton (tanned actor of a bygone era) would be envious of. Combined with other brown and black cosmetics that he smeared on his face and hands, Clint was able to attain total concealment of his character.

As expected, the redheaded dude was staking out the mail center. He was sitting in his car, a late-model Malibu, located on a side street off the main drag. The windows to the car were open and he was listening to a hard rock station on the radio. Clint approached, dressed in his derelict disguise. He stumbled toward the car, holding a folded piece of paper, finally coming to a halt at the driver's side of the Malibu. He took a moment to find his equilibrium, and then he finally spoke while pointing. "Th ... that g ... uy over there paid ... paid me to gifff you thish."

The punk grabbed the note then flung the door open, almost hitting

Clint. He jumped out and began looking around frantically. "Where? Which guy?"

Clint swayed back and forth for a moment then using both hands pointed his index fingers in opposite directions. "Th … that way."

"You drunken asshole!" The punk took off, running trying to get a bead on the Black Stallion. He ran down the street to his left, then reversed course and ran in the opposite direction. There was no one who could have been mistaken for the notorious hit man. The dejected punk returned to his car where Clint was still standing.

"Gotch any shpare change?" asked Clint, upbeat.

"Get the hell out of here, you stupid drunk."

"Y-y-yeah … wup shores," replied Clint in drunk speak as he stumbled off.

The note was then unfolded and read by the punk. It was computer generated giving directions, an address, room number, and a 10:00 a.m. time designation for their meeting the following day. It also mentioned that he was under twenty-four-hour surveillance and to come alone. Clint had placed a satellite homing device on the car so he would know if the punk decided to go early and case the joint, but that was the extent of his surveillance. Sometimes just the thought of being watched was enough to instill compliance.

Inside the car a nine-millimeter Glock was pulled from the glove compartment as the aspiring killer looked around trying to spot the surveillance team he knew was watching. He would be there tomorrow with his gun loaded.

The rays of the sun were just peeking through the planks on the windows in the ancient Hollywood building when Clint arrived. The satellite tracking device on the Malibu showed movement to a Silverwood location, but no change after that. Clint assumed that his opponent had gone home and stayed there for the evening.

A cohesive battle plan had been worked out then reworked in Clint's mind. From a past interview with the representatives from the Total Submission League, Clint recalled his antagonist was considered most likely to win the Ultimate Fighter Championship. He had gone from a weight of two hundred fifty pounds to 170 and purportedly kept the strength of the higher weight. His standup skills were lethal. Supposedly his body strikes felt like bricks hitting your body. The televised fight that Clint had observed didn't reveal much in the way of wrestling skills, however. The opponent was dazed from the standup fight and his wrestling moves proved ineffective once on the ground. The punk got on top and pulverized his face. The match was over within two minutes.

Clint was confident in his standup fight. He was a past Golden Gloves champion. That fact combined with his martial arts expertise made him lethal in his own right, but his true potential displayed itself in his wrestling skills. In high school he had won the state final in his weight class at the same weight he was now: 168. Obviously the two were evenly matched weight wise, but there was no wiggle room in this fight. One man would subdue the other and literally beat him to death.

The time had passed quickly since Clint's arrival. It was now 9:45 a.m. It was interesting the thoughts that cross your mind before a physical duel. There was documentary footage of a general who led the Korean conflict in the fifties featured on the History Channel; his words came to mind as Clint contemplated the struggle. The general, when he awoke in the morning and surveyed his communist enemy across the plain, said, "It's a great day for a fight."

Those were Clint's sentiments as the motion detector at the back entrance began beeping. He checked his handheld monitor. The cameras showed that his opponent had arrived, and by all observation, he was alone.

He buried the monitor and other tools not needed under a floorboard he had loosened for just that reason. Clint grabbed the three-foot black rope and pulled himself into position on the thin platform above the door. Clint was clothed in drawstring black pants synonymous with martial arts and was bare above the waist. One hand clutched the black rope, and the other held his HK .45 Mark 23 fitted with a silencer.

He could hear the floorboards on the stairs squeak as the punk climbed closer to his position. He began visualizing his domination in the struggle. He saw himself pounding the face of his adversary and finally breaking his neck. Then for a fleeting second, he saw the face of Stacy. Clint quickly subjugated that image, once again focusing on his ultimate victory; when he saw the barrel of his purser's gun break the plane of the doorway, it was showtime.

The punk had his arms extended as he directed the aim of the Glock in quick sweeping movements to his right and left. Once he passed through the door opening, he leaned his back against the door, shoving it to the wall. Convinced there was no one lying in wait behind it, he proceeded forward. Clint was impressed by that move; it showed smarts. After two more steps forward, Clint's aggressor stopped in his tracks as he felt the barrel of the silencer on the back of his head. Clint's body was fully extended, standing perpendicular to the wall, one hand holding the fully extended three-foot rope and the other holding a gun against the punk's head. He never saw it coming.

"One sudden move and your brains will be scattered on the floor. Bend down slowly, and I mean slowly, place the gun on the floor, then take four steps forward and lie down on your stomach, hands stretched forward," commanded Clint.

The punk followed the orders as instructed. Clint jumped from his perch and walked over to where the Glock had been placed. He picked up the gun, placing his pistol inside the waistband of his pants.

"All right, you can stand up now," said Clint. He took the magazine clip from the Glock and began unloading the bullets inside. The sound of the ammunition hitting the floor resonated through the room. After rolling over and standing, his opponent faced him.

"You're an ultimate fighter in the Total Submission League?" stated Clint.

"Yeah … I'm Red Phillips," responded the punk who was now regaining his composure after almost pissing in his pants from Clint's initial surprise attack.

"Well Red, what we're going to do here is have our own ultimate fight … to the death. Winner takes all, so to speak. You up for that?"

The punk took a moment to contemplate Clint's proposal.

"Oh yeah," replied Red, smiling broadly.

This was his domain. He couldn't believe this stroke of luck.

Red pulled off his jacket, took off his T-shirt, and slipped out of his black leather shoes as Clint drew the HK from his waistband and began unloading the ammunition from his pistol. Once emptied, Clint slid his gun over near where the Glock had landed.

Standing opposite each other, Clint and Red took a few seconds to size up each other. Red's upper body was strewn with tattoos; some of the words and symbols were in bold block letters while others were in smaller script. Clint had never been a big fan of tattoos. He felt the male physique and female form, when in perfectly fit condition, were a work of art. No human scribbling could improve on the sculpted canvas we were born with, but to each his own. Red seemed more ripped than he remembered in the televised fight. Clint then went into battle mode, working through his mind's fight strategy.

Red, in the meantime, was attempting to get a bead on this guy he was now facing. He had to be a little psycho to want a physical confrontation when he could have just shot him dead. The guy had the guns (muscles); he obviously trained for hours. Why would this Black Stallion guy want a one-on-one battle? Was he that lethal?

The next few minutes would tell.

The challengers then worked their way to the center of the room. Clint gave Red a slight nod (a martial arts gesture) and approached, his fists guarding his face. Red flashed a cold stare in response and stepped forward into the fray. They both stalked each other flat-footed.

Clint was the first to spot an opening. Red's fists were spread apart about six inches too wide, leaving Clint a clean shot to his face. Throwing a straight kick, Clint was able to connect with Red's chin. It was a powerful kick and connected hard, but Red just shook it off with a big smile as if to say, "OK, you got one off."

Red, not finding an opening, just began throwing punches. The first one hit Clint in the shoulder, and the next found its mark in the solar plexus. They struck with a force that was hard to humanly fathom. Clint had never felt pain like that, and he could take a punch. They were take-your-breath-away strikes. This guy did not have bricks for fists; he was swinging anvils. The power of the stomach punch was so penetrating that it caused Clint to drop his guard, leaving his head an appealing target. Red figured on this reaction and threw a haymaker that struck Clint right above his left eye. The skin above the eyebrow ripped and blood gushed from the wound. The blow shook Clint to the core. A few inches lower and the strike would have knocked him out.

Clint was dazed and began backing away from his aggressor to buy precious time to regain total consciousness. Red, sensing victory, charged forward. Clint ducked out of range from any head punches, but he could not blunt the exploding body shots that Red threw.

Clint's vision blurred from the blood, his senses were dulled from the pummeling, and the pain was racking his body; any thought of conquest began to slip from his grasp. In his stupor, the only sustaining thought he could conjure was the face of Stacy. He would have to survive if not for himself then for Stacy. If he died in the abandoned house, they might never find his body, and if they did find his corpse, he had no identifying ID. Stacy would be left to assume he had forsaken her in the harshest manner without even a call or note.

He had to go on so he reached into the depths of his spirit, a place where champions go to find the inner strength to survive and conquer. Suddenly it seemed crystal clear what he had to do. He needed to take this asshole to the mat. Clint could not beat Red in a stand-up match, but he might prevail on the ground using his wrestling skills, and he was in a perfect position for a takedown. He charged, wrapping his arms around Red's legs, then using all the strength he could conjure, Clint lifted Red off the ground and threw him to the floor. Red hit the ground with a loud thud landing on his back with Clint on top of him. A lesser man would have been stunned at least momentarily by the fall, but not Red. He instinctively swiveled his body, rolling on top of Clint. Then he elbowed Clint on the right side of his face, swelling his cheek almost instantaneously.

Even though Clint was on the bottom, he could at least wrap his arms around Red's neck and draw him in close so he had no room to punch.

They grappled on the ground for at least ten minutes with Red always able to stay on top. Then extraordinarily, Clint was able to use his legs plus an arm hold and begin to work his way on top. Red, sensing he might end up on the bottom, flipped himself over on his back, landing against Clint's chest. It was an unwise maneuver. Red lay wide-open for a hold that Clint had never used and only seen in ultimate fighting matches. It was called a "rear naked choke." Clint slipped his right arm around his neck and with his left hand locked the wrist. There was no escaping.

Red's face immediately turned a scarlet color, and his eyes bulged from their sockets. Clint could feel the live force draining from his body. Then the unexpected happened. Red began slapping the floor with his hand, trying to tap out. In ultimate fighting contests, that was a sign of defeat and the referee would immediately stop the fight. Clint thought, *What is he doing? This isn't a childhood playground fight. It's a fight to the death. No, you would kill me in a New York minute if roles were reversed. It ain't going to happen.* Clint tightened his hold.

"Please … Please," in a choking whisper pleaded Red as his hand continued to hit the floor.

No! Clint was not going to buy into the weak, bullshit, forgive-and-forget philosophy. This asshole was going to kill him. It was going to end here and now. Let an enemy go and he'll turn around and kill you. It's the law of the jungle, the law of life.

Red no longer had the breath to speak and his effort to tap out was just an intermittent feeble strike now.

"Damn!" shouted Clint as he released the choke hold. He shook his head in disgust at himself. *This is going to come back and bite me in the ass,* thought Clint. Hell of a hit man he was. Clint pushed Red's body off his.

Red rolled over onto his stomach, gasping for air. The wheezy, panting sound of Red gulping for air filled the room. Finally Red worked his body into a seated posture, still struggling for air. Clint sat up from his sprawled-out position as he also tried to regain his breath and composure. A long moment of silence ensued.

Red was the first to speak. "Thanks."

"How much did Darso give you to kill me?" asked Clint.

"I don't know this Darso guy, but it was 10,000 … I got a thou up front and supposed to get the rest when the job was finished. The whole deal went down by way of a kid."

"Ten thousand … uh." Clint shook his head in amazement at how little his life was worth.

"I had to have the money … My girlfriend needs a boob job."

*"You were going to kill me over a set of hooters?"*

Red stared at him incredulous that he would even ask that question. "Sure."

Of course he would. What was Clint thinking? It was a momentary lapse in male clarity.

There was another long period of silence as the men continued to catch their breath.

Clint finally broke the silence. "Talk about tits to die for." That got the two men laughing.

"We've got to figure a way for you to get your money. We can't have your girlfriend going around feeling self-conscious about her chest," said Clint.

"Yeah, that'd be great," replied Red.

"What would sell Darso that you got to me?" stated Clint aloud but meant more for himself. Clint was looking out on the expanse room when his eyes alighted on his pistol.

"My gun! Yeah, he would buy that. He would know enough about guns to believe the HK was my weapon of choice and … But do I want to give it up?" said Clint, again more to himself. The HK (completely untraceable) was like an old friend, and it was a $1,400 firearm. He owned another HK, but it was an older model. It would get Darso off his back. He could concentrate on protecting Peter. Geez, giving up his gun though.

"All right this is what we're going to do. I'm going to give you my gun and we're going to come up with a story on how you killed me."

Clint worked out three or four different scenarios in his mind and finally settled on one that dealt with his disguise as a derelict. Red would say that he had gone inside the PO box center to check out the place. When he returned to his car, he found a note under his windshield wiper telling him about the meeting in the abandoned house, giving directions, the surveillance setup, and the warning that he should come alone. When he arrived at the house and was making his way toward the back, he noticed a dirty, grubby, derelict passed out near the back entrance. The house was in an area of town that was home to many homeless people so he almost passed by the bum without a thought, but there was a small detail he noticed that didn't add up. The vagrant had all the accoutrements of a homeless drunk: the greasy filth, stained and ripped clothing, brown paper bag with a half-filled bottle of cheap wine, long slimy beard, a dark tan, and even alcohol and urine smells that were there. However, Red had noticed a small anomaly: the derelict's fingernails were neatly clipped. It's not that they were manicured, but it was obvious that they were well maintained. This was the one major flaw that Clint had overlooked when he first wore the disguise. He was meticulous about his hygiene, especially his fingernails, and he only realized his mistake when he returned home after a reconnaissance mission. Red would say he lay in wait for the bum near the back entrance and got the drop on him. He was able to catch him from the back with a choke hold that eventually suffocated him. His potential killer had no identification on him, only the HK. The time continuum would change. Red would say he got to the house late in the day and that once it got dark, he laid the derelict's body sprawled out near the road, still holding his brown bag of wine. When discovered, the authorities would attribute the bum's death to alcohol-related health complications.

Clint thought Darso might be skeptical; however, the fact that he had the gun and that Red had never been informed about the Black Stallion's use of disguises, it would work.

The other advantage that Clint had was the story would be told to a twelve-year-old boy (Banger) who would in turn relate it to another contact who would finally relay it to Darso. The facts would get clouded and Darso had other problems to deal with. He would want to believe it.

"Sounds good to me" was Reds final comment when he got all the details straight in his mind. The two were standing near the door. Red, with his T-shirt and jacket on, was now holding Clint's HK and his Glock pistol. There were no bullets in either gun.

"Do you want to keep my Glock?" continued Red.

"No, that's OK. You keep it. I will hold on to the ammunition though," said Clint with a smile.

"You should think about joining the league. You're one hell of a fighter. We could have a rematch!"

"My plate's kind of full right now. Maybe later."

Red had stuck the two guns into the waistband at the back of his pants.

"Thanks again, man, for everything," said an emotional Red as he gave Clint a big bear hug.

Clint thought, *Aw geez, not a hug … Come on, guy. Get it together.* He stiffly gave Red a couple pats on the back.

"OK, all right, time to go. Take care," responded Clint after what seemed like a half-hour hug. Mercifully Red ended the hug and Clint saw what he thought was a tear in his eye. No, it couldn't be. Probably just irritation from all the dust that got kicked up. Red finally exited.

Clint cleaned up the blood from his face and body as best he could with some wet wipes he had brought. He would sew the wound closed with some thread he had at the house. He began to pick up the bullets from the floor, reflecting on the day's events. He'd forgotten childhood battles and the aftermath of those fights. Every kid he fought, win or lose, had become his friend afterward. There was a camaraderie among warriors that transcended the battle. The fact that you would put your wellbeing at risk to confront another drew respect and honor, even from your combatant. His concern that Red would retaliate after his release was unfounded. He was pleased that he had not killed Red. Sure, he was out a gun, but now he was free of Darso.

# CHAPTER 17

IT WAS NOT THE FIRST TIME THAT CLINT HAD SEWN UP HIS OWN WOUNDS, but the cut on his brow was the first major injury to his face. Combined with the swelling on the right side of his mug from Red's elbow hit, Clint was not ready for his close-up. Once the wound healed, Clint figured there'd be a scar, which was cool. Any remnant of the gash would serve as a badge of honor, a reminder of the heroic struggle.

The sun was setting as he walked into his bedroom. With the magnitude of the energy expended in the fight, Clint thought he would be bone tired, but that was not the case. His senses seemed on high alert so he walked out of the bedroom into the living room, where he spotted the three books Stacy had given him. He picked up the paperback titled *Mere Christianity* and began reading. In the foreword, it mentioned that C. S. Lewis was an atheist before accepting Christianity as his faith. That piqued Clint's curiosity.

Reading on, he was impressed by the simple logic Lewis used to explain universal concepts and the rudimentary beliefs of Christianity. His theory about the "law of nature" and the acknowledgment of right and wrong behavior in all cultures he found fascinating. The purpose of Christ's birth, life, death, and finally resurrection became clear. It all came together through Lewis's unadorned explanations. He finished the 227 pages of the book in just over three hours.

Next he tackled *The Purpose Driven Life*. The book was to be read in forty days, one chapter a day. Clint threw caution to the wind and riffled through all 319 pages that night. (What a rebel.) The premise of the book denied the trend of self-examination as a way to find one's purpose, for a Creator-driven awareness. Like Lewis, Warren agrees that we were created for eternal life and our present daily routine is only a temporary assignment. He postulates that we are all here for a reason; there are no mistakes to our existence. Warren concludes that our purpose is to serve God by ministering to others and forging our character to become more Christlike.

The two books read back-to-back caused Clint to take a cold, hard, introspective look at his own life. The reality was that Clint had fallen far short of the mark. He used hatred of his father to commit murder for hire then spent the blood money on a lavish lifestyle. His first-rate material possessions attested to that fact. Knowing Peter and Stacy had opened his eyes to a new way of life. For the first time he found an awareness of God. He was still a neophyte lost in a tunnel, searching for the ray of light that radiated at the end of the passageway, but at least he was in the tunnel.

It was midnight when Clint closed *The Purpose Driven Life*. The physical strain of the day had taken its toll, and he was ready for sleep. Nonetheless, he still reached for the last book on the coffee table, the King James Bible. He indiscriminately opened the book to a page where a verse from Philippians (3:13–14) caught his eye. It read, "This one thing I do, forgetting those things which are behind, and reaching forth unto those things which are before, I press toward the mark for the prize of the high calling of God in Christ Jesus."

Clint wondered if God had a higher purpose for his life. A mission only he could accomplish. Could taking another life, killing Darso, be considered a Christian act? Christians are supposed to battle evil. Was that legitimization enough to go after him? The decision had to be made soon. It had already been three days since the shoot-out with the Gangstas and Darso would move quickly to find other avenues to get to Peter. He would save that determination and battle the theological war on another day. Slumber beckoned.

—⋘—

Fortunately, the swelling on the cheek that Red had elbowed subsided by the next morning, but there was a large black-and-blue mark left in its place. Combined with the black stitches above his right eyebrow, Clint looked like he had been beaten, not so much with the ugly stick but with the ugly two-by-four. (Hey, they can't all be winners.) He ran his fingers through his hair, straightening the locks, as he stood in front of Stacy's door. The doorbell could be heard from inside her apartment as Stacy rushed to the entryway. She opened the door and stared in wide-eyed shock at Clint.

*"Honey, what happened?"* asked Stacy.

"I made a new friend yesterday," said Clint with a smile.

"I don't want to know, do I?"

"No."

Clint stepped inside the apartment then wrapped his arms around Stacy, pulling her body into his. His senses went into overdrive as his cheek touched hers. The smell of her perfume, Opium, flowed through his olfactory sense into every cell of his being. Clint found it interesting that she would use a perfume named after a drug, but that narcotic euphoria seemed to best capture the sensation he was encountering. The warmth of her body kindled the fire within his heart. He had come so close to losing her in his confrontation with Red that he wanted to lock forever into his memory bank this moment. He held her tightly for a prolonged period, which raised Stacy's concern.

"You all right, sweetheart?" Stacy asked.

"I am now." Clint stared into her ocean-blue eyes and wanted to tell her how much she meant to him. He wanted to tell her he loved her, but words of affection were foreign to him. There was an uneasiness that overwhelmed him when he attempted to say loving words. His family had never shared those feelings.

"I must have done something right in my life to have you in my arms," said Clint tenderly. Close, but no cigar.

"You're sweet," said Stacy as she kissed him. What was meant to be an affectionate peck on the lips turned into a passionate French kiss. Clint would add the kiss to his memory bank as well.

Stacy had prepared dinner so the two adjourned to the dining room. While taking intermittent gulps of food, Clint regaled her with the knowledge he had garnered from his theological readings the night before. She was impressed that Clint would read both books in one night and how much he retained. He told her of his newfound faith and how the two authors provided clarity and an understanding to Christianity he never realized existed, answering many of the nagging questions that plagued him.

"Those two books put everything into perspective ... I mean it all makes sense," said Clint excited.

Stacy extended her hand, placing it on top of his. "I'm so proud of you," she replied as she clutched his hand.

"I am pretty cool, aren't I?"

"You might have passed over, in your reading, the part about being humble," said Stacy, smiling.

"Yeah. I need to work on that."

"I'll keep you in check," commented Stacy with a grin.

After dinner the two ended up on the couch in the living room. The conversation was to take a serious turn. Clint had come to a decision in regard to killing Darso. He was going to put his life on the line one more time. Peter deserved to live, if not only as a fitting testament for his courage to testify. He was the lone defender of the truth, the dead little boy's advocate, his voice beyond the grave.

"Hon, it's a Christian ideal to put your life at stake for another person, especially another Christian, right?" asked Clint.

"Sure … Giving up your life for someone else is basically what Jesus did for us. He died for our sins."

"This would be more like attempting to save someone's life."

"What are you trying to tell me?"

"I have it in my power to prevent someone's death."

"This has to do with that doctor, Peter, you told me about, doesn't it?"

"Yes."

"This thing you're going to do would put your life in danger?"

Clint shook his head yes.

Stacy took a deep breath and exhaled slowly. "If you've prayed on it and truly believe this is what God wants you to do, I'm behind you," responded Stacy with an urgency in her voice.

"I haven't really prayed on it, but I do feel this is what God would want me to do."

"Give me your hand." Clint slipped his hand into hers. Stacy gripped his hand and bowed her head as she began to pray. "Dear Lord, have mercy upon us, Your servants. Clint is trying to do the right thing in protecting his friend Peter. Give him Your strength in this struggle and make him ultimately come out victorious. Father, we ask this in Christ's name through the power of the Holy Spirit."

Stacy looked up into Clint's eyes. "Thanks for sharing your struggle with me. I'm sure it's been weighing on you."

Clint was truly impressed at this woman sitting across from him. She had such depth. He couldn't believe she was backing him on his mission to save Peter. Most women would have discouraged him, worried about his safety and ultimately their own personal loss if something fatal transpired. Stacy's beauty not only resonated on the outside but from the inside with her spirit as well.

"Yes, it's been on my mind … Thanks for the prayer. I can't tell you how much it means that you're backing me on this."

"I love you. I'll always be there for you, and I'm glad you told me. Now I can keep it in prayer."

"They broke the mold with you, sweetheart," said Clint with a smile as he leaned over and kissed her.

Stacy knew that encouraging Clint in his defense of Peter was the right thing to do, but heart of hearts, she wanted to stop his involvement. His conversion to Christianity was only in the infant stages and the honesty in their relationship was only now on strong footing. He hadn't even prayed on his decision to face the gangster in a life and death struggle. It was so like Rod—Clint. That darn name change was tough to get used to. Whatever. The love of her life was going to risk his existence to save another man.

Stacy admired him for it, but she feared for him. Sometimes God allows someone to give up their life for another. It was the mission of His Son to die for others. It could be feasible that Clint's possible death was part of a divine plan. His life had gone through an amazing mental and spiritual transformation; was this to be the final chapter? The thought sent chills up her spine. Stacy could identify with the wives and girlfriends whose loved ones fought in foreign wars in defense of ideals. Yes, they were fighting against tyranny, and for freedom, peace, and even justice, but what really drove home the sanctity of the endeavor was their loyalty to their fellow soldiers. They were protecting the man or woman fighting next to them. That did not make the ideals wrong but gave them a tangible reality and a biblical purpose. There is no greater sacrifice than to give up your life for another. Stacy's circumstance, however, was different from the wife or girlfriend of the soldier; she would know the outcome of the struggle within hours, days, not wait months or years for the results. She embraced these concepts.

After Clint left, she walked into her bedroom to pray. There was power in prayer. The power to overcome fear, change destinies, and ultimately find serenity engulfed in the loving arms of God.

On the way home from Stacy's apartment, Clint mulled over the events of the evening. He couldn't believe the sense of freedom he felt now that he had Stacy on his side. There would now be clarity in his planning. Her approval added an inspirational element to his endeavor. He had underestimated Red. That mistake could not be repeated when he faced Darso. He would attempt to smuggle a gun inside the home, but if that failed, he'd have to be at the top of his stand-up game. Wrestling Phil was out of the question. At a muscled 250 pounds, with most likely a 3 percent body fat quotient, Phil would outweigh him by almost eighty pounds and be a deadly opponent on the mat. It was unknown to him if Darso had martial arts training, but he would have to assume he did. (A correct assumption.) At six foot, five, Darso probably had a reach advantage of four or five inches, which was daunting and would favor him in a stand-up fight. Clint would have to use the room to his advantage, utilizing the objects in the room as weapons. Even a hard-covered book can be a deadly fighting implement in the right hands. Finally, he would need to make a worst-case scenario plan. Stacy would play a dominant role in that realm. She would need to be contacted if success eluded him.

Clint pulled into the driveway of his house as these concerns raced through his head.

—✴—

The sun was shining and the sky was blue without a wisp of a cloud as a cool breeze drifted through the air, producing a perfect, brisk, California fall day. It was a Thursday, the day following Clint's revelation to Stacy of his upcoming battle with Darso. Stacy had the day off and Clint invited her to join him for lunch at a Mexican restaurant located near the beach. Given the numerous cuisines of the world, Stacy had to admit that Mexican was her favorite. Whether it was the spices or the overabundant use of tomatoes in the sauces, she was not sure; all she knew was that she loved Mexican food.

Clint removed the top from the corvette and rolled up both side windows, enabling them to enjoy the sun without being blown out of their seats on their way to the coast.

The restaurant had a rustic, woodsy feel with colorful tile floors and large plants and foliage scattered throughout. The two shared chips with salsa and a large fajita plate and rinsed it down with tropical-flavored tea. They both agreed that the food was excellent, and after they finished, Clint suggested a walk on the beach to help accelerate its digestion.

Stacy sensed that Clint seemed slightly on edge. She attributed his jumpiness to his upcoming confrontation. At sixty-three degrees, both were wearing warm clothes. Stacy was adorned in a beige ribbed turtleneck that complemented her blonde tresses combined with a caramel suede jacket and worn fitted jeans. Clint was also wearing faded jeans, but with a blue T-shirt and a dark brown leather car coat. The restaurant was only a block from the beach so within moments of leaving the café they were standing against a steel metal rail and gazing at the ocean. The Pacific that day was a beautiful shade of blue, almost a match to Stacy's eyes. Her luscious blonde hair was lifted by the wind and rippled in the breeze like the proud mane of a thoroughbred. Clint was enraptured by her beauty like never before.

"It's so beautiful, isn't it?" said Stacy as she sighed.

"Yes, almost as beautiful as you."

"Cut it out," she replied with a bashful smile.

"It's true ... You know I'm crazy about you."

"And?" said Stacy, searching.

"You're the best."

"You never tell me you love me ... I love you."

"And that too," said Clint with a smile.

"See!"

"It's hard for me ... My family never said that word," added Clint with seriousness.

"Try ... Please, for me."

After a pregnant pause, he said, "You make my life whole ... Your gentle kindness has changed me in ways I never could have imagined ... And you're beautiful, not only physically, but you have an inner beauty that blows me away. I get high just being around you. I love you with all my heart, my soul ... my being ... Will you marry me?"

Clint pulled from his coat pocket a small velvet box with the word "TIFFANY'S" embossed in gold lettering on the lid.

He opened the velvet package to reveal a four-carat diamond set on a brilliant gold ring. Stacy did not see this coming. She looked up in shock from the ring into Clint's moisture-laden eyes and smiled.

Clint continued. "I'll do whatever it takes for us to be together forever."

"Yes, I'll marry you."

Clint cupped Stacy's face in his hands and kissed her, first gently then with more passion, and finally he engulfed her in his arms. As they kissed and embraced, Stacy jumped from the ground, wrapping her legs around his waist. And on that beach, in their small corner of the world, time stopped for two lovers who committed their lives to each other.

After leaving the beach, they arrived at Stacy's apartment, and she immediately requested that they select "their" song. This would be the first song they danced to after they were married.

"What about the classic fifties tune 'Great Balls of Fire'?" said Clint with a smirk.

"Clint!" responded a disturbed Stacy.

"Just kidding … Geez."

"It's supposed to be something romantic."

Stacy retrieved her cell from her purse and scanned the internet for melodies.

"There are a lot of great songs to choose from," she added.

"I don't mean to throw out negative vibes, but I don't know how to dance."

"What?" responded Stacy, irritated.

"Shoot me for being honest."

"I … I can teach you."

"All right."

They both slipped off their shoes. Stacy then positioned them in the traditional dance pose, placing Clint's right hand on her waist, one of her hands on his shoulder, and both their free hands were clasped together. That left about a two-foot space between them. She had brought up a Michel Bublé song on her phone, and they started to dance. Stacy began with the classic box step.

"Count one, two, three," stated Stacy.

Clint mumbled the numbers as he moved awkwardly, eventually stepping on her feet, completely out of sync with her movements and the music. Clint thought, *This isn't rocket science. What's my problem?*

"You're too far away," he said as he pulled her body into his. They began again, and in an instant, he was moving with the grace of a ballroom dancer. With her body against his, he could anticipate her next move. He could sense it through her body.

Clint added, "That's better."

"You're good!" responded Stacy with elation. She rested her head on his shoulder, placing her arms around his body. It was just a slow dance but was monumental given it was their first memory as an engaged couple and a beautiful slice of life.

They finished the dance and Stacy picked up her phone to search for the perfect wedding song. Initially she suggested the Etta James classic "At Last" as a possibility. Clint liked the song but wanted something different, but he wasn't sure what. Eventually it boiled down to two songs: one an oldie, Rod Stuart's rendition of "Have I Told You Lately (That I Love You)?" and the other Ed Sheeran's captivating "Thinking Out Loud." Stuart's song had Van Morrison's enticing lyrics "Have I told you lately that I love you … you fill my heart with gladness … take away my sadness … ease my troubles, that's what you do." Sheeran's lyrics were brilliant as well, but "Have I Told You Lately?" was the song finally selected because Stacy liked the line "at the end of the day we should give thanks and pray." She respected the fact that they mentioned praying in the song, and that truth decided the question.

Stacy played the selected song, and holding each other tightly, they slow danced to their song before Clint had to go. (Tomorrow he would face

Darso.) By the end of the song Stacy was in tears. It was all Clint could do to hold back the tears himself. His last words to her before he left were "I love you, sweetheart." And those words felt as natural to say as if he had repeated them a thousand times before.

# CHAPTER 18

The sun had just broken the horizon as Clint arose to take on the day. He did not do his typical workout routine, just some stretching exercises in an effort to preserve his strength for the rigorous confrontation that lay ahead. The stitches above his brow had been removed three days earlier, leaving a red scar that would illicit attention. Drawing on his vast experience with cosmetics, he was able to cover the cut to the point that it was undetectable. The swelling and discoloration on the left side of his face had completely vanished. He was thankful that he was a rapid healer. There would be no disguising his facial features with prosthetics today. The time for false identities was over. He checked and rechecked his older model HK pistol and was satisfied it would perform when needed.

Next he moved on to clothing. The identity he would assume was that of a popular delivery service provider. The trucks and delivery personnel were identified by their distinctly colored uniforms. Clint cloned the outfit worn by the organizations staff. He had the baseball cap, shirt, pants, and jacket all with the corporation's logo. His belt was black, the one notorious for the five-inch knife hidden within the leather. The shoes he wore were black athletic trainers. Clint stuck the HK gun inside the back waistband of his pants; the handle was covered by the jacket. He looked into the mirror and was satisfied with his appearance.

Props were next on his list of necessities. The delivery item he chose was an eight-by-twelve manila envelope sent supposedly by the US Treasury Department. He had researched the government seal and script, mimicking in exact detail the label of the real organization. He figured that the recipient would definitely accept an item from the treasury department.

The last item on his agenda was the electronic box that the customer signed when receiving the merchandise being sent. It had the correct look but did not function, which was part of the ruse. Whoever answered the door would be asked to sign the electronic box as a verification of receipt. The box would not function, and Clint would ask them to sign a paper facsimile. He would pull out a pen that had no ink. Once it was discovered that the pen was unusable, another useless pen would be presented to them. Finally, the customer would be forced to leave the door and find a suitable writing implement, allowing him to sneak into the house. It sounded good on the surface; Clint just hoped his plan worked. He double checked his props and all items functioned as predicted. He placed Stacy's phone number along with his correct identification in his wallet in case he was killed. She would need to know the outcome, good or bad.

If the worst-case scenario occurred, the paperwork had already been submitted for her to inherit his entire holdings and fortune. He figured she would probably give it away because it was tainted by death, but that was her choice.

It was eleven o'clock and time to go. Had he forgotten anything? No, everything was in order. He took the items he needed and locked the door to his home.

Once outside, he pulled the tarp off the truck that had been painted and signed to resemble the vehicle used by the company he was impersonating and then drove off toward the Darso residence.

However, he had forgotten something, something very critical to the success of his operation. He had forgotten to pray.

—◊—

The HK Mark 23 was one of the finest guns he had ever seen. That was the conclusion Darso came to as he examined Clint's pistol. Phil was seated at his desk, scrutinizing the weapon, when Caesar entered the room.

"Piz'on, check this out … That ultimate fighter guy got to the Black Stallion. I wouldn't have believed it, but this is his gun … I have no doubt," said Phil.

"That crazed-looking punk with the red hair killed him?" responded Caesar, surprised.

"I know … Hard to believe, but look at this forty-five. It's a work of art."

Caesar walked over and retrieved the gun from Darso. He inspected the weapon, checking the weight, sites, and empty clip, then handed it back.

"Definitely the kind of weapon a hit man would use. How'd the kid get to him?"

"These stories come via twelve-year-olds so you never know exactly what happened, but supposedly the fighter guy saw through the Stallion's disguise as a skid row drunk, something about his fingernails, and got the drop on him from the back, choked him to death."

"That would make sense. The guy is an ultimate fighter."

"I know, but with that dyed red hair, he seemed like such a yahoo. That's why I only gave him a thou up front."

"Sometimes even the best make mistakes."

"I guess. all I know is no killer would give up this beauty unless he was dead. So I paid the guy the other 9,000, and now we have one less asshole to worry about. And speaking of getting rid of assholes, you get the cash to Jake and Max?"

"I told you, boss, it's a done deal."

"They know wounded isn't an option? I want that doctor dead."

"Boss, this is Jake and Max … They know."

"That's what I like about using old-school guys. They've got the drill down … It's cutting it close though, only three weeks until the trial."

"They'll get it done."

"If they don't take him out in the next week, I'll want to talk to them myself … You know the secured line we've used in the past?"

"Gotcha, boss."

"Ya wouldn't think it would be that difficult to take out one guy." Phil raised the HK, aiming it at an empty wall.

"Bam! It's as easy as that," continued Phil.

Caesar had remained upbeat when hearing the news about the Black Stallion's demise, but secretly he was saddened at the revelation. Both Phil and Caesar assumed that Clint had switched sides, for whatever reason, and was ultimately responsible for stopping the Gangstas in their quest to kill Peter. Red's unexpected success meant that the doctor no longer had a champion to guard against the onslaught of Phil's minions. For his part, Caesar had done the unthinkable. He had not contacted Jake or Max about the hit on Peter. It was his way of rebelling, a small defiant stand against the tyranny that epitomized Phil, but now it looked like it might get him killed. He had not expected Phil to want to contact Max and Jake. Caesar would need to make the necessary calls that night and arrange a rendezvous for tomorrow evening to deliver the cash. Yes, it was the cowardly way out and he was letting Jimmy down once again, but his life was at stake.

After leaving the office, he walked into his bedroom, shut the door, and locked it. Caesar went to his wardrobe closet looking for a heavyweight fall coat he possessed. He found the coat and removed both the hanger and jacket, placing them on his bed. The hanger was the wide, thick variety. Hidden within the label was a lock. He pulled out his key ring and, using a small key located there, opened the cover to the inner compartment. Jammed inside were two white envelopes containing $100 bills. Caesar examined the contents then returned envelopes to their original location, locked it back up, and finally put the coat and the hanger back into the closet.

His next task was to call the intermediary who would arrange the hit and dispense the cash to Max and Jake. Phil would not allow him to record or save important numbers, so he had devised a plan where he used the page numbers in a book as a nonwritten reminder. He would dog-ear the pages with the correct numbers on them. Caesar went to his desk and pulled out a small paperback. Reviewing the dog-eared pages sparked his memory and he was about to make the call when the doorbell rang. Phil never answered the door, so he quickly put the book back inside the desk drawer, unlocked the door to his room, and headed for the entrance of the house.

Caesar opened the front door to discover a delivery man holding a large manila envelope.

"Sir, you have a parcel. Would you sign here please?" said Clint. He offered him the electronic box and pointed to the area he needed to sign.

Caesar examined the packet. He noted the return address from the US Treasury Department with accompanying seal, which prompted him to sign in the space provided. He took the attached pencil-shaped writing implement and signed as requested; however, nothing appeared on the small screen.

"Aren't I supposed to see my signature?" asked Caesar.

"Yes, you are." Clint took the receptacle from him and examined the signature area. "Darn it. This happened yesterday too. It looks as if it's malfunctioning again. Would you mind signing a paper receipt?

"No, that's all right."

Clint presented him with a pad containing paper receipts and a pen. Caesar attempted to sign the paper receipt, but the pen wouldn't perform. He tried scribbling on the top of the form to see if he could get the ink to run but was unsuccessful. He looked up at Clint with an angered expression.

"That isn't working either? I'm so sorry. Here try this one." Another pen was handed to Caesar. The same scenario ensued as was previously experienced.

"Like I need this crap!" blurted out Caesar.

Clint tested the second pen by writing on his hand, attempting to get the pen operational. He was unsuccessful.

"I'm sorry, sir, but I can't leave the package unless I have a signature, and I don't have any other pens," stated Clint in an apologetic tone.

"Damn it," said Caesar frustrated. "Wait here. I'll be right back."

Security was a high priority at the Darso residence, and on any other day, Caesar would have shut and locked the door while acquiring a pen, but on this day his thoughts were occupied with contacting hit men. He left the door wide-open.

Clint smiled at his good fortune as he stealthily made his way into the house.

Caesar headed for the kitchen where he knew he could find a pen in a counter drawer.

After making his way through the large foyer, Clint headed down a nearby hallway. He observed an open door halfway down the passageway, and as he neared the room, one of his steps caused a wooden floorboard to squeak. From inside the room, he heard a deep voice proclaim, "Caesar, who was at the door?"

Clint had heard the voice before; it was the unmistakable baritone utterance of Phil Darso.

Observing the doorknob was Clint's first priority. He took one step closer to the entrance and the door handle came into view. Auspiciously he found that it had a key mechanism installed inside. He quickly pulled the gun from the back of his waistband and entered the room. While facing forward, he quickly shut the door behind him and locked it. Phil was seated behind the desk and Clint immediately targeted him with his HK.

"Put your hands on the desk where I can see them," commanded Clint. Phil complied with his request. "Now you make one move and I'll kill you," continued Clint.

Phil gave him a steely stare. "Who the hell are you?"

"I'm the Black Stallion."

Enraged, Phil slammed the desk with his hand. Clint's finger tensed on the trigger of his gun.

"Damn it. I knew that redheaded asswipe didn't get to you. Shit, and I paid him!" yelled Phil, furious.

The comment elicited a smile from Clint. *Some girl out there is going to have one heck of a rack*, he thought.

"The gun was a good con," said Phil begrudgingly.

"I thought it might work."

"What made you change your mind, send the money back, then defend that asshole doctor?"

"You wouldn't understand."

Suddenly there was a loud banging from the door behind him.

*"Boss, are you all right?"* yelled Caesar.

The sound of Caesar's fists hitting the door momentarily distracted Clint's gaze from Darso. In that instant, Phil managed to flip the desk over, take cover behind it, and reach for the gun in his ankle holster.

Clint considered charging the desk but could see from the reflection off a glass curio cabinet that Darso had his hand on the grip of the small automatic. It was now imperative Clint find cover. An oversized, thick, mahogany coffee table was six feet from where he stood. He dove for it as Phil got his first shot off. After turning the table on its side, Clint was able to hide his entire body behind the wood barricade and return fire.

Once Caesar heard the gunfire, he pulled out his key ring, searching for the correct one to unlock the door. The problem was he had about twenty keys on the ring and had never used the key he needed before. He fumbled with a couple of keys, trying them in the lock to no avail. He stared at the key ring bewildered. Finally, he resorted to the only thing he could think of. He began ramming the door with his massive body.

Inside the room, the gun battle raged with neither of them getting the upper hand. Clint had chosen well with the coffee table. The table's wood was absorbing the shots, leaving him unscathed. Phil's huge desk likewise provided great cover. Working on the lip of the desk, Clint had fired repeated shots in the same area, splintering away some of the wood, but not enough to give him a clear shot. The only substantial target visible was each other's bobbing head. Clint had been shooting off the right side of his wooden shield, but he was ambidextrous. Using his left hand and peeking off the other side of the table, he surprised Phil, who was aiming to the right. A bullet connected, grazing the top of Darso's skull. The flesh wound drew blood immediately.

"You son of a bitch!" screamed Phil. Seething, he raised his body above the plane of the desk and fired five consecutive shots. On the sixth shot, the sound of an empty clip resonated across the room. Clint tossed the coffee table aside and rushed the desk, coming around on the right.

Phil was in wide-eyed shock as Clint fired at point-blank range. The sound of an empty clip once again broke the eerie silence in the room. Then the powerful thud of Caesar's body hitting the door could be heard. He was still working on the door with his commanding frame. The hinges were just beginning to show subtle movement.

Clint pistol-whipped Darso. Falling back stunned, Phil shook off the strike as Clint charged again. Though he was on his back, Phil was able use his legs to kick Clint against the curio cabinet. The glass shattered, producing small cuts on Clint's face.

Phil was quickly on his feet on the offensive. With feet planted, he threw a devastating punch that Clint averted by weaving to his right. Then Clint countered with an elbow to ribs. He could hear Phil gasp for breath. An uppercut and a solid right hand both connected with Darso's jaw. Two more punches, one to the temple the other to the forehead, hit their mark. Then a straight-up kick caught a reeling, groggy, Phil in the chest, driving him to the ground.

The tide of the fight was going Clint's way. He rushed over, lifted his leg to stomp Phil in the solar plexus, when to his surprise Phil grabbed his foot. He twisted it, throwing Clint off balance and to the ground. Phil rolled on top of him. This was exactly what Clint wanted to avoid. He grappled trying to escape Phil's grasp, but to no avail. Clint, however, was able to entwine Darso with his arms to prevent him from elbowing or striking him in the face. From the corner of his eye Clint spotted a large, glass, crystal ashtray. He squirmed over in that direction and was able to grab it. Phil, whose vision was blurred by blood, was late in spotting the object. He tried to control Clint's hand, but unsuccessfully. Clint twisted free and, using a backhanded swing, struck Phil in the eye with the corner of the crystal receptacle. It was not a particularly powerful jab because of the confining physical constraints of the situation, but it was to the eye and hit with catastrophic results. The strike immediately blinded Phil in that eye, and the pain was excruciating.

"Ahhhh!" Phil shrieked.

In that moment, Clint was able to shimmy his body two feet out from under Phil's weight. Only his legs were left caught in his grasp, but he was ultimately unsuccessful as Phil recovered quicker than expected and grappled his way on top once again. Clint's movement of two feet brought one unforeseen misfortune. Five inches above Clint's head was the spot where Phil's letter opener had fallen. Like everything Phil owned, it was an ostentatious piece of work. It was a huge steel implement coated with eighteen-carat gold. The knife itself was sixteen inches in length. The handle was two inches in diameter and spanned six inches of the knife. Carved into it was a rope design that circumvented the handle. The ten-inch blade, which in any other household would have been left dull, was purposely sharpened. Phil liked the dual functionality of a sharp blade, for whatever situations might arise. A wise decision on his part as he swiftly reached above Clint's head and grabbed the knife. In the confusion of battle, Clint had not noticed the letter opener. If he had known it was situated right above his head, he might have made more of an effort to prevent Darso from accessing it. Ah yes, hindsight.

Within seconds of Phil's possession of the knife, Clint was struggling for his life. Darso managed to get both of his hands wrapped around the handle and had the blade angled, at the ready, to pierce between the ribs of his chest. Two hundred and fifty pounds of Phil's body straddled Clint, making it impossible for him to move. Clint was in the disadvantageous situation of having to maintain a bench-pressing effort for an elapsed period of time with gravity working against him. Darso's face loomed above his. It was a horrific sight. His head was bloodied from top to bottom, initially by the flesh wound to the head then by the damage inflicted by the ashtray. One eye was completely swollen shut.

Darso stared down at him and spoke. "Did you really think you could kill me? You don't know who you're screwing with … You ain't bad enough to get to me." He smiled with an ear-to-ear grin.

The sound of Caesar ramming the door punctuated Phil's comment.

While still focusing on Clint, Phil yelled out, "Paesano, I've got it under control!"

With that revelation, the ramming momentarily stopped, then it resumed with seemingly more intensity as Caesar continued his onslaught of the door.

Clint's strength was fading as the blade came to within an inch of his chest. He finally closed his eyes. The face of Darso was not the last image he wanted to take into eternity. The point of the blade pierced his skin, producing immediate, intense, pain. Then as if out of a dream, the serene, compassionate face of Christ appeared before him. Clint yelled out, "Jesus, help me! I don't want to die! I'm sorry for the harm I've caused others! Please give me another chance! Give me more time with Stacy!"

Clint opened his eyes to Darso's ugly mug. Phil's knife had sunk into his chest two inches by this time, puncturing a lung. Somewhere Clint found the strength to hold him back from going deeper.

The sound of a loud crash rippled through the air as the hinges broke loose from the office door and it fell to the floor. Caesar stormed through the door and saw Phil with the knife in Clint's chest. He ran over to him, wrapped his arm around his neck, and pulled him off Clint.

"Caesar stop! You don't know what you're doing! He's the Black Stallion! He was going to kill me!" yelled Phil.

Clint, moving on instinct, immediately reached for his belt buckle and the knife it held. In a second, he had it dislodged from the belt as he worked his way to his feet. He saw the two men standing a few feet away. Phil was flaying his arms, the knife still in one hand, as Caesar continued his choke hold. He rushed over to Darso and plunged the five-inch blade into his body three times. The first strike was into his stomach. Next, he sunk the blade into his neck, slicing part of the carotid artery. Finally, he drove the knife into Darso's chest, slicing into the heart. Clint left the knife in his chest with the buckle protruding out then immediately collapsed to the floor.

Caesar let Phil fall to the ground then surprisingly jumped on top of him and began punching his already bloodied face.

"You killed Jimmy, you son of a bitch. All he wanted was to be loved." Tears were streaming down Caesar's cheeks as he continued to punch.

"He was just a little boy and you killed him," Caesar blubbered as he kept swinging away. "You killed my Jimmy."

Darso's last few minutes of consciousness were spent in confusion trying to figure out why his only friend would turn on him. Jimmy was an irritating little brat. What was the big deal? Phil's life force bled away, and after another barrage of punches, Caesar realized the demon of a man he had called boss was dead.

Caesar stood up winded after his ordeal. He looked around and spotted Clint unconscious on the floor, bleeding profusely from the chest. Working quickly, Caesar ripped off his shirt—he was wearing a T-shirt underneath—bunched it up, and placed it over the wound. He then slipped one of his arms under Clint's back shoulders, the other under his legs, and lifted him off the ground. Caesar used his chin to keep pressure on the shirt that covered the cut. Moving as fast as he could, he carried Clint out the front door to his car. Clint was placed in the front seat, and with one hand on the wheel and another placing pressure on the shirt covering Clint's chest, Caesar sped toward the hospital.

The electronic doors opened to the entrance of the emergency room as Caesar barreled through with Clint in his arms. Peter was standing near the reception desk working on charts. Nick and Darrel were standing in close proximity to him. Swiftly and with urgency in every step, Peter approached the injured man. Sliding his arms under Clint's body, he helped Caesar cradle him.

"I need a gurney here!" yelled Peter at the top of his lungs.

It took only a few seconds before two nurses and a mobile metal stretcher appeared. In moments they had Clint on the gurney with Darrel and Nick standing at the side of the cart.

Peter turned to Caesar. "What happened?"

Nick interjected, "Who is he?"

"He's the man who killed Phil Darso," said Caesar.

Peter, Darrel, and Nick exchanged startled looks at each other.

"Let's go … We've got to get him up to surgery," commanded Peter.

Just as the cart began to move, Clint opened his eyes. He focused on Peter's face first and then recognized Darrel and Nick.

"Peter, Darrel, Nick, what's going on?" asked Clint, dazed.

Peter quickly pushed as he spoke. "You've been hurt, and we're going to fix you up."

Darrel was the first to recognize Clint. "He's the guy from the shoot-out."

"Yeah!" exclaimed Nick as he connected the face with the local.

"He's got to live … Come on! Let's move!" shouted Peter as he speedily helped push the gurney into a waiting elevator.

—⁂—

Peter hoped to be in attendance during the surgery, but they were short-staffed in the emergency room so he kept tabs on Clint's condition as best he could between rounds.

Darrel continued to escort Peter during his shift. Nick, however, joined Caesar (after he cleaned up a bit) in the waiting room, where he inquired about the events that transpired at Darso's house. Police officers and an ambulance were immediately sent to the residence. Access was possible because the front door had been left ajar when Caesar left. The story that Caesar imparted to Nick was awe-inspiring. Of special interest was Clint's identity as the Black Stallion and his role as a hit man turned protector. Nick found that fascinating. Caesar's admission that he had not called the additional hit men came as a great relief. This meant that Peter was no longer in danger. He would still be protected by Nick and Darrel until he was officially deemed safe, but for all practical purposes he was free from harm. Nick was anxious to share the information with Peter and Darrel, but he knew he would not get that chance until the end of Peter's shift.

—◆—

A nurse intercepted Peter as he was filling out the chart of his most recent patient.

"Dr. Kalos, there's a Stacy Hendricks here to see you. She's in the waiting room," stated the nurse.

"Who?"

"Stacy Hendricks."

"The name doesn't ring a bell, but thanks." Peter said as he walked off to meet Stacy. Peter was unaware that Clint had listed Stacy and her phone number as the emergency contact in his wallet. Darrel followed him to the waiting room.

Stacy was pacing the floor as Peter approached.

"Are you Stacy?" inquired Peter.

"Yes, you must be Dr. Kalos. They called me because my fiancé, Clint Wolf, was brought in hurt from some kind of altercation."

"Oh yes!"

"Is he alive?" The concern was evident in her voice.

"He's doing fine. It was a little touch and go there for a while. He came in with a collapsed lung and traumatic pericardial effusion of the heart."

Peter realized he lost Stacy with the pericardial effusion line. "I'm sorry. He had bleeding in the pericardium. It's a sack that surrounds the heart … It was cut. Fortunately, the intrusion didn't reach the heart. The lung has been inflated and the repair on the pericardium was a success."

"Thank God. Can I see him?" said Stacy, relieved.

"He won't come out of anesthesia for another hour or so … Do you have a moment to talk?"

The two found empty chairs and Stacy recounted the history of her relationship with Clint. She revealed his identity as the Black Stallion and his occupation as a hit man. Peter was genuinely moved when she told him that Clint's conversion to Christianity and his decision to be his protector were due to the example he set in his life.

"How did he come to know me so well?" asked Peter.

Stacy did not want to reveal the presence of the video cameras located in his home (Clint, undetected, would at a future date eventually rid the house completely of the equipment) so she stated only that Clint worked in disguise as an orderly named Pano.

"Pano!" was Peter's shocked reply.

The incredulous story that Stacy revealed caused Peter to examine the events of the last few months that commenced with his decision to testify. The hand of God had certainly been present in his life and influenced people beyond the scope of his understanding. Peter felt a kinship to Stacy that was hard to explain. Beyond the fact she was a Christian, their lives had crossed paths in such a dramatic, personal, special way.

They talked for a half hour then Stacy went and sat in the recovery room waiting for Clint to come out of the fog of anesthesia. Peter shared with Darrel the details of his and Stacy's conversation during down time between patients and all the facts were made known when the two met up with Nick.

Lost in sleep, there was a peaceful illumination that resonated from Clint's face, thought Stacy. She sat next to his bed and placed her hand over his. The horrendous struggle was over, and he had survived. Stacy took a moment to thank God for saving his life. There was always an open line of communication between her and the Lord. It was like talking to an old childhood friend who knew your history and could relate with your adversities and joys. The comfort that resulted from her association with God was profound. She looked forward to making plans with Clint and their future together. Yes, there would be roadblocks. Clint had circumvented the law for so long that the repercussions of his actions would eventually catch up to him. One day at a time, one difficulty dealt with at the moment, and leaning on the Lord for help was how she would deal with the circumstances of her existence. She would trust in God, in His abundant love.

Clint's eyes opened and he immediately saw Stacy. "Hi," said Clint with a smile.

"Hi," responded Stacy as she squeezed his hand and smiled back.

"I made it."

"Yes."

"It was tougher than I thought it would be."

"I know; that's the way it is when you fight evil."

"How did someone so beautiful become so wise?"

"I had a good teacher. I learned from you."

"I missed you. I want to feel your lips next to mine."

Stacy leaned over the bed and kissed him. It was a soft gentle kiss. Clint savored the touch of her moist velvety lips on his. Stacy pulled away from his face a few inches, they exchanged heartfelt looks, and simultaneously both spoke the words "I love you."

# CHAPTER 19

PETER COULDN'T WAIT TO GET HOME AND TELL STEPH THE NEWS THAT Darso was dead and that they were free of danger. Stephanie, however, had already been made aware of the gangster's demise. Detectives Kathy and Cecelia had seen a segment on the six o'clock news about Darso's death, the anchor labeling it a gangland slaying. They even gave a secondhand account describing the blood and carnage found at the crime scene. When Peter walked into the house followed by Nick and Darrel, Stephanie rushed into his arms, giving him a tearful kiss.

"It's true, isn't it? We're out of danger!" exclaimed Steph.

"Yes, sweetheart, Darso's dead and we're safe now."

Their little boy John began jumping up and down then spinning in circles, somehow keying in on the elation of his parents. The four detectives gave each other knowing looks and smiles as if to say, "Our job is done here." It was bittersweet for them. The officers had become fond of Kaloses. When the assignment officially ended, it would be like saying goodbye to family members.

The future would bring a weekly luncheon get-together for the two male detectives and Peter, affectionately named "Tuesdays with Nick and Darrel." Stephanie would have her own weekly reunion with the girls. They would go out for a bite or take short shopping excursions.

The tension level for Peter and Stephanie would return to normal instead of the high alert, wartime, "Where's the suicide bomber?" mentality, and a new element would be added to the Kalos evening prayers. They would forever, on a nightly basis, thank God for their safe passage through the valley of death.

—◊◊◊—

Caesar was seated in Max Freeman's office with the chief, District Attorney Vince Darelli, and a stenographer. Nick's report from the hospital of Caesar's revelations was not legally binding as a confession. Figuring he had already spent time in hell living with Darso, Caesar worked out a plea agreement to stay out of prison before he talked. Today he would go into specifics. This day, by his testimony, Caesar would break up the largest drug distribution ring in the history of Los Angles. He gave them names, addresses, drop-off points, and all information related to Phil Darso's empire. The knowledge was priceless, and both the chief and Darelli were in a state of euphoria as a result of the revelations. This information was offered in a no-nonsense manner by the big Italian and comprised the first half of his interrogation. The next day the police would make a citywide sweep of the locations provided by Caesar and completely dismantle the drug cartel.

The second half of the interview dealt with Jimmy's death. Caesar began with the loving bond that he and Jimmy experienced, stating, "I was more like a father to him than Phil ever was … I loved that kid. He called me Unkey CeCe because he couldn't pronounce Uncle Caesar. I'd take him to the zoo and the park. He was a lot of fun to be with. Phil never saw his good points. He'd go off on him for the smallest things. He was a great kid … He'd tell me that he loved me."

The tears started to flow as he continued. "If I had been in the room while Phil was beating him, I hope I would have had the courage to stop him, but I don't know if I could have. I've seen firsthand his cruelty, his brutality, and the pain he could inflict … He was a huge powerful guy and good fighter. I personally saw him beat and nearly kill a big, muscular, three-hundred-pound drug dealer, and that was in a manner of minutes. Combine that with a guy who's crazy, and it's pretty hard to defeat someone like that. The Black Stallion gave him one hell of a fight though."

Caesar also mentioned his one act of defiance in his refusal to contact the hit men. After a review of the facts and realizing the great benefit derived from his testimony in dismantling the Darso drug empire, Vince agreed to the plea bargain. They did hold him until after the police raid in case he had provided false information, but he spoke the truth and was released after the police action was successfully completed.

Caesar walked out of the station a free man, but actually his greatest freedom came as a result of Darso's death. He no longer had to live in fear of him. It was true he had not been there for Jimmy when he needed him most, and he would have to live with that for the rest of his life, but he could move on. He would be a better man in the future and make up for his past mistakes by leading a more exemplary existence. The life of the Black Stallion was saved because of his intervention; he did have that.

Suddenly the craving for a big plate of spaghetti and meatballs hit him hard. There was a great Italian restaurant in walking distance, so Caesar headed for the culinary comforts provided by way of his native land.

After being hospitalized for seven days, Clint completed his recuperation at his home under Stacy's care. Then arrangements were made to meet with Max Freeman, the chief of police. It was not a meeting he was looking forward to. Clint was going to reveal the truth about his past. He would go into detail about the myriad of hits he had committed in his past and the natural kill method he used to commit those crimes. Caesar, he was sure, had revealed his identity as the Black Stallion, but that's not what spurred him to tell the truth. He was going to tell the truth because he would otherwise be caught in a web of lies. Peter, Darrel, and Nick could place him at the scene of the shoot-out. He could not be sure what Caesar would say, and he wanted his past sins behind him.

Clint had talked it over with Stacy, and she was of course proud of him saying it was the Christian thing to do. The reality, to his admission of so many kills, meant he would spend the rest of his life in prison. He and Stacy would be apart permanently, yet she still embraced his decision, saying, "God will provide." There was a part of him that screamed, *"Are you nuts?"* and another that whispered, "It's going to be all right." In the end, he prayed on it, and while reading his Bible, he came across Psalm 34:4. "I sought the Lord, and He heard me, and delivered me from all my fears." So he would leave it in God's hands. This was Clint's last thought on the matter as he made a right turn out of his driveway in route to his rendezvous with Max.

—⁓—

Max was cordial and actually seemed pleased to see him. They shook hands and the chief invited him into his office.

A few pleasantries were exchanged, and then Max asked, "Why don't you start at the beginning and tell how this whole hit man thing began?"

He had two unused yellow legal pads on his desk, and as Clint started to speak, he pulled a pen from his pencil holder and began to write.

Clint started with his childhood and the violence he experienced at his father's hand. He followed this with his military career and experience as a US Army Ranger. Finally, Clint recounted his introduction into the underworld and his career as a hit man. He told about his alias as the Black Stallion and the innovation of the "natural kill." Clint gave him the names of every person he had slain. Max recognized many of the victims. They had been on the LAPD's most wanted list.

Clint paid particular attention to one victim, Wendy Brennan. To his knowledge, she was the only hit who had not been involved in crime. She was an innocent victim targeted by her mechanic husband for her inheritance money. He had killed her by placing a strain of botulism in what looked like an undamaged can of tuna.

Clint finished his story with Peter and his road to transformation through the influence the doctor's example had exerted on him. He included his recent conversion to Christianity, his relationship with Stacy, the shoot-out in North Hollywood, and his confrontation with Darso.

When Clint eventually came to the end of his tale, he had spent over three hours talking.

"That's quite a story. I'm going to investigate the names you gave me and see what I come up with."

"I guess you're going to take me into custody now."

"No, I don't see you as a flight risk. Why don't you go back to that pretty fiancée of yours and I'll be in touch?" Max ripped a sheet from the legal pad and passed it over to Clint. "Give me a number where you can be reached."

After writing down his cell number, Clint said, "Are you going to exhume the bodies?"

"We'll see ... For now, just go home. I'll call."

Clint had been prepared for jail and was now shocked he could go home.

"OK ... Thank you, Chief." He stood and extended his hand to Max. The two shook hands.

He exited the office a little unnerved, expecting to be rushed by a couple of officers on his way out and carted away to a cell, but that was not the case. Clint got into his car and drove home.

The fateful call that Clint had been dreading came four days later. Vince Darelli, the DA, was on the other end of the line when he accessed the call on his cell phone. Darelli wanted to arrange a meeting as soon as possible. A 2 p.m. appointment was set for the next day. It was not a good sign that the second interview would be with the district attorney. There would probably be some sort of an indictment waiting for him dealing with the death of Wendy. When he revealed his background history as a hit man to Stacy, Clint had not mentioned her death. He truly regretted killing all his past victims, but Wendy's death at his hands was especially hard to deal with. She was not part of the crime world like the others. This was not a drug dealer's vendetta on a rival king pin. This was an innocent girl being killed for inheritance money. Should he tell Stacy about Wendy and his involvement in her death? He knew what was right. It would be better for the story to come from his lips than for her to gain knowledge of it from some newspaper account, but Clint just couldn't bring himself to tell her. They had gone through so many ups and downs in their relationship that to go to jail with her once again being disappointed in him was too much to bear. There was a possibility they would get him for the other killings, and she would be a small footnote in the case with only her name mentioned and no other details provided. That was the outcome he would pray for.

Clint had seen pictures of Vince Darelli in the paper. In the depictions, he looked distinguished, but in person, nobility radiated from him. His youthful appearance, premature gray hair, and dynamic personality played into this stately image. He genially welcomed Peter into his office and shook his hand. Vince immediately got down to business.

"I had a long meeting with Max yesterday, and we reviewed the results from the investigation related to your allegations and we've come to a determination."

"Did you exhume many bodies?" interjected Clint nervously.

"Max mentioned you brought that up in his meeting also … I'm not sure I understand the relevance of your question. I thought the whole basis of your style of killing was to kill in such a way that the death was of natural means and medically undetectable?"

"Yes, that's right." In an effort to be completely honest, Clint was losing track of reality.

"Literally 90 percent of the people on your list had autopsies performed, and of those, all showed cause of death as natural circumstance. We have no evidence to prove otherwise except by your admission, and it's hard to ignore the fact that almost to a man these deaths were of dangerous criminals of one kind or another."

"What about Wendy Brennan?"

"There was an autopsy performed on her body, and it was determined she died of an aneurism to the brain as a result of her deteriorated condition due to cancer."

"*She died of cancer?* What about the tuna with the botulism?"

"We were able to connect with her caregiver who was there near the end, a close friend of hers. She was asked about the tuna and actually remembered a can in the cupboard that had been so badly warped and swollen that she tossed it out."

Clint was never able to get inside Wendy's house to set up surveillance. He had been given so little time to accomplish his mission that most of his intelligence in relation to her was done by physical surveillance. He tailed her whenever she left the house. It was at the supermarket that he saw firsthand her attraction to tuna and devised the plan of planting a tainted can in her grocery bag. He had been so proud of himself for the way he had rigged the can with botulism. Placing a minuscule hole in the can with a needle, Clint had used a syringe to inject the botulism into the tuna then sealed the opening with super glue covered by tin-colored paint. Thank God his plan failed. He remembered that Wendy did not look well and never left the house the two weeks before her death. Only one person came to visit her, and she stayed those last few weeks prior to her demise. Clint assumed it was an old friend from out of town. The only reason he thought he had accomplished his mission was the arrival of the attendants from the mortuary and the resulting death notice, but the news blurb did not state cause of death. The mechanic husband, who had suddenly become the repentant loving spouse, was out of town for three weeks taking an advanced automotive course in Detroit. Clint was to complete the job within that window of opportunity.

"What about the husband? Did he get the inheritance?"

"No, suspecting his motives, she must not have told him that she was dying and changed her will. From what I've been told, she left everything to her church. Dick Shore, the husband, was found a month later with a bullet in the back of the head. My guess is that he got the money to pay you from loan sharks; when he couldn't pay them back, well those things happen."

"I didn't do it?"

"No ... And that brings me to my decision. If it was up to me, I'd pin a medal on your chest ... First, for getting rid of those scumbags that terrorized the state and attempted to rape your fiancée. And second, ridding us of Darso, which ultimately destroyed his massive drug ring."

"What about those other guys I killed?"

"I don't believe in circumventing our legal system to rid ourselves of the criminal element within our city. What you did you should be punished for, but because of your 'natural kill' procedures, I have no evidence."

What Vince wasn't saying was the monetary ramifications of opening the homicide cases of almost forty deaths from botched investigations would be astronomical for the city and would surely affect any thoughts of his reelection. Why ruin everything? With the demise of the Salvadorian gang and the death and subsequent demise of Darso's drug empire, Vince was looking "big" in the eyes of his constituency. Let sleeping dogs lie.

"So you're not going to punish me?"

"As long as you don't go running to the *LA Times* with a confession, which would then force me to toss you in jail and start an indictment."

Vince could see the dumbfounded look on Clint's face.

"Look at it this way: you put your life on the line to save a good man, Dr. Kalos, the only witness who could right a young boy's murder, and almost died trying to keep him safe. Darso was the toughest and the most diabolically shrewd criminal this city has ever seen. You defeated him and with that paid any dues you think you might owe."

Clint smiled. "You mean I'm free to go?"

"Yes … Now get out of here … And take care," said Vince Darelli as he smiled, stood, and extended his hand.

"Thanks," said Clint as he shook Vince's hand. He then exited the office.

Out in the street as he walked to his car, Clint felt like the prodigal son who had come home to a father who greeted him with open arms and whispered into his ear, "All is forgiven, welcome back." On a higher plane, it could be said that Clint had given his confession to Max Freeman and found absolution from Vince Darelli.

—m—

There was rejoicing at Stacy apartment that afternoon. God had come through for them. Not that Stacy ever doubted He would, but when the hope, the prayer, becomes reality, the result is awe-inspiring. The fact that Clint totally escaped prosecution for all his killings was nothing short of miraculous. They could now make plans for the future.

First, they dealt with financial matters. Stacy was adamant that Clint tabulate the money he earned from his years as a hit man and find a way to compile the equivalent of that money, which would be given to charities. The figure Clint derived was a little over $2 million. He had created a shame business to launder his cash, a laundromat. That seemed appropriate. The bookstore was more a front for his hit man activities and its recent closing was not an issue financially.

He had funneled a major part of his earnings into investments, tech stocks, real estate, and energy shares. With shrewd investments, he had more than quadrupled his initial stake. If he was to liquidate, his take after paying brokers and taxes would be just under $5 million. Clint's house in Encino was paid for as were his car, the motorcycle, and the ring from Tiffany's. He would cash out the blue-chip stocks and a large portion of his certificates of deposit. After selling off the business, real estate investments, and dumping his stocks, he would use almost the entirety of the money for donations to worthy charities as requested by Stacy. That would leave him with a $150,000 CD and just over $100,000 in savings. Those assets would be the grub stake for his future with Stacy.

Even though he was giving back more than double what he had made being a hit man, keeping the remaining money was a concern. Was it the right thing to do? Should he give it all to charity and start from zero? Clint prayed on it, finally deciding to keep the fresh-start money. He hoped God would understand and forgive him if that was not His will. Stacy signed off on his decision once he told her he had prayed on it.

Included in the charitable contributions was money to be allocated for their religious institution of choice. In this regard, they needed to decide as to what church they would attend. Stacy belonged to one of the larger Evangelical congregations. Even though Clint found the services inspiring, his heart and soul found sustenance at St. Sophia Cathedral. It had been the first church he had attended; he sensed that in the grandeur and solemn beauty of its interior, the spirit of God dwelled. Combine that with the angelic voices of the choir and the exhilarating sermons of the priest, Clint was sold, but he still needed to persuade Stacy.

One look at the stirring giant fresco of the Christ Child and Virgin Mary that spanned the dome above the altar, and Stacy began to embrace the Orthodox Christian perspective as her own. After a few visits, she quickly perceived the same attributes that had captured Clint's soul, and the glittering heavenly magnificence of the cathedral was a girl's dream come true for a wedding. The decision was made; Stacy would convert, and Clint would be baptized at St. Sophia Cathedral. The two went through religious instruction under Father Costa's tutelage, learning the history, creed, and sacraments of the church, which reinforced their initial decision to accept Orthodoxy.

Ten weeks later, Clint and Stacy were accepted into the Orthodox faith through the sacraments of chrismation and baptism. Their sponsors, or godparents, were Peter and Stephanie Kalos. The four were drawn together by past experience, and Clint and Stacy gravitated to them in church because of their amiable godly presence. A lasting friendship would eventually ensue between the two couples.

Stacy did not want to completely abandon her prior church and friends so they would attend one Sunday a month and gave sizeable donations to both denominations. Two hundred thousand went to the Evangelical church and 300,000 to St. Sophia. It was not long before the gregarious congregation at St. Sophia's embraced their presence, and when they were married six months later, many at the wedding were new friends they had met in church.

Ah yes, how did the wedding turn out? Stacy chose red for her bridesmaids. She felt red best captured the passionate spirit of love. Contrasted against the black tuxedos of the groom, best man Peter, and the groomsmen, the look was impressive. Her white gown was a fabulous Vera Wang creation purchased for her by Clint, who made price no object in making the occasion unforgettable. The beautiful, stirring, Orthodox ceremony, full of symbolism and steeped in tradition, was intensified by the glittering gold interior of the cathedral. The magnificent giant mural of Christ on the top dome of the church made it seem to Stacy that the Lord was looking down upon them with divine pleasure at their joyous union as man and wife. From the exchange of flowered crowns to the final walk down the aisle, the wedding was a glorious picture-perfect event. Clint reconciled with his mother and sister, who attended the wedding.

How was the wedding night? Clint spoke briefly on the subject, saying only, "It was the best two minutes of my life." Seriously, what he was unable to verbalize was that their physical union went beyond description: a sensual experience that seemed almost out of body. The consummation of their love broadened, deepened, and enhanced the affection they already felt for each other. They lost themselves in the soulful exhilarating splendor of each other's bodies. Two of God's creations became a singular holy presence.

—∞—

Attending a Greek Orthodox church meant the congregation was largely made up of people of Greek ancestry. He found the Greeks to be bright, sociable, warmhearted, and passionate about life. Clint's association with this nationality brought some unexpected changes in his life. He began to drink alcohol, moderately of course, but it all started at a Greek festival sponsored by the cathedral. One of the parish members asked him, "Have you ever had Metaxa? It's a Greek drink."

"No, I … I don't drink alcohol," responded Clint.

"Oh, then you can have Metaxa," replied the church member as he handed him a plastic cup full of the mixture. Clint took one large gulp and started coughing and gasping for air.

"I thought you said this didn't have alcohol in it?" said Clint in a raspy whisper.

"Well, it's not really considered alcohol; it's more like high-octane rocket fuel … It's Greek brandy."

Once Clint's eyes finally became uncrossed and he could focus, he replied, "You know it's good when you finally get past the first gulp." Clint displayed a groggy grin as he took another sip.

This small memorable incident would add to a long, pleasurable, heartfelt relationship with the Greek community and church that would last long into the future.

The wedding was everything that Stacy had hoped for, and Clint was pleased he could provide her with an unforgettable experience, but now Clint needed to start generating some income. Pondering and analyzing his strengths and weaknesses, he finally alighted on a bold idea. He would provide a computer-activated security system for homes and small businesses. He configured a high-end software package using advanced encryption techniques that could be controlled and accessed by cell phone. It took him only two days to create, and he already possessed modified state-of-the-art cameras. He negotiated with the appropriate vendors, packaging the five minicameras, remote hookup, and a backup computer battery system together into one large box, with a handle provided for carrying. He called his new venture Black Horse Security Systems Inc. The name brought a kind of continuity to his life. After building a web site for internet activity and placing advertising in some of the top security periodicals, he was set for business. In our safety-obsessed society and at a cost of only $1,500 per kit, it was not long before the orders flooded in. Clint quickly hired a small staff and rented a large warehouse to process and fill requisitions. The irony was that in his first year, Clint tripled the income he made in his best year as a hit man. Literally, crime didn't pay, at least not as much as his new visionary occupation.

# CHAPTER 20

A LITTLE OVER A YEAR HAD PASSED SINCE CAESAR WAS INTERROGATED by the police chief and district attorney. It was Thanksgiving Day and he was having dinner with Gina, his girlfriend, and her extended family. A lot had changed for Caesar from that day at the police station. Living with Phil, in the presence of evil, had smothered his intrinsic kind nature. With Darso he was involved in drug trafficking to the point that young children were getting addicted. Caesar didn't use drugs and despised himself for being part of something that was harmful and dangerous to youth. Those were years of self-loathing; now he was among loving, caring people and for the first time in his life felt contentment.

He had met Gina at the restaurant he patronized after the inquiry. It was an eating establishment not only renowned for their great Italian cuisine but the singing waiters and waitresses they employed as well. Caesar had an amazing baritone voice that he kept cultivated in private by singing along with famous Italian vocalist and traditional American artists. He was a big fan of Josh Grogan, who seemed to epitomize the best of both worlds. Fate intervened that day when he noticed the posted sign in the restaurant window advertising their need for servers who could sing. Gina was the hostess who had seated him, and he inquired from her about the position.

"Can you sing?" was her response.

Caesar belted out a few verses from one of his favorite Italian songs, and the rest, as they say, was history. Even though he had no restaurant experience, they hired him on the spot and started training two days later.

Gina was a classic Italian beauty in her early forties with dark hair and a round, attractive face. A little on the chunky side, she carried most of her excess twenty-five pounds in her breasts and hips. She was not the model-thin call girl type that Caesar was accustomed to, but his attraction to her hit immediately. They were both Italian and in the same age range; the nonstop flirting between the two began on his first day on the job. Within a month the two were dating. Gina was blessed with a great personality, possessed solid values, and had a strong Catholic upbringing. Caesar began attending church with her on Sundays, recommitting himself to early childhood beliefs. Somewhere between their hourlong talks, laughter, and intimate moments together, he fell in love. Those feelings were reciprocal on Gina's part as well. In fact, she was the first woman to say the words "I love you" to him.

After a phenomenal Thanksgiving meal at her parents' home, Gina and Caesar retreated to the gazebo located at the far end of the property. It was there, on one knee, that Caesar proposed to her. With tears in her eyes, she accepted his proposal of marriage. He slipped a two-carat diamond on her finger, and the two went back into the house, where Gina broadcasted the news to her family. There were congratulations from all and a lot of drinking. In fact, in front of the entire family Caesar, serenaded Gina with an Italian love song bringing cheers and another round of drinks.

Later that evening, Caesar took a moment to reflect on the day's events and became choked with emotion when he realized that Gina's family would now become his. He truly loved her parents and the sometimes quirky relatives. The years spent with Darso had now become just a vague nightmarish memory. Gina knew about his past and only accepted him into her life on the requirement he swore never to return to criminal endeavors.

The only physical objects retained from that time were his car, clothes, and $80,000 in cash that he was to give to the hit men. The police ripped apart Darso's house looking for his money from his drug trafficking. They discovered all Phil's hiding places and the lone one of Caesar's containing $10,000. Darso's holdings in cash netted the police $750,000. The vehicles he possessed were valued at $500,000, while the house and furnishings came to $4 million. They allowed Caesar to take his clothes besides keeping the car. The police actually looked through the pockets of the coat that hung on the hanger containing the cash but overlooked the safety deposit hanger. Yes, it was tainted money, but it would be put to good use.

Caesar used $5,000 of that money to buy the ring for Gina, and a large portion of the rest would go as a down payment on a house. The money he earned at the restaurant was decent. He netted about $40,000 a year from wages and tips, and with Gina's money from her work as a hostess, the two would have a comfortable life.

The future would bring changes, however. Caesar would hear another voice telling him, "I love you," this time from a younger girl, his daughter. With this second chance, he would not fail to protect the ones he loved. After Maria's birth, he accepted the job as manager of the Italian restaurant, putting his salary at over $70,000. He became a well-respected man in his church, an exemplary father, husband, and an esteemed member of the community. Caesar would be forever thankful to God for his many blessings and changed existence.

—⁂—

Another Thanksgiving celebration was in full swing, this time at the Kalos residence. Joining the Kalos family were Nick and Loretta, Darrel and Chelsea, Clint and Stacy, and detectives Cathy and Cecelia. In life, the days, the weeks, the months tend to fly by, and so it was the holidays had arrived. Assembled in front of Peter at the dining room table, spread with a sumptuous feast, was his family. A family formed by marriage and procreation, and a family created by divine intervention. The detectives as well as Clint and Stacy came into his life in such a dramatic fashion, and now here they were all gathered together, at peace, to give thanks for the sustenance before them and their many blessings. The group joined hands in anticipation of the blessing.

Peter began the prayer. "Lord, I'm truly a blessed man seated here are my family and friends who I love dearly. We have all been through rough times together and are thankful for a tranquil year. May You continue to bless us with Your grace. Thank You for this food, our health, and the bond of love we share. We ask these blessings in Christ's name. Amen."

"Great prayer, Doc. I've said it before; you got a way with words," blurted out Nick.

Peter shook his head and smiled; Nick was such a character.

Seated next to Nick was Loretta, who was looking vibrant. They had been dating for almost a year and Nick still had made no overtures of marriage. Deep down in the recesses of his ego, Nick considered himself a player, a kind of Hugh Hefner with a badge. Even though he was completely faithful to Loretta, there was always the possibility! Darrel would chastise him, saying, "She's the best thing that ever happened to you. Don't lose her with your knucklehead idea that there are greener pastures."

Nick would later that day bring up the subject of commitment with Clint, who he viewed with admiration as a worldly streetwise guy. His union with Stacy seemed so solid. Even her newly discovered pregnancy did not seem to faze him. He was so devoted to her and still infatuated; Nick hoped for some sound advice.

Clint responded with candor, "I think you should marry Loretta. I want you to suffer like the rest of us." He produced a wide smile and patted Nick on the back. Stacy was standing nearby, out of sight, but in earshot of the conversation. She walked up to Clint with a smile and a twinkle in her eye and said, "So you're suffering?"

"Aw geez, you heard that." Clint quickly turned to Nick and said, "But remember suffering builds character."

Stacy, shaking her head, said, "I better get the rowboat. It's getting deep in here."

Six months later, Loretta would give Nick an ultimatum. "You make some sort of a commitment or I'm out of here." He would one week later propose and give her a ring. He was a little thick at times, but Nick was no fool. Loretta was special and would be a terrific wife. His pasture was a lush green. There would be no regrets.

Paired next to Nick and Loretta were Cathy and Cecelia. Working as partners provided the perfect environment for building a friendship. Cecelia had a more serious demeanor than Brenda's infectious free spirit, but she would stand tall in the face of danger and cover her back. Cathy was pleased and surprised to find that Cecelia had a clever, dry sense of humor. It was that quality that eventually broke through the wall of despair built by Brenda's death. The two over time formed a close bond.

Darrel and Chelsea were adjacent to the girls. It was somewhat of a momentous date for them. Thanksgiving Day marked the two-month anniversary of their engagement. They were head over heels in love with each other but contrasted to the initial euphoria early in their relationship, there were difficult moments. Chelsea stayed sober; however, there were bouts of depression and a few emotional outbursts that dotted her recovery. Darrel hung in there through the ups and downs, solidifying the love that was building in their hearts. His quiet, steadfast devotion broke through the dark, gloomy days, and slowly Chelsea grew stronger. She was being healed not only of her drug addiction but of the psychological scars of her past as well. Darrel had stood firm in his vow not to have premarital sex. They would consummate their love for each other on the wedding night. It had not been an easy decision for either of them, but they held true to that conviction.

That day Darrel related to the group fond details of his first date with Chelsea. "I even remember what she ordered that day at the restaurant."

Chelsea interrupted. "Don't give him credit for that. We had lunch at

Roscoe's Chicken and Waffles. It doesn't take a rocket scientist to figure it out what I had."

There were laughs and chuckles from the group. Peter looked fondly upon his sister. It was good to see her healthy and happy. Chelsea had come home again. He thought of his mother and father, knowing they would be gratified as well while looking down from their celestial resting place.

Situated close to Chelsea were Clint and Stacy. With Clint's business taking off in such a big way, the two were making plans to build on property with an ocean view.

Marriage for Clint was everything he hoped it would be. Spending undisturbed time with his best friend and lover was a dream come true. Sure, they had disagreements, but mostly it was a joy to experience the day with Stacy. Now that she was pregnant, they were both eagerly awaiting their child. Spiritually he had grown as well. God became that all-knowing, loving friend that he could talk to at a moment's notice. Stacy would say when touching the scar left from the knife wound that Clint had something in common with Christ, who had also been pierced in the chest. She never told him though that what he had done to save Peter's life was the most courageous selfless act she'd ever known and paralleled Jesus's actions in many ways.

After an hour and a half of eating, friendly conversation, lighthearted teasing, and laughs, the men excused themselves from the table, grabbed some beers, and headed for the family room to watch football. The women cleared the table then congregated in the kitchen to kibitz and wash dishes.

Peter settled into his favorite leather rocker with his son in his lap to watch the Lions play their traditional pigskin confrontation. As he looked at the men seated around him, he prayed, thanking God for friends who would put their lives on the line to save his. It was a privilege to be in their presence. He focused on Clint, who had sacrificed the most and whose life had so profoundly changed. When Peter thanked him for preserving his life, all Clint said was "You live a life that's worth saving." Peter smiled at the thought of being Clint's *nono,* the Greek word for godfather. He was related by God to a man who initially tried to kill him. How ironic. Such was life. Almost on cue, Clint turned, gazed at Peter, and smiled, tipping his beer as if to say thank-you for the good time.

Clint relished the moment. He had never spent Thanksgiving with a group of friends. He had always been the loner. His Christian conversion brought so much unexpected joy from unforeseen places. If a man is judged by the friends he keeps, Clint figured he scored off the Richter scale being there.

At that moment, his cell phone rang, drawing the attention of the group.

Clint shrugged his shoulders in bewilderment and said, "Got me. What could be so important to interfere with Thanksgiving?"

He put the cell phone to his ear. "Hi," Clint responded when hearing Max, the police chief, on the other end. The chief was hoping he would come into his office for a meeting; he could use his help with a "situation" he was dealing with. A time was agreed upon, Thanksgiving salutations were exchanged, and then Clint ended the call.

*"Who was that?"* exclaimed Nick.

"Just a friend calling to wish me a happy Thanksgiving," replied Clint.

Suddenly the Black Stallion had come galloping back into his life. He looked at the unexpected call with clarity born from his faith. He thought, *It is what it is. I won't be alone out there. I've got Jesus covering my back, and if God is for you, who can be against you?* Whatever the challenge, together they could take on anything.

A serene peace enveloped him. He looked over at the TV as the Lions scored on a long pass play.

Milton Keynes UK
Ingram Content Group UK Ltd.
UKHW011028240624
444593UK00010B/136/J

9 781665 759052